ALSO BY THE AUTHOR

THE PULPIT IS VACANT
DEATH OF A CHAMELEON
A CHRISTMAS CORPSE

FRANCES MACARTHUR

COURTING MURDER

To Ros
love
Frances

Frances MacArthur

ACKNOWLEDGEMENTS

I would like, once again, to thank my proof-readers, Leela, Margo, Jean and Ivor my husband. The latter is improving with practice!

Thanks too to all my friends who purchased my first three books and to those who have even asked to be put on the list for Number Four.

My biggest thanks for this book go, however, to my friends at my tennis club. No, not for providing me with details for a murder but for buying all my previous books and making me determined to set one book at the place where we enjoy playing tennis.

None of the fictional members are modelled on any real ones.

CHAPTER I

"Why have you brought me here?"

"I've got something to show you. No don't put on the light till we get into the changing room."

The couple moved on down the narrow corridor, the young girl in the lead. She put on the light and looked into the face of her companion who smiled back then softly traced the girl's face with one hand continuing down her neck to where the v of her sweater pointed to the valley between her small breasts.

"That's nice," murmured the youngster. She closed her eyes then opened them and moved away slightly to ask again, "What is it you want to show me?"

"I don't want to show you anything, Norma. I just wanted an excuse to be with you."

Flattered, the youngster let herself be led towards the bench seat where she once again closed her eyes as her neck and then her breasts were stroked.

After a few minutes, lulled by her acquiescence, her would-be lover brought her to a standing position and caught the hem of the short skirt and pulled it upwards, revealing a pair of childish white panties. Still the girl did not demur, simply moaning slightly as a finger inserted itself under the panty leg. Further emboldened, the finger tried to insert itself into the virginal opening but here it had to stop as the girl wrenched herself away.

"I'm sorry...I can't...you shouldn't...I'm going home."

"Don't be silly. You'll love it. You're not a child now. Don't make me angry."

The girl pulled away but was caught roughly by the shoulders and pushed to the floor. This time gentleness was missing. A hand tugged the skirt up and pulled the knickers down and off. She felt the rough floor covering scratched her legs and her bottom. Her assailant forced her legs apart and there was a sharp pain and some grunting then she was let go.

She stumbled to her feet and ran along the short, dark passageway towards the door. She had not gone far when she felt two strong arms pulling her back towards the dressing room.

"Please, no. It's wrong. It's wrong. I'll tell my mum...I..."

The voice, raised to a cry of indignation, altered. It became a cry of terror as she felt two hands round her throat.

Saturday morning was glorious for April, a perfect day for the junior tennis coaching session. Avril Smiley counted her young tennis hopefuls. There were twenty-four, a good number, she thought. .She told them to go over to the other side of the net and come up one at a time to try to return her shot. This kept them occupied for some time then she took one at a time along with her on one side and showed each one how to hold the racquet correctly for a forehand return shot. Wanting to make it fun, she then put four on each side of the three courts and told them to hit balls back and forwards, trying to keep the ball within the outer lines.

The coaching lasted an hour. They had all come dressed to play and apart from two, all were happy to go home in the same clothes except Patsy Cowan and Alice Pearson who were going into town with Patsy's mother straight after the coaching.

"Mrs Smiley, where can I change?" Patsy asked.

"The female changing room's the room at the end of the corridor, Patsy. The toilet's there too for the girls if anyone wants to go. Boys, your room is this first one here," she said, opening the door to the first room.

Patsy and her friend Alice went up the corridor. The changing room was in darkness and Patsy fumbled to find the light switch.

The scream reached Avril where she stood at the outside door. She ran down the corridor and met Patsy and Alice coming towards her. Both were white-faced and Patsy was still screaming. Avril had to slap her face to get her to stop.

"What is it? Tell me."

"In there," Alice pointed back towards the girls' changing room, "in there. There's a body." Patsy dived outside and was violently sick. Alice, feeling sick herself, comforted her friend.

Avril had reached the changing room and had seen the body with its purple neck and protruding tongue. She made herself look at the face before turning away and reaching for her mobile phone.

"Police please...My name is Avril Smiley. I'm at Greenway Tennis Club in Stamperland. There's been a murder."

Looking at his rota sheet, the PC at the desk of the police station, noted that it was DCI Davenport who was scheduled for today's business, a pity really, the man thought, as Davenport had only recently wound up a murder investigation. He liked Davenport who seldom stood on ceremony and often had a joke with him. Never mind. It could not be helped. He rang through to Davenport's room.

"Sorry, Sir but a call's just come in from a Mrs Smiley, Avril Smiley, reporting a murder at Greenway Tennis Club in Stamperland. Yes, she knows the victim. It's a Norma Lawson, a young member of the club. She's been strangled, Mrs Smiley thinks. I've told her to wait there till you arrive."

Picking up his jacket from the back of his chair and calling out for DS Fiona Macdonald to accompany him, Davenport made for the car park where his silver grey Audi was parked. Even at a moment like this, he felt a moment of delight at seeing it, his new car purchased last week.

He got in and had just switched on the ignition when the passenger door opened and Fiona Macdonald got in. Quite short but slimmer than she had been some months ago, she had become his good friend as well as a valued colleague.

"A murder, Fiona, at a tennis club in Stamperland. A young girl… strangled, I think."

"Who found her?"

"A Mrs Avril Smiley. Don't know who she is or any of the details. We'll soon find out."

It took them about fifteen minutes to reach the club which was situated not far from the main road. The car, pulling up suddenly, sent a spray of gravel through the wire netting into the middle court and came to a stop a few feet from what appeared to be the back door of the clubhouse. A young woman in a navy tracksuit was standing in the doorway, her arms round two girls who were also dressed in tracksuits, one in black and one in grey. All three looked scared.

Davenport introduced himself and Fiona.

"I kept Patsy and Alice. They found the ...body, Inspector. I've phoned their parents. They were supposed to be going into town with Patsy's mother who hasn't arrived yet but is on her way. I didn't think you'd want bystanders so I sent everyone else away."

Davenport thanked her and told her that she had done the right thing.

At that moment, another two cars swept into the car park, one behind the other. A man got out of the first one, a red Passat, and a woman got out of the back one, a grey BMW. They hurried towards their daughters who threw themselves into the arms of their parents.

Davenport let them hug the girls for a minute or two then stepped forward.

"My name's DCI Davenport and this is DS Macdonald. There's been a murder and your daughters unfortunately found the body. I think it would be best if you brought them to the station. It's in Govanhill. I have to see what has happened and get my men in to start our murder process then I'll ask you to follow me. Mrs Smiley, would you come too please."

On the way over in the car, Fiona Macdonald had contacted the police surgeon, Martin Jamieson and the head of the SOC team. Both had promised to be at the scene as soon as possible.

She and Davenport went along the corridor and bending down, inspected the body, being careful not to touch anything. The young girl lay on her back, naked from the waist with her legs splayed, Davenport could see dried blood at the top of her thighs. Even without Martin Jamieson's expertise, he could see that the girl had been strangled as her face was purple and her tongue protruding. He looked round but could see nothing which could have been used to strangle the girl.

"Nothing here, Sir, just an anorak hanging up on a peg. No bag. No sign of her underwear."

"Right, Fiona. You wait here for Martin and SOC. I'd better get these youngsters down to the station. Their parents will want to get them home."

"OK, Sir. I'll ask Martin for a lift when he's finished."

Davenport went outside and got into his car.

The little procession set off.

Sergeant Salma Din, a striking looking woman in her late twenties, was standing in the doorway of the room she shared with constables, Frank Selby and Penny Price. She had heard Davenport calling out for DS Macdonald and had wondered what was happening.

Seeing her, Davenport said quickly, "Another murder, Salma. I'll want you and Frank and Penny in the Incident Room shortly. Find them for me please."

He ushered the three adults and two children into his own spacious room.

He brought forward chairs and sat himself on his desk. He spoke to Avril Smiley first.

"Mrs Smiley, would you tell me what happened please?"

"I had just finished my hour of coaching. Patsy and Alice had to change and asked where they should go. All the youngsters are new members and don't know the layout of the club. Sorry, I'm wittering. I told them to use the female changing room at the end of the corridor. They went down the corridor, and then I heard a scream. I ran down to the changing room. The girls were coming out. They said they had found a body. I went in and saw a half-naked body on the floor."

Alice started to cry. Her father put his arm round her.

"Did you recognise the girl, Mrs Smiley?"

"Yes. It was Norma Lawson. She is...was one of our intermediate girls, a very promising tennis player."

Davenport looked at the two girls.

"Can I have your names please, girls. Don't worry. I won't keep you long."

"I'm Alice Pearson," said the taller of the two, a slim girl with light brown hair tied back in a ponytail. She had stopped crying.

"I'm Patsy Cowan," said the smaller girl. She was darker haired and had short hair held back by a red band.

"Now, Alice and Patsy. I have to ask you this. Did you touch anything at all in the changing room?"

"No," said Patsy.

"Yes you did," argued Alice, "you switched the light on."

"Sorry. I did put the light on. I forgot."

"Anything else?"

"No."

They spoke in unison.

"Did you see any clothes lying on the floor?"

"I didn't look anywhere else but at ...her," said Patsy.

"Me neither," echoed Alice.

Patsy had started to shiver and her mother leant over and put an arm round her.

"Is that all, Inspector?" she asked.

"Yes thanks. You can get the girls home now. I suggest that you get their doctors to see them as soon as possible. Maybe get them something to help them sleep tonight."

The youngsters were led away by their parents and Davenport spoke to the woman who remained.

"Did you see any clothes lying around, Mrs Smiley?"

"No. She had nothing on below the waist, Inspector. The skirt was pulled up. Was she raped?"

"Sorry, we won't know that till the police surgeon has seen her."

He got up from his desk.

"That's all for now. Thanks for your help. I'll get a police constable to run you back to the tennis club or home if you prefer."

"I live next door to the clubhouse, Inspector and would be grateful for the lift."

"I'll be in touch again. Just have a think and see if you can remember hearing anything from the clubhouse either earlier today or last night."

Promising to do her best and to ask her husband, the woman left and Davenport made his way to the Incident Room to let his team have all the information he had right now.

CHAPTER 2

"Right team," said Frank Selby standing out in front of the others in the Incident Room. He pulled on his left ear lobe the way his boss did when perplexed or annoyed. Penny Price shook her dark curly head at him but laughed at the same time. Salma Din, looking elegant as usual, her black hair shining and her eyes too, shook her head at Frank who was always looking for fun. He had been keeping them entertained over the last six months by imagining a romance between DS Macdonald whose name was Fiona and DCI Davenport who was Charles, nicknaming them Bonnie Prince Charlie and Flora Macdonald and whistling such tunes as, "The Sky Boat Song" whenever he thought he could get away with it.

"Frank! Come and sit down. They might catch you," Salma said.

Frank had just taken a step towards them when the DCI and Fiona entered the room.

"Catch him at what, Sergeant?" asked Davenport.

"Nothing, Sir," Salma muttered. She felt her cheeks hot and for once was grateful for her dark complexion.

Luckily for Frank, Davenport's mind was on other things and he did not press the point.

"Right team..."

Penny had to turn her giggle into a hasty cough. DS Macdonald threw her a stern glance.

"There's been a murder at Greenway Tennis Club in Stamperland. A young girl aged fourteen, called Norma Lawson, was found this morning by two youngsters who were at the club for pre-season coaching. The girl had been strangled. It's my opinion, having looked at the body, that she was strangled manually. There was no mark from a ligature round her neck. DS Macdonald contacted Martin Jamieson and the SOC team and they are there now. Is that right, Fiona?"

"Yes, Sir. Martin, as usual, said he'd contact you as soon as possible, probably later today as he has nothing pressing to do right now. I waited while he made a quick inspection before allowing the body to be removed. SOC were dusting the room for fingerprints."

"Did you check the other rooms?"

"Yes. The gents' changing room had only an empty tennis racquet cover lying on the bench and in the room upstairs where there was what I imagine is a committee room or where they have refreshments after games, there was nothing except the furniture, some old, plastic chairs and a couple of tables. There was a very small kitchen. Nothing unusual in there either."

"Had she been raped, Sir?" asked Frank.

"Obviously we won't know till Martin gets in touch but she was bare from the waist down and there was what looked like dried blood on the inside of one thigh."

Fiona who had noticed this too, nodded in agreement.

"I got the address and phone number of the membership secretary from the coach who phoned us," said Davenport. "Penny, get along to her house and collect a list of members from her. Either the girl herself or her murderer had to have had a key to the premises unless it was left open, in which case the murderer was just lucky and I think it's very unlikely that he brought the girl to an out of the way clubhouse hoping to find it open. Local knowledge on the girl's part or on the murderer's, I would think, for them to have gone there."

"Do you think they went together, Sir?" asked Penny.

"Either that or she went and he followed her, Penny. I don't know when the murder took place but it was either early morning before the youngsters came for their lesson or last night. If it was last night, the two surely came together."

"Why, Sir?" asked Frank.

"Well, what reason would a fourteen year old have to visit the club house at night by herself?"

"What I meant Sir was that they could have arranged to meet."

"Oh I see, sorry, Selby. Yes, that's possible."

"Do you want us to find out who her friends are...were, Sir" asked Fiona.

"Yes but right now I want you to come with me to see her parents. I don't relish having to break this news."

"Can Frank and I do anything, Sir?" asked Salma who as usual had remained quiet throughout.

"When Penny comes back with the list... Penny ask if she has separate lists of juniors, intermediates and seniors, please... make three copies of each list and then you all start on the intermediate list. Visit them and try to find out if Norma was seeing anyone, any male friend. Find out who her best friends are. Ask who she spoke to at the club."

"It's possible, Sir, that it was an older boy," said Fiona.

"Yes, I'm aware of that but we'll start with the younger ones who should know her better. When we get back from visiting her parents, we can start on the senior male list. I just hope that the membership secretary has separate lists. If she hasn't Penny, ask her to tick the intermediate members and score out the juniors."

Penny left. She drove to Muirend to where Anne Scott, the membership secretary, lived. It being Saturday, Anne was at home and had been contacted by Avril Smiley with the bad news. Avril had forewarned her that the police would be paying her a visit for lists so she had them ready. There were six lists, male and female of all three sections, junior, intermediate and senior with addresses and phone numbers. Penny thanked her and asked her if she knew who Norma's friends were.

"Sorry, I can't help you. Norma's a comparatively new member. She only joined last April. She played at a club over in the West End I think, before they moved here. Her wee cousin's a member too. He's in the junior section."

"Would he have been at the coaching session today?"

"Might have been, though I've heard people talking about what a good wee player he is so maybe not. Sorry I can't help more but I work so I only play in the evenings and with the senior women on Saturday afternoons and I don't come into contact with the younger ones."

Penny thought of something.

"Maybe you could get in touch with as many of the senior women as possible. There won't be any tennis for them this afternoon I'm afraid."

"I guessed that but you're right. Avril may have done it already but better that they hear twice than not at all."

Penny thanked her and left, making it back to the station as Salma and Frank were setting out for the staff canteen so she joined them. It would be better, Salma said, to eat now as they might not get time later.

Over a snack of baked potatoes with various fillings - even Frank was being persuaded to eat more healthily these days - they discussed this new murder.

"Poor wee girl," said Penny. "Only fourteen. What a waste."

"I know, it always seems worse when it's a child somehow," said Salma.

"Wonder if she knew and trusted this murderer or only met him that night," Frank mused.

Lunch over, they went back upstairs and got on with the job of photocopying the intermediate lists. It was decided that Penny and Salma should make a start on the girls and Frank would get another PC and visit the boys.

CHAPTER 3

Charles and Fiona went off to Waterfoot and found the house they were looking for. It was at the end of a terrace of white-washed houses. They walked up the path, side-stepping a child's red and yellow tricycle. The garden was untidy but the house freshly painted. The front door was open so Davenport called into the house and a woman came to the door. She was in her mid-thirties, with lanky fair hair and she was dressed in denims and a grey shirt blouse. She looked tired and frazzled.

"Hello. Can I help you? You're not Jehovah's Witnesses are you because if you are, we go to our own church?"

At another time Fiona would have found this funny. They were in suits and smartly dressed so she supposed the mistake was understandable. However this was not a time for smiling.

"No, we're not Jehovah's Witnesses, Mrs Lawson. We're..."

"I'm not Mrs Lawson. I'm Mrs Gilbert."

"Sorry, we're looking for Norma Lawson's mother. I'm DCI Davenport and this is DS Macdonald."

"I am Norma's mother. What's happened? Has she been in an accident? She was staying overnight at a friend's house."

"Mrs Gilbert. May we come in please?"

The woman stood back to let them enter then went past them and led them into a room, sparsely furnished with only a settee, two chairs and a piano. There was a picture on the piano, two small boys, one with curly fair-hair, the other dark, with straighter hair and chubbier than the boy who was obviously his twin.

"Sorry about this room. It's the last to be decorated. We sit in the family room at the back. We moved in about a year ago."

"So you are Norma's mother. I take it that you've remarried?" said Davenport.

"Yes, five years ago to Gavin. We have twin boys, Rory and Donald who are three but Mr Davenport, what's happened to Norma?"

"Please sit down, Mrs Gilbert."

The woman sat on one of the chairs. Davenport sat on the settee and Fiona sat beside him.

"There's no easy way to tell you this so I'll just tell you bluntly. Norma is dead," Davenport said, hating this part of his job. The woman cried out and put her hands up to her face.

"Dead! How?"

"I'm afraid that she's been murdered. Her body was found in the tennis club at Stamperland."

The woman's shoulders shook and Fiona moved across to put her arm round her.

"Who would want to kill my Norma?" Mrs Gilbert turned a tear-stained face to Davenport.

"That is what we have to find out, Mrs Gilbert. Where is your husband? It would be good if he could be here for you right now."

"He's at the park with the boys. He should be home soon. We haven't been getting on, me and Norma. She didn't like me getting married again. We'd had five years by ourselves after her dad left us. She's a bit jealous, thinks I spend too much time with the boys. They're only wee, Inspector." The woman was speaking in jerky sentences with shock, already making excuses for herself.

"How did she get on with Gavin, your husband?"

"Not very well. She resents ...resented him I think."

There was the sound of footsteps in the hall and two small boys catapulted into the room flinging themselves on their mother. A man followed, a stockily-built man, dark-haired and smiling. His smile faded when he saw the two strangers.

"Jan, what's the matter? I saw the strange car outside."

"It's Norma, Gavin. She's been murdered."

"Murdered!" the man sounded shocked. "Where?"

"At the tennis club."

"But I thought that she was staying overnight with a friend from school."

"So did I but I didn't check. I should have checked."

The man moved quickly to stand behind her. He put his hands on her shoulders.

"Jan, she often stayed over at Mary's. How were you to know she didn't this time?"

Probably glad to get rid of a sullen teenager, Fiona thought. It could not have been easy having Norma around, resenting the new family.

She rose to her feet, offering to make them all a cup of tea. When no one said anything, she left and having found the kitchen, returned with a tray with four mugs of tea which she handed round, insisting that Mrs Gilbert took two spoonfuls of sugar in hers.

"It'll help you, Mrs Gilbert. Sweet tea is good for shock."

"I'm sorry folks but someone is going to have to identify the body," said Davenport.

"But you said it was Norma. Could it be someone else?" Mrs Gilbert's head came up quickly.

This was a common occurrence, Davenport knew, the bereaved wanting to disprove that it was their loved one who was dead.

"I'm afraid the body was seen by one of the tennis club members and she knew Norma."

"How was she killed, Sir?" asked the man.

"I can't say till we have the report back from the police surgeon, Mr Gilbert."

"OK then, I'll come with you," the man replied.

"I want to come too," said the woman.

Knowing that it would probably be better if Norma's mother could see her daughter and have some sort of closure, Davenport agreed, asking if there was a neighbour or member of family who would look after the two boys who were still clinging to their mother's knees, oblivious of the tragedy which had struck the family but sensing something was wrong.

Mr Gilbert got up and went to the phone in the hall, spoke to someone and came back to the lounge.

"My sister will come round," he said.

"Right," said Davenport. "I'll get back to the station and DS Macdonald will accompany you to the city mortuary once your sister gets here."

He got up. Fiona rose too and, leaving the couple alone, they went out into the hall.

"Hope you don't mind, Fiona."

"Not at all. I'll get them to bring me back here and then come on to the station by taxi."

Norma's stepfather had come out into the hall behind them.

"Would you please give me a recent photograph of Norma," Davenport asked him.

The photograph given to him was obviously a school photograph and showed a pretty teenager with long reddish fair hair and dressed in school uniform.

At the city mortuary, Martin Jamieson slid the trolley holding Norma's body out of a cold drawer. Brushing his fair hair out of his left eye, he quietly pulled back the white sheet and stepped back to let the girl's mother and stepfather look at the body. Jan Gilbert staggered back, ashen-faced. Gavin Gilbert looked a while longer, then, putting his arm round his wife, he drew her towards the door.

Fiona was waiting outside. She raised an eyebrow at the man and he nodded,

"Yes. It's Norma," he said.

Fiona, taking a second to go back into the room and say to Martin that they would await his diagnosis, led the husband and wife out to their car. Back at their house, she suggested that Mrs Gilbert saw her family GP as soon as possible, then she phoned for a taxi to take her back to the station.

At the station, she found only Charles who was looking at the list of senior males. She looked over his shoulder.

"How many, Charles?"

"Fifteen. I suppose we should be thankful for the fact that it seems to be a reasonably small club. The others have left copies of the lists. There are even fewer intermediate boys, only seven. Salma left me a memo. She and Penny have gone to interview the intermediate girls - there are six of them and Frank's gone off with PC Grey to do the same with the boys."

"What about us?"

"A very late lunch first I think. We'll go to the Redhurst. It's quite near Stamperland, unless you'd rather go to a tearoom."

Knowing that Charles did not like what he called 'eenty' tearooms, Fiona chose the hotel.

Over a lunch of macaroni and cheese for Charles and chilli con carne for Fiona, they discussed their tactics.

It being Saturday afternoon, they might be lucky and find some of the men at home although some might be at football matches or in town with wives and families. The seniors who were still at school might be at home studying for coming exams.

Davenport rang Salma on her mobile and, hearing that she and Penny were being quite successful in finding the intermediate girls in, told her and Penny to work on till 5pm then come back to the station. He did the same with Frank who was not having much luck. Davenport guessed that the boys would be reluctant to use the weekend for exam revising. He told Frank to leave his investigations till the evening and come back to the station now.

"I'll let Bob Grey get home to his wife and kids and I'll come out with you this evening, Frank. I want to get the boys of Norma's age seen first."

"What about me, Charles?" asked Fiona. "I thought you and I were going to make a start on the seniors."

"Think, as I said to Frank, that there's not such a rush with them. You and I can see them tomorrow night. I hope that won't spoil your Sunday evening. You can have tonight free."

He had remembered that Fiona had her engaged friend and her friend's fiancé coming round that evening and had decided to make use of her the next night instead. He just hoped that the younger members of his team did not have prior engagements but if they had, they would have to cancel them. It was one of the downsides to their job.

As it turned out when he met them later, only Penny was going out, with her boyfriend Gordon Black and she said he would understand. As a vet, he too often had callouts at awkward times and understood that Saturday nights could be cancelled at short notice.

Thanking his lucky stars for loyal staff who did not moan and complain when things were rough, Davenport told them to try to finish off as many of their visits as possible and to try to do as many as possible early in the evening before the youngsters went out. Luckily most young ones went out much later than they had done in his young days, he thought.

"I've changed my mind. I think we'd better do the interviews, one man, one woman. Penny, I'll go with you. Frank you accompany Sergeant Din."

"Stop around 8pm and get off home. Meet tomorrow at 9 am sharp in the Incident Room and we'll exchange information then."

CHAPTER 4

Penny and Salma only had six girls on their list. The first house they went to was an imposing building set back from the main Glasgow Road. The path wound through immaculate gardens and the trees and bushes thick with unopened buds promised a riot of colour in a few weeks.

"Wow!" said Penny. "Bet they're not short of a bob or two."

Salma looked nervous. She had found that well-to-do Glaswegians tended to be a bit more racist than their poorer cousins. As they approached the front door with its magnificent stained glass panels, she straightened her shoulders.

A young woman answered their ring. Dressed in off-white trousers and a pale blue tee-shirt she did not look as if she belonged to this house. She confirmed this by replying to their request to speak to Miss Georgina Laird, that the family were out in the back garden and would they come through please.

Aware of possible dirt on their shoes, they stepped onto a thick, cream carpet which in Penny's view had no right to be laid down in a hall. She saw Salma also treading gingerly and sent her a conspiratorial grin.

The young woman was obviously foreign, from her hesitant English, and she said very little as she escorted them through a beautifully appointed lounge to French windows which led not only to a vast garden but to a swimming pool.

"I wonder how often they swim in that," thought Penny with memories of Scottish summers, then noticed that there was a recessed roof which could obviously be pulled across if needed.

A small group was sitting round the pool in various stages of undress, two women and three men. The men were all in swim-shorts, it being a reasonable day but the women were dressed more sensibly, the older woman in close-fitting white trousers which, when she stood on seeing the visitors, showed knife-edged creases. The other woman, much younger, wore denims and a cerise tee shirt. She remained seated as did the two younger men. The older man came towards them, motioning what was presumably his wife to sit down.

"Police? What's happened?"

He looked at Penny as he spoke but Salma answered him, smiling pleasantly.

"There's been a young girl murdered at your daughter's tennis club, Sir. We'd like to speak to her if possible."

"And you are...?"

"Sergeant Din, Sir and this is PC Price."

The man turned to the group at the pool.

"George! Come here please."

The young, blonde woman unfolded her lithe body from the lounger and came to her father's side.

"Yes, Daddy. What's the problem? Have I got another speeding fine or parking ticket?"

She laughed, a tinkling sound which somehow grated on Penny's ears.

"Miss Laird," said Salma, "I believe you are a member of Greenway Tennis Club?"

"Yes. Why?"

"Were you friendly with Norma Lawson?"

"That youngster? No I'm not. Why would I be? She's a junior..."

"Intermediate," said Penny more sharply than she had intended.

"Sorry. Intermediate. You should ask my sister. She's the same age."

"We're checking the people on the intermediate list and your name's on it."

"Guess there's been a typing mistake then. I'm a senior member. It's my sister Henrietta you're looking for. Daddy, where's Henry?"

"She's probably in her room, reading."

"There you go sergeant. You'll find my brainy little sister swotting in her room as usual."

With that the girl turned and made her way back to the poolside. Her father turned to the two policewomen.

"Better come inside. I'll call my younger daughter."

The three walked back through the French windows and into the hall. Mr Laird called upstairs, "Henrietta! Come down please!"

There was the sound of feet on the polished wooden stair and a plumpish girl came down towards them. She wore her fair hair tied back in a ponytail, had a book in her hand and wore glasses.

"Henry. These two policewomen want to ask you about someone from the tennis club."

"Hi," said the girl giving them a friendly grin. "Who d'you want to know about?"

"Henry. A girl's been murdered. What was her name again, sergeant."

"Her name's Norma Lawson. Were you a friend of hers, Miss Laird?"

The girl's face paled. She took a step towards her father as if for protection.

"Murdered? Norma?"

"I'm afraid so. Was she one of your friends?"

"We're all very friendly with each other. There are only six of us, you see."

"Did she have a boy-friend?" asked Salma.

"Norma? No. She's only fourteen. She's the youngest of us."

"You never saw her being especially friendly with one of the boys at the club then?"

"No. The intermediate boys are so immature. All they can talk about is computer games and football and the older ones wouldn't be interested in us."

"Thank you, Miss Laird. If you think of anything that might be relevant, please get in touch with the station at Govanhill. Shawbank it's called."

Penny gave the girl the phone number of the station and, thanking Mr Laird and his daughter for their time, they walked back down the path to where their car was parked on the main road.

"She seemed a nice kid, Salma," said Penny, getting in behind the wheel of the car.

"Yes, unlike the older sister," Salma grimaced. "She was a real snooty..."

"Bitch."

"Right."

"Who's next on the list? Hope there's no more mistakes on it."

The next on the list was a Samantha McMillan.

"I guess she'll be called Sam," laughed Penny.

She was indeed called Sam and she verified what Henrietta Laird had said, namely that Norma had not been interested in any of the boys at the tennis club.

It was not till they reached the last girl, Zoe Stewart, that they got any new information. Zoe lived with her Mum in a flat in Clarkston and she and Norma had been close friends.

She burst into tears when she heard about the murder and Penny had to make her usual cup of comforting tea for both Zoe and her mother before Zoe was fit to answer their questions. They sat in the lounge, Penny and Salma on the flowery patterned settee and Zoe and her mother on the chairs.

"Did Norma have a boyfriend?"

"I don't think so."

"But you're not sure?" Salma had noticed the uncertainty in the girl's voice.

"We've been good friends since she joined the club. We're the youngest of the intermediates. We're partners in the team but recently she's been a bit strange."

"Strange? In what way?" asked Penny.

"Well, she started wearing make- up. I mean to play tennis you don't need make up and we'd always said we wouldn't use the stuff. When I teased her about it she got quite... I don't know...quite grown up and said I would understand one day which I got annoyed at. In fact we haven't been speaking to each other since she said that. Oh, Mum and now I can't say sorry 'cos she's dead."

The girl burst into tears again and her mother got up and going across the room, sat on the arm of the chair, put her arms round her daughter.

"I'm sorry, Zoe, Mrs Stewart. Thanks for your help," Salma said and once more she and Penny went back to the car which this time was parked quite a distance away, in the parking space above the shops.

This time Salma took the wheel and having manoeuvred the car out of the tight space, headed for the station.

"Looks as if Norma had found herself a boy," mused Penny.

"And either at the tennis club or she was meeting him after tennis if the make-up was anything to go by," added Salma.

Glad that they had something to tell the others, they went back to the station.

CHAPTER 5

Frank and Bob Grey had only found two of the intermediate boys at home. One was what Frank privately marked down as a 'geek'. His mother said he was in his room studying for exams which were due in a few weeks' time. She called upstairs, "Robin! Come down please. There's someone here to speak to you."

The youth who came downstairs had bad acne and was extremely thin. He had longish, dark, greasy hair. It was hard to visualise him being sporty and impossible to imagine him attracting the attention of an attractive young girl, like Norma. Frank glanced down at the photograph of Norma which his boss had photocopied.

"Mrs Stevenson - Robin - I'm sorry to have to tell you that one of the girls at the tennis club has been murdered. Her name is Norma..."

"...Norma who?" interrupted the boy. It was not an auspicious start.

"Lawson. Robin, there are only six intermediate girls at the club. Surely you know who they are." Frank tried to keep the irritation out of his voice. Remembering himself at this age, he had known the names of all the half decent 'lookers' in any club or in school.

"I never play mixed doubles. I only play singles with my friend Gregory and we avoid girls. They're silly and giggle all the time."

"Robin's a serious boy," his mother added proudly. "He wants to be an accountant. He usually only goes to tennis after school on Fridays."

"Did you see Norma...any girls...at the tennis club yesterday after school?" asked Bob Grey.

"No."

Frank thanked them and the two constables left. It was no use asking if Robin had ever seen Norma with a boy if he did not even know who she was, nor asking him where he was on Friday evening.

As he expected, Gregory Browne was also at home studying. He was a plump, fair-haired boy who looked younger than his fifteen years and he answered the door of the second floor flat to their ring. He, however, knew Norma.

"Yes, I know who she is. She's friendly with Zoe Stewart who lives upstairs."

"Have you ever seen her talking to any of the men or boys at the tennis club?"

The boy thought for a moment.

"She partnered one of the senior men in last week's American Tournament. Why do you want to know?"

"I'm afraid that Norma's been murdered, Gregory." Frank knew there was no point in beating about the bush.

The boys' rosy cheeks blanched.

"Murdered?"

"Yes. Her body was found at the tennis club this morning. Now I need to know this man's name, the one she played with."

The boy hesitated.

"His name's Donald but I don't know his surname. We played against them, Pat and I. Norma called him Don."

"Pat who?" Frank nodded to Bob who took out his notebook.

"Pat Harper. She's a senior, about my Mum's age. I don't know her, our names were balloted."

"Did Robin, your friend, take part in this tournament?"

"No."

He shuddered.

Frank sighed. It was unlikely that a woman in her thirties would know much about a fourteen-year old girl. Still, at least he had two names to give Davenport. Feeling a bit silly, he asked the boy where he had been on Friday evening and was told he had been at home with his family. He looked puzzled about being asked this question.

Frank and Bob thanked Gregory, and Frank, remembering what his boss would do, told the boy to make himself a cup of sweet tea as he was obviously in a state of shock.

They tried five other houses with no luck, although one father, when told what had happened, said he played sometimes at the club and he and his son had played a game with Norma, a giggly girl, and her friend Zoe. He remembered them because his son had confided in him that he liked Norma who went to the same school as he did but she went everywhere with a girl called Mary at school and with Zoe at tennis and did not seem interested in him or any of the other boys.

"Mr Jenkins. Do you know if Peter ever did ask Norma out?"

"Don't think so. He's got a girlfriend at the moment, someone in his class at school."

"Do you play tennis at the same club, Sir?"

"Occasionally."

"Where were you, Sir, that night?"

"Me? I was at home - alone, constable."

"School!" Frank said to his colleague as they walked back out into the weak sunshine. "It could have been someone she'd met at school. She would have a key for the clubhouse but it doesn't mean that the boy or man had."

Bob groaned.

This might mean interviewing her school peers too unless they turned up something in their interviews of tennis club members.

The phone call from Davenport came when they had only one other boy to try but Bob was keen to get home so Frank made his way back to the station alone. He would see if Penny and Salma wanted to eat somewhere locally before they continued interviewing.

It was about 4.40 and Salma and Penny arrived back just after 5pm having seen all the girls except one, Lucy Collins who had been in town shopping with her aunt. Her father had said that she would be at home in the evening as they had her uncle, aunt and cousin coming to visit.

Davenport met with them in the Incident Room. He allocated Salma and Frank a couple of senior men to add to the intermediate boys whom Frank had failed to find at home and told Penny that he would accompany her to see Lucy Collins and then they would try to see some senior males too.

"Penny and I will try to see this Don you mentioned, Frank."

Frank would have liked to interview this man himself but he could hardly say this.

"Set off at 6.30. Try to catch them before they go out or have visitors," Davenport told them.

Penny was delighted. She had a great respect for her boss and always felt that she learned a lot from watching him at work.

Frank still felt a bit embarrassed at accompanying Salma. He liked her a lot now but did not want his friends to see him with her. She knew this and would rather have worked with Penny or Davenport. However, it was not their place to argue with Davenport.

The trio went off to eat at Battlefield Rest, one of their favourite eating places. Penny had rung ahead to book as, even as early as this, it was Saturday evening and the place was popular.

All three chose pizzas, only Frank having a bottle of beer though he could almost feel the girls' disapproval. Neither of them ever drank while on duty but Frank felt that it was Saturday night and he should be allowed one drink. It was silly really as he did not enjoy the drink, knowing how the others felt. They finished off with frothy cappuccinos, Frank stirring in three spoonfuls of sugar and the girls dropping in sweeteners.

"Got your Mum's official photographs yet, Penny Farthing?" Frank asked.

Mrs Price had got married a few weeks ago to her close friend Jack and was now Mrs Maclean. Penny had been her attendant and both Frank and Salma had been invited to the evening celebrations at The Brig O Doon Hotel in Alloway. The day had been glorious after a dull start and plenty of photographs had been taken, Penny had told them, on the auld bridge where Tam O' Shanter's mare had lost her tail to a witch in the poem, ' Tam O' Shanter' and also down by the river. Canapés had been served outside before the family and close friends had gone into the hotel for the meal. There had only been twenty guests at this part of the proceedings and another thirty had joined them later for dancing and a light supper. All the photographs had been taken at the hotel because the church where they had been married was in the heart of Pollokshaws and it was not very scenic round there. Jack had wanted a church wedding and Margaret Price had been delighted, as she was a churchgoer, as was her daughter when work did not interfere for Penny.

Salma had thought that Mrs Price - Mrs Maclean now - had looked stunning in a cream dress with matching coat, pink hat and shoes. Jack had been in a light grey suit with pink shirt and grey tie. Penny had also chosen to wear a cream outfit, a dress which had swirls of dark brown in it. She had a bolero in cream to wear over it and she and her Mum looked more like sisters than mother and daughter as they stood together waiting to walk down the aisle.

Salma usually wore a salwar kamiz for special occasions but knowing that she would be going with Frank, spared his feelings by wearing a long, pale blue skirt with a white blouse. This set off her shining raven-black hair and Frank had been delighted when he picked her up. He was wearing a dark grey suit and had teamed it with a lemon shirt and dark grey tie.

Now Penny told them that she would be getting the photographs back from her aunt this weekend and would bring them into the station on Monday.

Coffees finished, they made their way back to the station and the interviews which would fill their evening.

CHAPTER 6

It was Saturday evening and the two couples were finishing a meal in Richards on Ayr Road. It was a small restaurant and had only recently reopened after refurbishment.

"Missed this place when it was closed," said Stewart Bolton, looking round. They were the last to leave but the manager did not mind. He knew these three well, nice young folk who had been regulars and one stranger, a young man he had not seen before.

"Do you like the new decoration?" he asked them now, looking round at the white painted walls with psychedelic frieze about head high. He had replaced the steel framed chairs with ones made of heavy plastic which gave the impression of glass. The whole place was much more modern and he wanted their opinion.

"Yes, Jim, I like it," said one of the girls, "but I don't think my mum and dad will. They prefer comfort to style."

"But the seats are comfortable, Jane," retorted her friend.

"I know they are but they don't look it."

Jim looked worried. He wanted to attract the youngsters as they were the big spenders and drank more than the older clientele but he did not want to put off the older people either.

"Come on you lot. Time we weren't here. Have to get into the club before it gets too busy." Stewart was standing up. Looking at her boyfriend, Jane thought, as she often did, how handsome he was, with his almost platinum blond hair and his muscular physique. She never failed to be amazed that he had chosen her, with her mousy fair hair and thin frame.

"Who's driving?" she asked now. They had come in two cars with the girls driving but they had all drunk quite a lot already, even Jane who seldom did drink.

"I'll drive. I've still only got three points on my licence," laughed the other girl.

"George. Don't be silly, we'll get a taxi and pick the cars up tomorrow."

Georgina Laird's blue eyes flashed dangerously.

"Are you telling me what I can or can't do, Barry?"

Jane and her boyfriend Stewart could have told Barry he had made a mistake. Georgina was not one to be given advice, especially once she had had a few drinks. Stewart tried another tactic.

"George. Your new car's fantastic. What if it got dented or scratched in town?"

This worked. Georgina had been given a new white mini cooper for her twenty first birthday, a few weeks previously.

"Ok you guys. Who's phoning for the taxi?" she said now and Jane and Stewart looked at each other in relief.

On the way into Glasgow, the talk turned to the murder at the tennis club. All except Barry were senior members.

"The police came to our house," Georgina volunteered. "Dad thought it was me they wanted to speak to but I didn't know the girl. Anne had put my name in the intermediate list instead of Henry's."

"Who's Henry?" asked Barry.

"My young sister, Henrietta."

"What was the dead girl's name again, George?" asked Jane

"Norma something. Henry knew her."

"Pretty looking girl? Fair hair usually tied back in a pony- tail?" asked Stewart.

"That could be a number of them," laughed Georgina.

"But how awful! Where was she killed?" asked Barry, this being the first time he had heard the news.

"At the tennis club we think. The police didn't give Henry any details," said her sister, "but Anne

Scott phoned the senior women to tell us that there would be no tennis this afternoon so I imagine it must have been at the club somewhere."

"So you're a tennis player, George?" remarked Barry. This was his first date with the woman he had admired from a distance. They had been at school together but he had never been brave enough to ask her out then and only after gaining confidence at university had he become more self- assured and, meeting her coming out of the cinema last week with a girl- friend, he had plucked up courage to ask her out tonight. She had suggested a foursome with her friends, Jane and Stewart.

Tonight she had seemed quite cool and aloof, unlike her friend Jane who seemed at home with Stewart.

"Yes. I love the game. I'm in the first team, second couple but aiming to get to first," she informed him.

"What about you, Jane?" he asked her friend.

"Oh third couple only. I'm not as good as George."

Stewart laughed.

"Not as committed, you mean. You'll need to join the tennis club, Barry if you want to get anywhere with George."

"I wouldn't mind. I used to play at school. Would you like me to join, George?"

"Suit yourself."

Georgina was gathering her jacket and bag as the taxi was pulling up outside the club in Sauchiehall Street and did not see his look of disappointment at her dismissive reaction. However she stayed by his side all evening, seeming uninterested in dancing with any other boy except Stewart and the four left together around 3 am.

Barry had discovered that Stewart and Jane were an 'item' and had been for about six months. Jane had tried to reassure him about Georgina's apparent disinterest in him, telling him that the girl was focussed on both her tennis and her college course in physiotherapy.

"She plays tennis nearly every night of the week," he was told. "Her partner in the team is very keen too and she plays mixed doubles with Don Kinross at least one night a week."

"Does she fancy this Don?"

"Oh, no! He's married and a lot older than her."

This conversation had taken place during a dance and Barry did not get another chance to question Jane about her friend. Now they were almost home. Stewart declared his intention of walking Jane to her door but Georgina refused Barry's offer of an escort, saying that her house was on the main road so she was perfectly safe once the taxi dropped her off.

"I'll get Dad to run me to Richards to collect my car, Jane, in the morning then I'll pick you up and take you to get yours."

"Thanks, George. See you later. Bye Barry. Nice to have met you."

Stewart and Jane walked off arm in arm. George kissed Barry on the cheek. At five foot ten, she was almost as tall as he was.

"Thanks, Barry."

"Will I see you again, George?"

"Yes that'll be great. When?"

"Next Saturday? We could go to the cinema."

"I'd like that. Bye."

Giving him a wide smile, she strolled off up the main road, leaving Barry to get back into the taxi, feeling delighted that she wanted to go out with him again.

Her house was in darkness when she arrived at the top of the drive. Her parents had long since given up staying awake for her at the weekends. She opened the front door and closed it quietly behind her. At the top of the stairs, she switched off the downstairs lights and was on her way to her bedroom when she heard a muffled sound coming from her sister's room. There was a sliver of light beneath the door.

Opening the door, she looked in. Her sister was sitting at her desk and turned round. Her face was puffy and as she took off her glasses, Georgina could see that her eyes were red.

"Henry! What's up?"

The young girl stood up.

"Oh, George, I couldn't get to sleep for thinking about Norma. How could someone kill her? Why would they do that?"

Georgina walked over and took her sister in her arms. They were not usually demonstrative towards each other but her sister obviously needed comforting.

"Come on, Henry. Stop crying. I'm sure Norma wouldn't have suffered."

"How can you be sure? We don't know how he killed her."

Georgina was at a loss for words for once.

"I'll go downstairs and make us both a cup of tea," she said and received a weak smile.

When she returned with the two steaming cups, her sister had composed herself so she handed her one cup and, telling her to get to bed as soon as she had finished the tea, she went to her own room.

Once in bed, she thought about the murder then her thoughts turned to Barry. He seemed a nice guy and he had offered to join the tennis club. Maybe she would invite him home next weekend.

CHAPTER 7

A spotty-faced, gum-chewing teenager, wearing headphones, answered the door of a bungalow in Stamperland. He looked at total odds with his surroundings in his ripped denims and grubby white tee-shirt with "Death to Them All" written on it. Salma and Frank had walked up the short path through an immaculate garden which nestled behind neat hedges.

"Brian Hewitt?" Salma asked, wondering if the boy could hear her.

Casually the boy removed the headphones.

"What did you say?" he asked rudely.

"Brian, who is it?" came a voice from inside the house.

"It's the fuzz, Mum!" he called back,

Immediately a tall, thin woman with what Penny would have called 'wild' reddish hair appeared to stand beside the boy.

"Police? Whatever anyone's said, it wasn't my Brian. He's been in town with me all day."

"Mrs Hewitt?" Salma asked pleasantly.

"Yes and who are you?"

"I'm Sergeant Din and this is PC Selby. May we come in and speak to you for a few minutes?"

"Say what you have to say here."

Another figure appeared behind her.

"Who is it my dear?" enquired a gentle voice.

The woman moved to the side and Salma and Frank saw a tiny little lady with sparse white hair. She was leaning heavily on a Zimmer frame.

"It's the police, Mum," replied the younger woman. "I've just told them that it wasn't Brian as he's been with me all afternoon."

"What wasn't Brian, dear?"

Salma tried again.

"We're not accusing your son of anything, Mrs Hewitt. Please may we come in and I'll tell you what we're here for."

The old lady took charge.

"Of course you must come in. Jean dear, step aside and let them in and Brian pet, take those headphones off and give your ears a rest."

Rather sheepishly, the youngster did as he was told and led the way into the lounge where a large TV dominated the room. Luckily it was off. The old lady made her way to a chair by the fire, a gas one mounted on the wall. Her daughter and son sat down on the settee, leaving one chair for Salma. Frank leaned on a wall just inside the room.

"Mrs Hewitt, there's been a murder at your son's tennis club. We just want to..."

"...speak up dear. There's been a what at the tennis club?" the old lady enquired.

"A murder," Salma said loudly.

"Surely you don't think my Brian had anything to do with that. I know he's been in trouble with you folk before but..."

"Mrs Hewitt. Please would you hear me out. We're not here to blame Brian. We just want to ask him a few questions."

Slightly mollified but still looking protective, the woman sat back on the settee and Salma turned to Brian who was looking interested.

"Who's been murdered?"

His accent Frank noticed had become middle class suddenly and he wondered if the tough demeanour was an act. He imagined that this unattractive young lad might be bullied at school and had developed this front as a defence. Salma would have been surprised to know his thoughts, not expecting such insight from the normally cynical PC.

"Do you know a girl called Norma Lawson?" Salma asked the boy.

"She's in my class at school. Is she dead? Who killed her?"

"Don't you know her from the tennis club?" Salma queried.

The sullen look was back.

"I don't play tennis. Mum did you renew my membership? I told you not to. It's a sissies' game."

"Dear, I did it in case you changed your mind."

"Well I won't."

"OK, Brian. Can you tell me about any friends that Norma had in school?"

"She goes about with Mary McGregor all the time. Think they're God's gift, always eyeing up the older boys. Norma never used to be like that. She was good fun in first year."

"What about Zoe Stewart?"

"What about her?"

"Is she not a school friend of Norma's?"

"Naw. She's a Tim…"

"Brian! That's not a nice word," said the old lady.

"Sorry, Gran."

The boy looked across at the old lady and smiled. He was obviously fond of the old woman and really did look sorry.

"Zoe goes to a Catholic School," he said.

"You've never seen Norma talking to any boy in particular?"

"Nup. As I said, she and Mary try to chat to the older boys but I've never seen any of them looking interested."

"Thanks, Brian. If you remember anything else please get in touch with me at Govanhill Station. Sergeant Din's my name."

Thanking Mrs Hewitt and her mother, Salma got up and walked to the door. She heard the old lady say in a puzzled tone, "What does your tee-shirt say son? Death to whom?"

"Nothing, Gran. It's just a joke."

"Time the joke had a wash isn't it?" were the last words they heard before they were back outside and walking back down the path.

"Phew! What a dysfunctional group they were, Sarge. Wonder if there's a Mr Hewitt."

"Don't think so, Frank. I looked into the kitchen as we passed and the table was set there for three people. Mind you, he might be away."

"I'd be away if I was him," laughed Frank. "A shrew for a wife, a spotty weirdo for a son and a mother-in-law who's deaf."

"But wasn't she lovely?"

"Yes. I'll give you that and she has more influence over the boy than his mother has."

"No further forward are we? Except negative stuff like Norma hadn't a boyfriend at school."

They had no more luck with the remaining four boys. All went to the same school and all agreed with Brian that Norma and her friend had eyes only for the older boys. Peter Jenkins confirmed what his father had said, that he'd liked Norma but she wasn't interested in him, or any boys. Peter had been at BB on Friday evening. Frank noted one comment from the boy they saw last, namely that Norma had only time for the senior men at tennis too.

"Any man in particular?" Frank had asked him.

"She was annoyed when she got partnered with Don...Donald Kinross. I heard her say to Zoe that she had wanted one of the younger seniors. Didn't stop her flirting with Donald though and he's married and in his forties."

The youngster had sounded disgusted and Frank told Salma on the way to the next house that he thought that the lad had fancied Norma himself. He had been at home on Friday evening with his mother and sister. His sister confirmed this "Don't imagine he'd have had the strength to choke her to death Frank but put his name down anyway. We've little enough to tell as it is."

Frank duly noted the name Neil Smith in his notebook.

It was by now a little after 7pm and they still had two senior men to see. Davenport had given them two who lived quite close to each other in Barlae Avenue in Waterfoot which was a short drive from the last house which had been in Muirend. Frank drove as Salma preferred this to listening to him complain about her driving. Frank thought all women drivers should be banned from the roads. This incensed Penny but only amused Salma.

The first senior male was a young man in his early twenties. He was in the shower, his mother told them, getting ready for an evening out with his fiancée. When told what they wanted him for, she went into the hall and told him to hurry up, that the police were here and wanted to speak to him. He came into the room, towelling his hair dry on a large towel and wearing only a pair of jeans. His feet were bare.

"What's wrong?" he asked.

"Sorry to interrupt you, Sir," said Frank, taking his turn at the questioning. "There's been a murder at Greenway tennis Club. A young girl called Norma Lawson was found dead in one of the changing rooms this morning."

Salma made a mental note to pick Frank up on what he had said. He should not have mentioned exactly where the body had been found as sometimes a murderer could be trapped into revealing knowledge they should not have had.

"Norma! God, she's... she was a lovely girl. Bit of a flirt this year. Think she'd just discovered boys."

"Any boy in particular, Mr Bentley?" asked Frank, hopefully.

"Not really the boys, constable, more the senior men. She pestered me quite a bit actually. I had to be quite blunt and tell her I was engaged to Nancy."

The young man blushed.

"Anybody else, Sir?" enquired Salma.

"Nobody in particular, just everyone in general I would say, except the older men although I think she gave Don Kinross a hard time when he partnered her in an American Tournament and he's old enough to be her father."

"Sorry to have to ask this, Sir but where were you on Friday evening?" asked Frank.

"Out with Nancy, at the pictures."

"Interesting that, Salma," said Frank on their way to the next house. "Maybe what Norma was looking for was a father figure. Did the boss not say her Mum had remarried?"

"Yes. Wonder what happened to her father - dead? Divorced? Wonder if she still saw him."

They were unlucky at the next house as the man was at a meeting of the Round Table. His wife took them into the lounge and listened to their story. A woman in her mid- fifties, she laughed when they asked if Norma could have flirted with her husband.

"I love him dearly," she said. "But I doubt if he'd be a young girl's cup of tea."

She left the room and returned with a photograph album.

"These were taken last year on holiday," she said. "This is Ken."

Salma and Frank looked at the picture of a portly, completely bald man.

"Afraid he doesn't play much tennis nowadays. His tummy slows him down."

They thanked her, asked her to tell her husband to let them know if he had seen any particular man with Norma during any of his few visits to the club and left.

It was almost 8pm.

"Right, Frank, I think that's all we can do for now. Run me back to the station to pick up my car and we can get off home."

CHAPTER 8

Lucy Collins was a bubbly, likeable young girl. Davenport had explained to her father why he wanted to see Lucy and Mr Collins went to the living room door and shouted upstairs, telling her to come down. They heard footsteps running along the top landing and then clattering down the stairs and a mini whirlwind entered the room.

"Here I am, Dad. What is it?"

"Whoa, Lucy. Take your time. You'll fall down those stairs one day."

Lucy gave him a cheerful grin and looked questioningly at the two others in the room.

Her father introduced them.

"This is DCI Davenport and PC Price. Lucy pet, I'm afraid that there's been someone killed at the tennis club."

"Killed? How? Who?"

The youngster looked interested rather than horrified.

"Norma Lawson. She was found this morning at the tennis club," Davenport told her.

"Oh, poor Norma. She had an unhappy life and now she's dead."

"Unhappy? Why was her life unhappy, Lucy?" asked Davenport.

"Well, her Mum and Dad split up. My Mum died but Dad and I are really happy just the two of us. Aren't we Dad?"

"Yes pet, we are but Mr Davenport doesn't want to know about us." Mr Collins sounded and looked embarrassed.

"Sorry. Well, Norma and her Mum got on really well too but her Mum met another man and they got married and then last year they moved over here. Norma had to leave her school in Bearsden and all her friends and she didn't like her stepfather and she has two brothers, they're twins and they get all the attention, Norma says."

Lucy paused for breath.

"How do you know all this, Lucy? Were you friends with Norma?"

"I'm friends with everyone. She's special friends with Zoe Stewart but we went to the cafe one afternoon after tennis and she told me all about her Mum then. She said she couldn't wait to leave home. I asked her about her Dad and she said that her mother wouldn't let her see him - he's got a girl-friend."

"Lucy!"

"Sorry, Dad but he has. Where was I? Oh yes, I said I would want to see my Mum if she was alive and she said she wanted to see her Dad and that he came to the school gates one day and she told him to write to her and send it to Zoe's address and Zoe's Mum didn't mind 'cos she thought it was wrong that Norma couldn't see her dad and..."

She stopped, breathless and Davenport took the chance to ask another question.

"Did Norma have a boyfriend?"

"Don't think so. She goes around with Zoe at tennis and at school with a girl whose name I don't know. We're not in the same class in second year," Lucy explained.

Davenport got to his feet and Penny did the same. She smiled at Lucy and Lucy grinned back, then her face fell.

"I'd forgotten that Norma's dead. Who would want to kill her? Was it one of those ped...peda..."

"Paedophiles, Lucy? We don't know who killed her yet," said Davenport. "I don't suppose you've ever seen anyone hanging around the tennis club?"

"No, just those silly boys who drive past and shout, 'Anyone for tennis!' They think they're so funny and they all just say the same thing!"

The four of them walked into the hall. It was an impressive entrance with sweeping staircase.

As well as the living room, there were six other doors downstairs and, Penny guessed, about five bedrooms upstairs. The sound of voices came from one room. Mr Collins explained,

"My sister and her husband are here tonight. Lucy has her cousin Ben upstairs with her. He'll be on the computer no doubt."

"Can I go back up, Dad?" Lucy asked.

"Yes pet."

Lucy climbed the stairs, slowly this time, deep in thought.

"Mr Collins," Penny asked, remembering something, "you said *the* tennis club, not *your* tennis club. Are you a member too?"

"I am. I started with Lucy to give her someone to play with and I'm now part of the third couple in the gents' first team. She doesn't need me now but I enjoy it."

"Do you know Donald ...Don..."

"Kinross. Yes, he's in the gents' first team too. He's a nice guy. Why do you ask?"

"Just that he partnered Norma in some tournament recently."

"Yes, the American Tournament at the start of the season last week. He's a married man with two children, Inspector. Surely you don't suspect him?"

"Everyone's a suspect right now, Sir. That's what happens in a murder enquiry."

"I only play on team practice night, Tuesday, Inspector. I only saw Norma once at the tournament. Lucy mentioned her name."

"I have to ask, Sir, where you were on Friday night," apologised Davenport.

"Here at home and by myself, I'm afraid. Lucy was at her aunt's."

Thanking him for his time, Davenport and Penny walked back down the long driveway and out onto the main road where they had left Davenport's grey Audi parked half up on the pavement.

"Well we've learned a few things, Penny," said Davenport, settling in behind the wheel.

"Firstly, Norma's Dad was in touch,unbeknown to her Mum. We'll need to have a look in her room, see if we can find his address without asking Mrs Gilbert, if possible. Lucy said that Norma couldn't wait to leave home. Maybe she was pestering her Dad to take her and his girlfriend wouldn't have been pleased."

"But kill your own daughter, Sir? Surely not." Penny was horrified.

"I hope not. Penny, well done for picking up that Mr Collins was a member too. That's one senior we can take off the list."

Davenport looked at their list.

"He must be on Frank and Salma's list. Better give them a ring. Then we'll do three senior males and finish off. It's nearly 7 pm and I doubt we'll get many men in much later than this on a Saturday night."

They tried three more men. One was recovering from a bad dose of flu. He had been in bed since Wednesday and had only got up to watch something on TV. He was lying on the settee wrapped up in a blanket and looked very pale and wan.

He and his wife, both members of Greenway tennis club, expressed their horror at the murder. Mrs Hughes had been told by Anne Scott that afternoon on the phone.

The next man, Stewart Bolton, informed them that he had heard from Georgina Laird and his girlfriend Jane Green. Stewart told them what he said he had told Jane and Georgina last night, that he remembered her as a pretty, fair-haired girl with her hair in a pony- tail. He did not think that he had ever spoken to her.

"Too young for me," he had laughed, then looked as if wished he had not, when he saw Penny's look of disapproval.

"Where were you on Friday evening, Mr Bolton?" Davenport asked.

"Out at Jane, my girl-friend's," he replied.

"Was there anyone else there?"

"No, just us."

The one they really wanted to see, Donald Kinross, was out. His house in Netherlee was in darkness.

"Right Penny, home for us now."

They arrived back at the station. Salma's car had gone so she and Frank must have finished for the night. Davenport offered Penny a cup of coffee from his coffee maker. Pippa was at her Aunt Linda's so he had no need to hurry home. It was a big improvement from the canteen's excuse for coffee and over it they discussed the people they had seen.

CHAPTER 9

Charles had phoned Fiona Macdonald on Sunday morning to suggest that they did a visit to Norma's house during the afternoon and kept the evening for some more senior men visits.

"I'll drop Pippa off at Hazel's. She's having her meal with them. You and I can go and eat somewhere or go back to mine and have a carry-out and I'll pick her up after I drop you off later."

She looked out for him turning into her street in Shawlands and ran down the stairs quickly to prevent him having to try to find somewhere to park.

"Thanks for being ready. This place is a nightmare to get parked."

"Tell me about it! Try living here. I was parked round the corner but someone moved out this morning so I nipped out and re-parked."

Fiona settled back in the comfort of her boss's new car.

"This is beautiful, Charles, much better than my old Fiat!"

It took them about twenty minutes to drive to Waterfoot and soon they were once again walking up the short path to the door of number 51. Charles rang the bell.

It was Norma's mother who answered the door. If she had looked harassed the last time, she looked even worse this time.

"Sorry to bother you, Mrs Gilbert," said Davenport.

"No bother. We expected you but didn't know when you'd come. I'm afraid Gavin's out with the boys again but then maybe you prefer that. It'll give us some peace to talk."

Mrs Gilbert took them again into the sparsely furnished lounge and they took the same seats as before.

"Sorry to have to ask you this, Mrs Gilbert but did Norma see her father at all?" asked Davenport.

"No she didn't!" the woman said angrily. A tendril of hair slipped over her face and she undid the elastic band and secured the stray strand in the pony tail. Her face looked shut. She obviously did not like talking about her ex-husband but Davenport could not afford the luxury of pandering to her right now.

"Why are you so sure?" he asked her.

"Because I got an injunction to prevent him seeing her. The divorce was all his fault and when he took up with his fancy piece, he lost all rights to Norma."

"How did Norma feel about that?" Fiona questioned.

The woman looked uncomfortable.

"She wanted to see him. She was too young to understand but I think she grew to accept it. She hasn't mentioned him for ages, not since we moved over here in fact."

"I wonder if we could see Norma's room. There might be some clue as to who she was seeing or who she..."

"Fancied? I doubt you'll find any girlish diary entries about a hoped-for romance. Norma wasn't interested in boys. She told me that she and her friend Zoe didn't like boys and that she had no intention of every marrying. I hoped she'd change her mind and realise that all men weren't the rats her father and his sort are."

Mrs Gilbert got to her feet. Davenport and Fiona followed suit.

They climbed the stairs and the woman opened the door to one of the tiniest bedrooms Fiona had ever seen. Perhaps sensing their unspoken thoughts, the woman said, "We gave the boys the bigger bedroom as there are two of them."

Fiona wondered how often the two three-year olds stayed in their rooms. Bunk beds would have been adequate for them and Norma could have had the bigger space that befitted a teenage girl. She must have felt as if she was being pushed out of the new family circle.

"There's not enough room for three of us in here, Mrs Gilbert. Perhaps you would just leave us to look for ourselves," said Davenport.

Reluctantly, the woman agreed and they heard her go back downstairs.

"Poor kid. This wouldn't make her feel wanted," Charles echoed Fiona's thoughts.

There was a small single bed, wardrobe and chest of drawers squeezed into the space. Davenport opened the top drawer. It contained bits and pieces of makeup, hair decorations, writing paper and envelopes, a book of second class stamps with two stamps left in it, a couple of cheap, plastic bracelets in red and black and a small, square jewellery box. He opened it and found a gold chain with a gold teddy bear attached to it. A piece of paper inside the box read, "Love from Dad."

"What a shame. The best piece of jewellery she had and she couldn't wear it openly," said Davenport, thinking of Pippa and how she would have worn this proudly and shown all her friends.

He felt to the back of the drawer but there was nothing else. The next drawer contained underwear, childish cotton bras and what Fiona would have called 'serviceable' panties and the bottom drawer held three jumpers and one sweatshirt.

Fiona opened the wardrobe. There was not much in there: one school blazer, an anorak, two white school blouses, a pair of denims and a pair of white summer trousers and, on a skirt hanger, a navy blue pleated school skirt. On the floor of the wardrobe were three shoe boxes, one containing flat, black shoes, one containing a pair of sandals and an empty one. A holdall containing tennis clothes and trainers was on top of the shoes and Fiona noticed the tennis racket, lying against the wall between wardrobe and chest of drawers.

Davenport picked up a photograph which sat on top of the chest. It showed a young Norma in between a man and a woman, a younger, smiling Mrs Gilbert. Mr Lawson had his arms round his wife and daughter. He was a tall, slim man with a head of reddish fair hair, quite the antithesis of her stepfather.

"Seen enough, Fiona?" Davenport asked.

"Yes. Wait a minute, I'll just look under the shoes. I kept my diary under the tissue paper in my shoe box when I was young."

A search under the shoes did not turn up a diary but it did reveal a letter.

Fiona read it and passed it to Davenport who read it then put it in his pocket.

They went back downstairs. Mrs Gilbert met them in the hall.

"Did you find anything?"

Davenport toyed with the idea of saying truthfully that *he* had found nothing but the woman had the right to know.

He took the letter out of his pocket and handed it to her. She read it, getting more and more agitated as she read on.

"It looks as if Norma was in contact with her father after all, Mrs Gilbert."

"It says here that he'd love to have her stay with him but that his...woman wouldn't like it. Surely Norma wouldn't have left me."

Thinking of the tiny, cramped bedroom and the meagre supply of clothes, Fiona was not so sure.

Davenport put out his hand for the letter and, reluctantly, the woman handed it over. They thanked her for her help and telling her that they would keep her informed when they had any information, they left.

"At least we now have Norma's father's address," Davenport said as they reached the gate.

Fiona had opted for a take-away meal at Charles's house so they went across to Newton Mearns. Charles phoned the local Chinese Restaurant and ordered sweet and sour prawns for himself and lemon chicken for Fiona with one portion of boiled rice to share. Over this meal they discussed the case, and then the talk turned to more personal things. Charles, Pippa and Fiona had booked a holiday in Malaysia in July and when they were together, talk was often about this new venture.

"You'll need to come up for the evening soon, Fiona. Pippa wants to talk to you about what clothes to take."

"Do you want me to go shopping with her one Saturday? Has she to get new clothes?"

"Good idea. We could all shop and then I could meet up with the two of you for lunch and then you could come back here for the evening. I've still to show you my train set."

This was a standing joke as Charles knew of Fiona's hobby of reading Chalet School books and was always saying that he should show her *his* childish hobby.

Meal over, they visited two senior men who lived in Netherlee. Arthur Mackay was, he said, only an honorary member. He had been one of the club's first junior members and now, in his eighties, was always sent a membership card. The second man, Donald Kinross, was a good-looking man in his late thirties. He had been told about the murder and invited them in.

"Afraid we have only one public room, Inspector. I hope you don't mind my wife being here. She's not a member of the club but she knows what has happened."

Mrs Kinross, a plain looking woman with mousey-fair hair, smiled at them nervously from her seat by the fireside.

"Mr Kinross. You knew Norma Lawson quite well..."

"Not well, Inspector. I played in one tournament with her, that's all."

"I've heard that she had become a bit of a flirt. Did she try to flirt with you?"

"Not that I noticed."

"Don's a good-looking man, Inspector," said his wife. "I don't expect he notices being flirted with any more."

Was he imagining it, thought Davenport, or was there a touch of bitterness in that remark.

"Olive!" said Donald Kinross. "You'll be giving the Inspector the wrong idea."

Davenport laughed to lighten the atmosphere.

"I imagine wherever there are teenage girls, there'll be flirting and crushes," he said.

Fiona asked the man if he had noticed Norma paying any attention to any other men, young or old, at the tennis courts and looking rueful, the man admitted that he had not seen any signs of Norma chatting up any of the men.

"Not that I saw her very often. I played on team practice night usually, with my male partner, Harry Grey and sometimes with my mixed doubles partner, Sheila Ferguson."

At the sound of the last name, his wife gave a wry smile but said nothing.

"Where were you on the night of last Friday?"

"I left Carlisle at about 6.30 and got home around 9 I think. Olive?"

"A bit later I would say, around 9.30."

Davenport thanked him, saying the usual thing about getting in touch if he remembered anything which might be relevant and he and Fiona left the house. They had to walk quite a way to get to the car as the streets here were bumper to bumper with cars. Once inside, Charles asked Fiona if she had got any vibes from the interview.

"Think the flirtation, or more, was with this Sheila Ferguson if his wife's reaction to the name was anything to go by. I think she's got her work cut out keeping her husband by her side."

"Exactly what I thought, Fiona. I think he has a couple of kids so maybe he doesn't get all the attention he wants from his wife."

"Enough of a ladies' man to try it on with a fourteen-year old?"

"Perhaps."

It being after 9 pm, Charles said he must collect his daughter from her friend Hazel's and Fiona told him to do this before dropping her off as she had not seen Pippa for some time.

Pippa came out to the car and chatted happily about what she and Hazel had been doing then Fiona suggested some holiday shopping in town one weekend soon and Pippa readily agreed.

Charles stopped the car outside Fiona's close and she got out.

"See you tomorrow bright and early, boss."

CHAPTER 10

Charles was in the station early on Monday morning. Pippa was quite used to being dropped off early at school. Her young teacher, Miss Jackson, a farmer's daughter, was an early riser and was always in school by 8 am and she was happy for Pippa to sit and read in the classroom, on occasions.

He was putting his notes into the computer as he always did for himself, finding it easier to flesh out his jottings rather than give it to a secretary to do, when the phone rang and the sergeant at the desk informed him that he had Martin Jamieson on the line.

"Charles. I worked on the body yesterday. Kath was away for the day visiting her mother and she took the children so I had spare time."

He cut short Charles's thanks.

"I hate these cases involving youngsters and it would have been on my mind all day anyway."

Charles asked him what his findings were.

"Well, she was raped. Unfortunately like a lot of rapists, he did not ejaculate so there was no semen. She was a virgin as you might expect, being only fourteen. I found her travel-card in her pocket and that gave me her date of birth. She had bled but other than that there were no other injuries except round her throat of course where she had been strangled - manually, by someone who put his hands round her throat from behind.."

"From behind?"

"Yes. There were three indentations from the fingers of both hands. She had eaten about two hours previously, a decent sized meal, and from the temperature of the body, taken that it was a cold night on Friday, I would say that she died between 8 and 12 midnight. Sorry I cannot be more exact than that."

"Thank you for that, Martin. It's a pity about the lack of semen. Were there any other traces of anything that might help us?"

"Sorry, no. Her nails were bitten down so short that even if she had dug them into her attacker's hands they would not have made any impression and there was no fingernail to find any skin under. SOC might have found some tell-tale hairs but I do not imagine anyone hoovers in the changing rooms so the carpet will have all sorts on it."

"What was she wearing, Martin?" Charles asked.

"A white bra, a white blouse with most of the buttons undone, black mini skirt, denim jacket, high black socks and kitten-heeled black shoes."

"Were all the blouse buttons intact?"

"Yes, so maybe she did not struggle at first," Martin suggested.

"What about makeup?"

"She had eye shadow and a trace of lipstick. That is all."

Charles thanked him again for his speedy work and Martin rang off, promising to put all this information in writing as soon as possible. He wrote as he spoke, very grammatically correct. He was never as fast with his paper work as he was with his reporting but Charles preferred it that way. At least he had something to go on, now that the expected rape had been confirmed.

The sound of girlish voices talking and laughing came to his ears and he went to the door of his room. It was Salma and Penny.

"Hi, girls," he said.

"Morning, Sir," came the reply. "Do you want us to come into the Incident Room now?"

"It's only 8.40. You've got time for a tea or coffee in the canteen first if you want."

They went into their own room to remove their coats and hats then went down to the station canteen which was empty.

"I'll get it," said Penny. She knew that Salma liked tea at this time in the morning.

Carrying two mugs, she joined her friend at one of the Formica-topped tables which was clean and not covered in food and drink stains as it would be later in the day. Now that Penny had a steady boyfriend, the two women did not see so much of each other so they had some catching up to do.

"Is there any word of your flat yet?" Salma asked. She knew that Penny was moving in with Alec who had been a friend all through childhood.

"Alec's offered me an entrance date any time after Saturday. He's got his cousin staying for a few days."

Penny had hoped to be out of the house she shared with her mother, before the newly-weds got back from their honeymoon but Alec had reneged on his offer of a room in his flat when it appeared that his boyfriend Phil was going to move in. However, at the last minute, Phil had opted out, realising what a big commitment he was making and Alec had sheepishly approached Penny to ask if she was still interested, which she was.

"Need any help with the move?" Salma asked now.

"Oh yes, that would be great. That is if we can get time off with this new murder."

"You have to get time off for a removal," Salma informed her.

"I know but maybe you wouldn't. I can always postpone the move. Alec will be happy as long as I'm paying rent!"

Salma looked at her watch. It was almost 9 am. She got to her feet. Penny followed suit. They took their empty mugs back to the serving hatch and were thanked by the canteen worker.

"Hope Frank's on time," said Penny as they climbed the stairs. Frank was not noted for his punctuality. However, as they rounded the corner, Frank was coming along the corridor, in deep conversation with DS Macdonald. The two couples headed for the Incident Room.

Davenport was waiting for them. He was standing by a white board on which was an enlarged picture of Norma Lawson's prone body.

"Grab seats, team and let's get started. Thanks for being so punctual." He looked at Frank who reddened.

"Right, firstly I've heard from Martin Jamieson. Norma was raped. There's no chance of getting DNA from sperm as there wasn't any. As Martin reminded me, a lot of rapists don't actually ejaculate and this one didn't. It's true, Frank," he added, as this young man was looking sceptical. "She was strangled manually, from behind. Either she arrived with no pants on or the rapist took them away."

"Did she have make-up on, Sir?" asked Penny who could never wait to be given details.

"Just a little. Why, Penny?"

"It's just that her friend Zoe Stewart said that Norma had started wearing make-up, much to Zoe's disgust as previously they had said they weren't going to wear it. I wondered if Norma had planned to meet the rapist."

"Seems like she may have," Davenport conceded. He wrote the name Zoe Stewart on the white board and continued, "Now that you've started telling us what you and Salma found out, maybe you'd like to continue with your findings."

Penny looked at Salma who opened her notebook.

"We saw Henrietta Laird. She lives in a big house in Waterfoot. Actually we got her big sister at first as the membership secretary had Georgina Laird down as an intermediate. She pointed out the mistake and we spoke to her young sister who said all the intermediate girls were friendly but I don't think that's strictly true as two of them told us they only played with each other twice a week after school and had refused to make up the numbers for an intermediate team."

Salma looked at Penny who continued.

"Henrietta - Henry - Laird said that Norma didn't have a boyfriend but Zoe Stewart who lives in a flat in Clarkston and seems to have been Norma's best friend at tennis, wasn't so sure about that because of the makeup. She and Norma had kind of fallen out over that."

"That leaves one girl." said Davenport. He now had four names on the board alongside that of Norma.

"Actually it's two, Sir. Think whoever said six intermediate girls must have meant six apart from Norma," said Salma. "We saw a Samantha McMillan who didn't think there was a boyfriend."

"And Sir, you and I saw the last girl," chipped in Penny.

"That's right. May as well mention her now and that finishes with the intermediate girls. Go on Penny."

"Lucy Collins, a lovely, friendly youngster."

"Just like you," Salma thought, looking at her friend whose red cheeks were glowing with health. Penny talked to everyone she met.

Penny was continuing.

"She mentioned that Norma was getting letters from her father."

"Thanks, Penny. DS Macdonald and I visited Norma's home yesterday afternoon and found a letter from her Dad in a shoebox in Norma's room. It was obvious from the letter that Norma wanted to go and live with her Dad but that his new woman wasn't happy with this."

"It was obvious that Norma's mother knew nothing about this," said Fiona. "Norma also had a chain which her Dad had given her, still in its box in her drawer and we think she would have worn it if her Mum knew about it."

"What about the intermediate boys?" Davenport turned his attention to Frank.

Bob Grey was busy on the desk and had left his colleague to do the reporting for both of them.

"One boy didn't even know Norma's second name. His name was Robin Stevenson. Another, Gregory Browne, knew her because she visited Zoe who lives upstairs from him. He mentioned that Norma had partnered one of the senior men in an American Tournament last week."

"That's Donald Kinross, Frank," said Davenport. He began a new list headed intermediate males.

"Yes, Sir. Another boy quite fancied Norma, according to his Dad, but didn't do anything about it because he thought that Norma wasn't interested in boys."

"What was his name, Frank?" asked his boss.

"Peter Jenkins. He was at the BB on Friday night."

This name was written on the board.

"We interviewed another boy but he said he had given up tennis though his mother had paid his fees for this year," Salma added. "He did know Norma from school though and said that she and her friend Mary tried to chat to the older boys."

"We'll need to see this girl, Mary. Anyone know her surname?" asked Davenport.

There was a chorus of, "No Sir," and he added Mary ? to his list of names on the board. "What was this boy's name, Salma?"

Salma glanced at her notebook.

"Brian Hewitt. Oh sorry, Sir. I've written Mary's surname down. He said it was Mary McGregor."

Davenport rubbed out the question mark and replaced it with McGregor.

"He said that Zoe was Catholic and didn't go to the same school as he and Mary and Norma did," Frank added.

He continued, "Salma and I saw four more boys."

He gave their names to Davenport.

"There was nothing new from them except one, Neil Smith, who agreed with what Brian Hewitt had said about older boys and that Norma had flirted with Donald Kinross.

"Do they all have alibis for Friday evening, Selby?"

"Neil Smith was at home with his mother and sister, Sir. His sister was in and confirmed that. David Bentley was at the pictures with Nancy, his fiancée. He said that Norma came on to him and he had to tell her he was engaged to Nancy."

Davenport thanked Frank. He looked at his own notebook.

"Stewart Bolton was at his girl-friend Jane's house and ...

"...so he said," chipped in Penny. "There was no one else in to confirm that."

"...and Kevin Collins whose daughter Lucy is a member and is Norma's age, was in alone. He's a reserve for the first team and only plays on team night which is Tuesday and that finishes the intermediates," said Davenport. "Now let's do the senior men."

He wrote SENIOR MEN on the board and underlined it.

"First, Donald Kinross. Fiona, take it from there."

"The DCI and I visited his home yesterday afternoon. We got the impression that he was a bit of a ladies' man but that he was paying attention to one of the senior women rather than Norma. Not that that means he was immune to a teenager fancying him. He was on the way home from Carlisle and got there around 9.30, according to his wife."

"You can rule out Kenneth Ross. He's balding, in his fifties and plump and seldom plays tennis nowadays," said Salma.

"And Arthur Mackay. He's in his eighties and only an honorary member," said Fiona.

"And Mr Hughes. What was his name, Sir? I forgot to write it down," said Penny. "He's been ill in bed since Wednesday."

"Bill," said Davenport adding the name to his list.

Penny had one more comment to make..

"Stewart Bolton, Sir, I didn't like him much. He seemed to be amused about Norma flirting, said she was too young for him."

"Don't be hard on the guy, Penny," said Davenport. "He looked quite embarrassed after he said that."

Frank gave him the final name to add to his list.

"Peter's dad, Mr Jenkins, said he'd played one game against Norma and Zoe at the end of last season and Norma had just been a giggly teenager. She certainly hadn't flirted with him or his son, he said. I asked where he had been and he was at home alone, Peter being out."

Davenport added up the list.

"That's eight men altogether so we have seven still to see."

"Do you think she was maybe looking for a father figure, Sir?" asked Frank.

"I might have thought that, Frank, if we didn't have proof that she had seen her father at the school gates not that long ago. Penny didn't tell you all that?"

"Sorry, Sir," Penny said.

"My fault too." He smiled at her.

"Maybe Donald Kinross's partner..." Penny turned over a page in her notebook "...Harry

Grey, might be able to tell us more about Norma's flirting with Donald."

"Right, team." Davenport rubbed his nose.

"Maybe he's worn away his ear," whispered Frank to Penny.

"Maybe he's what, Frank?" asked Davenport.

"Nothing Sir," mumbled Frank.

Luckily for him, his boss was thinking of other things and did not press the matter.

"Right, as I was saying, we've another seven to see. Frank, you and Penny go tonight and see this Harry Grey and then visit the next three men. Salma, you and Bob can do the remaining three on the list. I'll go to the school this afternoon and talk with Mary McGregor. Meanwhile, get your notes written up, everyone."

CHAPTER 11

Davenport, having typed up his notes, went back to his room for his coat. It was still quite cool being mid- April. He knew that as soon as he left them alone, Penny's first job would be to sort out Frank's notes. He was good on the computer but his notes got into a mess and Penny helped him put them into a sensible order for typing. Sure enough, as he passed the room which Frank and Penny shared with Salma, Penny was scribbling away in a notebook with Frank looking over her shoulder. As he continued on down the corridor, he missed Salma telling Frank off for making fun of their boss's habit of pulling on an ear lobe when concentrating.

"One of these days, Frank, he'll catch you and then you'll be in big trouble."

Frank just shrugged his shoulders, nonchalantly. He was incorrigible but he really had been trying with his timekeeping and his uniform was always neat now and his shoes polished.

Davenport could not find a space in the school car park so he drove back out and parked on the road. He walked towards the door and had to buzz the janitor to let him in and show his identity card once in. He was glad to see that this school at least was still being careful about letting strangers in. In the aftermath of the Dunblane shootings, all schools had been very vigilant but he suspected that some would be a bit more lax now.

He walked toward the sliding window of the office and one of the office staff opened it. Once again he showed his card and asked if he could see Mary McGregor who was in S2. He was asked to take a seat and shortly a young man came along to speak to him.

"DCI Davenport?"

"Yes."

"My name's David Greaves. I'm depute head in charge of S1 and S2. I believe you want to talk to Mary McGregor. I'm sorry, she's absent today."

"Have you had a phone call from Norma Lawson's family today?"

"No."

Davenport was in a quandary now. Should he inform the school about what had happened? He thought not.

"Norma won't be in but I should really let the family contact you, Sir," he said. "Thanks for your time. If you would just let me have Mary's address, I would be very grateful."

The young man went into the office and returned with a slip of paper which he handed over. Davenport thanked him and left. Once back in his car, he rang Fiona Macdonald at the station and informed her that he was on his way to Mary McGregor's house.

Mary lived in Waterfoot, in a street which led off from the main road. An elderly man came to the door, leaning heavily on a walking stick. He had a shock of white hair and a white moustache.

Davenport showed his credentials once more and was invited in. The man looked unsure about what to do and his words confirmed this.

"Mary's upstairs, Mr Davenport. She had a phone call from Norma's mother last night. Mrs Gilbert didn't want her to go to school and maybe get the news there. She knew it would be a terrible shock. I don't know if my daughter –in-law would like you to speak to Mary without her here."

"Can you contact her, Sir?" asked Davenport.

"Of course."

The man went into the hall. There was a silence then he could be heard asking to speak to June McGregor.

"June. Dad here. The police have come to speak to Mary about Norma. What do you want me to do?"

There was the sound of the receiver being replaced then the old man returned. He was very frail and quite shaky on his legs.

"My daughter-in-law realises that you want to speak to Mary as quickly as possible but she's a doctor and can't get away till about three. Could you come back?"

Davenport could do nothing except agree to do this so, thanking the old man, he took his leave. There was no point in going back to Govanhill so he drove up to Clarkston and was lucky to get parked on the main road there. He went into a small delicatessen cum tearoom and ordered a cappuccino and a chocolate chip muffin. He was trying to diet but was easily tempted by the array of cakes and tea-breads on display. Someone had left The Daily Mail and he picked it up, wondering how soon it would be before the press got hold of the murder. The paper, not his favourite, did not hold his interest for long and he ended up people-watching, one of his favourite pastimes and one which annoyed his daughter Pippa. At the thought of Pippa, he realised that he might not be able to pick her up from school so he rang his sister and arranged for her to pick Pippa up and take her to her house as she often did in these circumstances.

A young woman was sitting nursing a cup of something steaming and looking out of the window. Her face lit up as she saw a man coming towards the door. He came towards her and gave her a kiss on the cheek. She was a good-looking girl with auburn hair falling in a shiny curtain to below her shoulders. The man was verging on plain, stockily built and dressed in a well-worn suit. From where he sat, Charles could not hear them talking so he amused himself with inventing a story about them. They were having an affair and grabbing an opportunity to meet in the middle of the day. The man ordered a drink but when the girl finished hers, he left his and they went out together, fuelling Davenport's fertile imagination. They were going off to a hotel, he thought.

Laughing at himself, he looked at his watch and noticed that it was 2.50. He put the paper back where it had been and left.

This time it was a young woman who answered the door.

"Hello, Inspector. I'm sorry I had to make you come back but I really had to be present when you interviewed Mary. She didn't sleep much last night and is very upset. I had to give her something to make her sleep and she was still asleep when you came earlier, so Dad said. I couldn't have asked him to cope. He's just out of hospital after having had his hip replaced and is still quite shaky."

Davenport reassured her and asked if Mary was now awake. By this time he was in the lounge. It was one of those lounge and kitchen downstairs and two bedrooms upstairs' houses which had been popular as starter homes in the seventies. The room was empty.

"Dad's gone for a lie down. I'll get Mary."

She left the room and he heard her footsteps going up the stairs and then two sets of footsteps coming back down.

The girl who entered the room ahead of her mother was quite a plain youngster. She had short hair and was small and quite plump. She was in her dressing gown which was pink with white rabbits on it, quite a young style for a fourteen year old. If Norma and she were wearing makeup, Davenport guessed that Norma had been the instigator.

"Sit down, Mary. Don't be frightened. I'm sorry about Norma and just want to ask you some questions."

The girl and her mother sat side by side on the settee and Davenport took a chair.

"Did Norma have a boyfriend?"

"No, Sir."

The reply was almost whispered.

"But she liked boys?"

"Not in first year, she didn't but after Christmas she changed."

"In what way did she change?"

"She was always dragging me off to groups of older boys and trying to talk to them. She started wearing make-up..."

"…yes and getting you to wear it too, love," said her mother. "I tried to make Mary see that she was too young for it, Inspector, but she was always easily led and Norma led her by the nose."

"Mum! Norma was my best friend. Don't talk about her like that. She's dead!"

Mary started to sob and her Mum put her arm round her.

"I'm sorry, pet. That was thoughtless of me."

"Mary, were any of the boys interested in Norma?"

Mary hiccupped and said, "Not really. I felt that they were making fun of her."

"Did she ever talk about a boy at the tennis club?"

"She told me that the older boys liked her. She partnered an older man at some match and she said he fancied her."

"And do you think that was true?"

"Well if it was true, she never went out with any of them. When we weren't together, she was playing tennis matches. She was in one of the teams, I think."

"One more question, Mary, then I'll leave you in peace. Did Norma see her Dad?"

Mary's face reddened. She looked at her Mum.

"I think I can help you there, Inspector. Norma got her dad to write to her at this address. I put a stop to that. If her Mum didn't want her to see her father, I didn't want to be part of a secret correspondence. Only one letter came here."

"Is that true, Mary?" Davenport asked her.

"Yes, Sir."

"So the letters stopped?"

Mary looked apprehensive.

"They didn't, did they?"

"She got another friend's address for him to write to."

"Do you know which friend?"

"Zoe someone at the tennis club," Mary replied.

"What kind of parent would be party to that?" asked Mrs McGregor.

Davenport made no response. He had noticed that Mary was looking nervous and wondered if she knew more than she was telling.

"Mary, I know she was your best friend but we really need to know anything that might help us to find who killed her. Do you know anything else?" Davenport's voice was gentle.

The girl's hands were tightly clenched, the knuckles white.

"Mary, you must tell the Inspector everything. Please, darling. I won't be angry whatever it is - I promise."

"Once she went to stay with her Dad when his girlfriend was away. She told her Mum she was a staying overnight with me."

"Oh, Mary!" her Mum sounded aghast.

"And I guess she told her Mum she was visiting you on Friday night, Mary. Am I right?"

Mary nodded.

"She didn't say she was staying the night on Friday though."

"Are you sure, Mary?"

Mary nodded.

"She couldn't have Inspector." Mrs McGregor confirmed. Mary's cousin was staying over. My sister brought her across about 7.30."

"Yes but the girls would know that Norma's mother didn't know that."

"Honestly, Sir. Norma didn't ask me to say she was staying the night. She just wanted me to say she was seeing me in the evening, if her Mum rang here."

So, thought Davenport, Norma had not expected to be out all night on Friday.

Davenport remembered that Mrs Gilbert had assumed that Norma was with Mary all night and knew that this was going to make her feel even guiltier.

"Mary, think carefully. Did Norma say who she was seeing on Friday evening?"

"No, Sir but she was really excited all day at school."

Davenport thanked Mrs McGregor and Mary for their help and rose to his feet. Mrs McGregor did the same. Mary remained sitting. By now she was twisting a handkerchief in her fingers. Davenport was grateful that her mother was a doctor and would know how to treat her daughter. The least she needed was a cup of hot, sweet tea.

Back in his car, he rang the station and finding that his DS was available, he spoke to her and asked her if she would like to come up to Newton Mearns for a makeshift meal. She agreed so he picked up Pippa and made a detour to Morrisons in Newlands. He bought some chops and a frozen dessert, lemon meringue pie which was his daughter's favourite.

CHAPTER 12

Charles and Pippa went to work to set the table and get the meal ready and everything was well in hand by the time Fiona arrived, bringing with her a bottle of white wine.

"It's almost ready, Fiona. Pippa, get some paper napkins out of the sideboard drawer and the pair of you sit down."

"Napkins, Dad. How posh!" said Pippa, grinning.

"She lets me down all the time," said Charles laughing.

They sat down as they had been told and Charles brought their plates of chops, baked beans and oven chips to the table. Fiona had often had one of his hurriedly-prepared meals and he had stopped apologising for them.

"I brought the wrong colour of wine. Pippa's coke looks better," Fiona laughed.

The lemon meringue pie was voted good and really tangy and then Pippa dragged Fiona off to her bedroom for their customary talk about Chalet School books, leaving Charles to do the dishes. He had never invested in a dishwasher, thinking it unnecessary for two people.

"I'm on to 'The Chalet School and the Island,' " Pippa informed Fiona.

"Who's the main character in that one?"

"I think Annis Lovell and I think she's about to run away," Pippa informed her.

From her adult vantage point and having read all the books in the series, Fiona could have told her that this happened quite often but she didn't want to spoil her young friend's pleasure in the books so she kept quiet. She asked if Pippa had read any more Agatha Christie books as she had started on them a few months ago when she and her friend Hazel had been involved in a murder and wanted to become detectives like Hercule Poirot.

"Yes, I've read one with an old woman detective, a Miss Marple, in it."

"Who do you prefer, Hercule Poirot or Miss Marple?"

"I think I prefer him as he's so funny with his odd accent and the mistakes he makes in English. Have you read many of Agatha Christie's books, Fiona?"

"I've read them all, all seventy-six I think there are. She also has a couple called Tommy and

Twopence Beresford as her detectives in a few of her books."

"Who do you like best?" Pippa was keen to know.

"Well, since someone called Joan Hickson started playing the part of Miss Marple, I've reread some of those books and because I can picture her now, I prefer the Miss Marple ones."

"Have you got any of the books on DVD, Fiona?"

"I don't have a DVD I'm afraid but I have some on video, one or two. Would you rather read the books first or see the films?"

Pippa thought for a minute.

"Think I'd rather see them first then get more stuff from the book afterwards."

"More detail do you mean? Good idea. Sometimes the film is disappointing because it misses things out."

"Are you girls going to stay up there all night?" came a shout from the bottom of the stairs. Pippa shouted back that they were just coming and reminded Fiona that she still had to see her Dad's train set. They went downstairs and into the lounge.

"Dad, I want to see something on TV. You take Fiona up to the loft and show her your trains."

Charles looked at his watch. It was almost 8 pm.

"Only half an hour of TV, pet then bed for you. It's a weekday remember."

"OK."

Pippa turned to the TV, picking up the remote control.

"Well if you promise not to laugh, I'll give you a brief introduction to my hobby, Fiona."

"I promise."

Laughing, they climbed the stairs and Charles got the pole to hook the catch on the Ramsay ladder. He pulled the ladder down.

"I'll go up first and give you a hand at the top," he said.

Fiona negotiated the aluminium steps and Charles held her arm as she stepped onto the loft floor. Once she was safely there, he put down the trap door which closed the hole down to the upper hall. Fiona looked round. The loft had been carpeted, in a soft green and a velux window would let in a lot of light during the day or during the longer summer evenings. Tonight the loft was lit by a couple of spotlights. At waist height was a complicated network of train tracks. Charles had ducked under one section and now stood in the centre of the tracks. Fiona did the same and joined him.

"Well, here goes," Charles said, and pressed a switch. All along the track things came alive. Stations lit up and lights went on in miniature houses. He moved over to a set of levers and moved one. A tiny train, pulling goods' carriages set off along the track.

Fiona was delighted. One of her friends at primary school had had a train set and he had let her play with it in return for her letting him ride her tricycle but it had been a very basic affair compared to what she was seeing now. Charles moved across to another set of levers and moved one and another train, this time a passenger train, set off. He checked a set of points and the two trains passed each other safely. Fiona admired the scenery. It was almost like a model village in parts and had been very carefully set out.

"You must have had a lot of trouble transporting all this from your last house," she commented.

"Not really. Most of it was in boxes. I didn't have a room for it like I have here. My wife wasn't having a room cluttered with my 'toy' as she called it and the attic wasn't floored."

"Didn't she have a hobby?"

Fiona knew that Charles kept in touch with his ex-wife and that they had a friendly relationship now that they weren't living together so she didn't feel bitchy about commenting.

"Not really. She liked watching Soaps on TV and listening to music but nothing that really took up her time the way this can take up mine. She saw little enough of me with the job and wasn't prepared to have me engrossed in trains when I was at home. She felt the same way about my golf and hated coming to the golf club. It's perfect now because I have time when Pippa goes to bed. It'll be a different story when she stays up later I suppose; though she reads so much she probably wouldn't notice that I wasn't there!"

He smiled at Fiona. He was thinking that she was an avid reader like his daughter. Would she accept his hobby? Fiona's mind was going along the same lines, thinking that she would be quite happy to know he was contentedly relaxing with his hobby after a hard day at work.

"Would you..."

"I wouldn't mind..."

They both stopped and suddenly there was a charge in the air that had nothing to do with the electricity being used for the trains. Fiona was aware of how close they were, hemmed in by the rail tracks. Charles stepped towards her as she stepped towards him. There was no denying the attraction this time.

He cupped her chin in his hands and kissed her gently. The gentleness became firmness and then they were kissing passionately, his tongue exploring her mouth, her tongue playing with his. His right hand brushed her left nipple and she felt it harden. In her groin, she felt a responding tingle.

"Dad, I'm going to bed now. Will you bring me a mug of cocoa please?"

They stepped back from each other as if stung, Fiona bumping into a section of track which wobbled precariously.

"Oh s..s..sorry," she stuttered.

Charles ducked under the track and, opening the trap door, looked down to see his daughter's face looking up at him.

"OK pet. We're just finished up here. Get to bed and I'll come up with the drink. Do you want a couple of digestive biscuits too?"

"Yes please. Goodnight, Fiona!" she called up.

"'Night, Pippa. We'll have a trip into town soon to look for holiday clothes."

Fiona kept back from the trap door. She was sure that her face would be crimson.

"Great. Goodnight." called back the child.

Charles helped Fiona down the ladder. They made their way downstairs, Charles going into the kitchen to put a pan of milk on the stove and Fiona going into the lounge to try to compose herself. She heard the mug being stirred and a tin being opened, then footsteps on the stairs.

She was standing facing the blank TV screen when she heard him come up behind her.

"I guess things are on a different footing now, love," he said.

"It was the 'love' that made it suddenly all right. She turned round and gave him a light kiss on the lips.

"Yes but maybe it's right that we should go slowly. Maybe Pippa did us a favour. We have to work together."

"You're right. Let's not rush things. I want it to be special, not a frantic fumble in the loft with Pippa nearby."

She laughed, a happy carefree sound which delighted him.

"I think we're too old for frantic fumbles and on a serious note, we have work early in the morning so, my love, I'd best be on my way."

Like her, he thrilled to the endearment. He gave her a bear hug, let her go and went to get her jacket from the coat rack by the door.

CHAPTER 13

At first it had seemed perfect. She had her own house. There were no prying parents, no partner, no flatmates. Although older, she had a similar taste in music and a well-stocked drinks' cabinet. She was experienced in the art of love-making, had had a husband and several lovers and knew what she liked though she was also adventurous and willing to experiment.

But suddenly it had all gone flat and stale.

The affair now lacked spontaneity, had become almost routine, every Tuesday after tennis practice. The thrill of the chase was lacking. The absence of the need for stealth and secrecy lessened the excitement. The fact that she would do anything, thrilling at first, had become an irritation. It would have been better had there been a challenge, had she been reluctant and needed to be persuaded. It would have been titillating had she had to be punished for non co-operation. They pretended that she was disobedient in order to practise some sadomasochism but knowing that it was pretence had taken most of the thrill away.

Looking at her now, spread-eagled, face down on the rumpled bed, her mature body half-dressed in a school skirt and blouse, the feeling of revulsion came again.

"Get up. I've had enough. I think we should cool it for a while."

The petulant face turned round.

"What did I do wrong? You asked for school uniform. I'm sorry I couldn't get a gym slip but I did try."

The voice had become a whine.

"You didn't do anything wrong. It's my fault. I've gone off the notion, that's all. I'm going home."

"Will you still come next week?"

"Maybe not. Don't annoy me. You know how I hate to be pestered."

The face took on a hopeful look at the angry tone. The woman raised herself to her knees.

"Are you angry with me? Have I been naughty?"

At one time this asking for punishment would have been a turn - on but this time it merely disgusted and sickened.

"Get dressed. Don't be pathetic."

This time the voice was tearful.

"You don't love me anymore. You've found someone else."

The wailing started then it stopped suddenly.

"If you leave me, I could tell people about us. You wouldn't like that."

"Neither would you, you stupid cow. What would your children think of you?"

Silence.

The voice when it came again was silky smooth and spiteful.

"I could tell the police about you chatting up that young girl, Norma, at the tennis club."

"Don't be ridiculous. I don't chat up young girls."

"Yes you did. She's been coming down on Tuesday evenings and watching the seniors practise and you've talked to her each time. She obviously liked you."

The atmosphere had become charged with antagonism then there was a laugh. The woman on the bed lay back against the pillows, pleased that she had got command of the situation.

"You're right of course. I suppose I did chat her up. It was quite flattering to have a young girl flirt with me. But I would never give you up for a child like her. I'm sorry I was so bad tempered but you did annoy me you know so I think you have to be punished."

Seeing the fluffy pink handcuffs being taken from one of her dressing table drawers, the woman smirked and lying back, stretched her arms above her head.

"Turn over. I want you on your tummy first."

She turned over once again and the handcuffs were placed round her wrists and attached to the bed knobs. Her lover stripped her slowly and then taking a whip from the same drawer began to whip her. She knew that next she would be released, told to turn over and refastened. Then she would be straddled and when she had climaxed, she would be untied and they would change places. She closed her eyes and bit into the lacy pillow as the whip made contact again.

CHAPTER 14

Tuesday morning dawned wet and windy. Watching the forecast on TV, Charles noticed that there was the promise of better weather later in the day. He made breakfast of porridge for himself and Pippa then called up to her to get up. Pippa was not a morning person and he had to climb the stairs and put on the lights in her room before she surfaced from under her duvet.

"Come on, pet. It's eight o'clock and we've to leave in half an hour."

They sat together at the kitchen table. As always, his daughter put sugar on her porridge and then spooned out a 'moat' round the edge and filled it with milk.

He had told his team to be in for nine o'clock this morning, a bit later after their working weekend. He wanted to hear how the last lot of senior men interviews had gone the night before.

"Anything special happening at school today, pet?" he asked Pippa, as they drove down to

Shawlands. He had chosen a school near his work and near his sister rather than one in Newton Mearns although he knew that the school did not have such a good reputation as the ones nearer his home. His daughter had a strong character and he had hoped she would choose her friends wisely. She had done this, even befriending the school bully who being older was now in the secondary school. Her best friend, Hazel Ewing, lived in Newlands.

"Dad!" Pippa said. "I told you last night that we're going to visit Bradford High this afternoon."

"So you did. Sorry. I forgot. Are you going with Hazel?"

"Yes. It's alphabetical. The names A-F are going today, 6 of us."

"Why so few?"

"Because there are others coming from other primaries too. A-F too I suppose."

"Do you know what's going to happen there?"

"No."

Charles had met the head-teacher and most of the staff at the secondary school because of two murders there earlier in the year. He liked Angela Martin and her deputes and was glad that Pippa was going there.

It was 8.50 when they reached the school. Pippa leaned over and gave him a quick kiss before opening the car door and racing off across the playground.

All his team were in the Incident Room except Penny which was unusual and she rushed in, breathless and apologetic at 9.15.

"Sorry, Sir. My car wouldn't start. I had to get two buses."

"No problem. You don't make a habit of being late. What have you done about the car?"

"Nothing. Just left it. I'll phone the RAC at lunchtime, Sir."

"Right team. I'll fill you in about my visit to Mary McGregor, Norma's school friend, then you can tell me about your interviews."

Davenport told them about Norma trying to get her Dad's letters sent to Mary's house but Mary's Mum forbidding this.

"Mary said that the letters were sent instead to Zoe's house."

He told them that Norma had taken to talking to the older boys quite recently, that she had gone to stay with her Dad once when his girlfriend was away, that she had told her Mum she was staying with Mary that night.

"On Friday, she told her mother that she was going to visit Mary. Mary insisted that she wasn't going to stay the night and Mrs McGregor confirmed that as Mary's cousin was staying over."

"So, Sir," said Frank, "Norma intended going back home on Friday."

"That's right, Frank. That's all from me. Now, Penny and Frank, we'll hear about your interviews first please."

Frank opened his notebook.

"Well Sir, we saw Harry Grey first. As you know, he's Donald Kinross's partner."

"He's older, Sir," said Penny. "He's got married children. Sorry, Frank."

Frank smiled at her. He was used to his impetuous colleague. He continued.

"He said that he felt sorry for Don. He drew Norma in the American Tournament which the club has at the start of the season. They didn't know each other but Norma tried to flirt with him. Harry said it was immature stuff, like linking arms with him after each game and laughing up into his face. Harry said that Don kind of played along but moaned to him afterwards about it, saying that he would rather have had an older partner."

"What about the other three senior men you saw?"

"One had been away in Spain. He'd missed the opening day and hadn't been at the courts yet, Sir," said Penny.

"And the other two?"

"Brothers, Sir, new seniors, aged about eighteen and twenty. They only joined this session. They said that they didn't know the names of any of the women, old or young."

"Did you show them Norma's picture?"

"Yes, Sir. The older brother thought he remembered seeing her once on another court but the younger one was sure he hadn't seen her and they had only so far played together so one of them was wrong..."

"...or just less observant," said Salma.

"Thanks you two. Get those notes written up as soon as possible."

He added Harry Grey to his list on the board, plus the other three names, even though they hadn't offered anything important.

"Right, Salma. What did you and Bob come up with?"

Bob was only drafted into the team when there were large numbers of people to be seen or house to house visits and he was not present today. Salma opened her notebook.

"The first man we saw was Hugh Manley. He said he had joined with his wife this year and they had only ever played together on the occasional evening. We spoke to both of them and they remembered seeing two girls one evening, on the court next to the road. One was fair-haired but they couldn't say if one was Norma from looking at the photograph."

Davenport wrote the name Hugh Manley on the board.

"Our second man was the partner of Ken...," she looked down at her Notebook, "...Ross." He's in his fifties. They play together in a match for veteran players. He was at the American Tournament and was partnered with Henrietta Laird, one of the intermediate girls, Sir. He said he saw one girl "being silly" - his words Sir - with Donald Kinross. He said she was young enough to be his daughter. He recognised the photo of Norma."

"What was his name, Salma?"

Ian Fraser's name was added to the list.

"Your last man?"

"He was in his early twenties, name Mark Lang. He recognised the photo. Said she was a lovely girl. He admitted that he quite fancied her until he found out that she was only fourteen. He was at the BB on Friday evening. He's an officer there."

The last senior name went on the list. Davenport stood back and looked at it.

"I don't imagine the last young man would have admitted to liking Norma anyway if he had been the killer," said Fiona, musingly.

"I guess we're left with Donald Kinross and possibly Stewart Bolton and David Bentley, just because they're in the age bracket that Norma would have fancied and they only have a girlfriend or fiancée to give them an alibi."

"What about the two fathers, Peter's dad and Lucy's dad? They must be mid- thirties. If Norma made a play for Donald Kinross, she might have done the same to them," Fiona suggested.

"Yes, Sir and they were both at home - alone," Penny said. eagerly.

Davenport circled the five names.

"I don't see a fourteen-year old being at all interested in the older men, Sir," said Salma.

"What about the intermediate boys?" Davenport asked.

"Well, two were a bit geeky and young for fourteen, one had lots of spots and never went to the club, and two only ever went to play against each other. We should maybe check that, Sir" said his DS.

"Yes you're right."

"The others, Peter Jenkins and Neil Smith have alibis, Sir" said Fiona.

Davenport looked at his colleagues and pulled on his left ear lobe.

"Well that gives us five to concentrate on. I'm going to add Norma's father, Mr Lawson to the list. Is there anyone else?"

"Her stepfather, Sir?" asked Salma.

"Any reason, Salma?" asked her boss.

"Just that sometimes stepfathers abuse their stepdaughters. I know it was in the tennis club which is an unlikely place..."

"Unlikely for her father too, I would say," ventured Frank. "Do we know where he lives?"

"Well the letter was from an address in the West End of Glasgow, near Great Western Road," said Fiona who had noted this down.

"Unlikely that he would come all the way across the city to meet his daughter in a tennis club." Frank was determined to get his point across.

"Unless the murder was planned, in which case he would want to do it far from his home," said Davenport.

"Why would he want to kill his daughter, Sir?" asked Penny.

"No idea."

"More likely to have been Gavin Gilbert then," said Salma.

"I agree with Salma," said Fiona "but I guess we'll have to keep our minds open. What next Sir?"

"We'll need to talk with both Gilbert and Lawson. I suggest that we get them both over here. Take them from the security of their own homes. The other thing I'd like to do is talk with the senior women. Women often notice things men fail to see. Someone might have noticed Norma with one of the men."

Fiona had her lists with her. She was counting.

"There are thirty-two senior women, Sir."

"I think we should ask someone, maybe Anne Scott, which of these women came to the club regularly or were present at the American Tournament. We might be able to rule out some of them, in the same way we're doing with the men."

"Will I visit her, Sir?" asked Penny eagerly. "I know where she lives as I went the last time."

"Fine, Penny. Phone her first. Does she work?"

"I don't know, Sir."

Penny left the room and came back to say that she had left a message on Anne's answerphone.

"Ok folks, off to your own room and get your notes into some form of order. Fiona, come with me, please."

Charles and Fiona were having a coffee in his room when the phone rang and he was put through to the head of the SOC team. He listened carefully and put the phone down, having reminded the man to put his report in writing as soon as possible.

As Martin Jamieson had suspected, there were lots of hairs, nail clippings and fingerprints in the changing room. The only piece of interesting information was that SOC had found scuff marks from the hallway to the room, consistent with someone having been dragged into the room, not along the floor bodily but on the heels and this had been supported by an examination of the heels of Norma's shoes which matched the indentations in the carpet. The heels were scuffed down the backs. They were newish shoes and unmarked anywhere else.

"Ben Goodwin said that she had maybe made a run for it and been dragged backwards, possibly by a man who had put his arm round her neck."

"It would need to have been a strong person then, Charles?"

"Well, Norma wasn't heavily built so it needn't have been Mr Muscle though she wasn't short so the person must have been reasonably tall. You couldn't grab someone taller than you round the neck. Get up a minute and let me try it on you."

Fiona stood with her back to Charles and he crooked his arm round her neck. He was easily five inches taller than she was and without dragging her anywhere, it was obvious that he could have done just that.

Going into the corridor, he called for Penny who was smaller than Salma and Frank.

He instructed her what to do with her DS but she could not do it. Fiona could easily have resisted her. Seeing Penny's puzzlement, Davenport explained what they had learned and told her to tell the others.

"Fiona, ring Martin Jamieson and ask him what height Norma was."

Fiona did this and was able to inform Charles that she was five feet five and weighed 130 pounds.

"So we need to find out the height of the nine males and the two fathers. Get Salma and Frank on to that this afternoon, Fiona."

Fiona went down the corridor to give the sergeant and constable their instruction. When she came back, she was able to tell Davenport that Anne Scott had rung Penny. She had come home for lunch, prior to going shopping in town as Tuesday was her half day. She had agreed to wait at home for Penny and to have a think about the senior women and their likelihood of having known Norma or seen her at the club.

"I feel a bit guilty having the rest busy and us not doing anything," said Charles, " but there is nothing left for us to do, so how about lunch?"

CHAPTER 15

Pippa and Hazel had gone into school excited about their visit to what they called the 'big school'. After registration, their teacher Miss Jackson, told the six who were having the visit to Bradford High to go along to the janitor's box and wait for the head-teacher, Mrs Hobson, who was going with them. Pippa made a face at Hazel. Neither of them liked Mrs Hobson much. She had taken their class one week when Miss Jackson was off sick and they had found her strict and with no sense of humour.

She was waiting for them and hastened them into a double line.

"Now, Bradford High isn't too far away and it's a dry day so we'll walk there. Remember that you are wearing school uniform and I want you to be a credit to our school so heads up and walk smartly. Pippa, you and Hazel lead off please and follow me."

It only took about ten minutes to reach the front door of the senior secondary school.

Mrs Hobson held the door open for the six of them to walk through. In the foyer was a group of about eight children from another primary school, standing with a teacher. The youngsters stood silent, looking around in awe at the large foyer with its huge mural depicting the battle of Langside. The front door opened again and another little line of children came in, about nine this time. The doors swung shut just as another door opened and a black-suited, tall, fair-haired woman came out and walked towards them. She was accompanied by another woman, smaller and less formally dressed in a brown skirt and lemon coloured blouse.

"Welcome to Bradford High School," said the first woman. "I am Mrs Martin the head teacher. This is Mrs Turner one of the depute heads who will take you to the library, children. You'll be given a timetable for today and she will get some of our older pupils to take you to the correct rooms each period. At 3pm I'll meet you in the library again."

She smiled at them.

"I know this place looks very big to you but you'll get used to it very quickly, I promise you."

Turning to the little knot of teachers, she invited them into her room and Mrs Turner led her charges off to the library which was on the second floor. Once there, she sat them at tables and issued them with timetables.

"First you'll be going to English, then Science, and then you'll have a break which we've made at a different time from the older pupils so that you won't be swamped in the canteen. Then you'll go to French and Geography. Lunch is next but not in the dining room. In the afternoon you'll go to Home Economics and Maths."

The library door opened and two tall pupils came in.

"Hi, Mary and Peter. Children, these are two of our prefects. They're going to come along every period and take you to the next room. Do you have any questions?"

"We were told to bring our own lunch, Miss," one of the girls said.

"That's OK. You can eat it in the same room as the others who will be having school lunch."

There being no other questions, the children followed Mary and Peter out of the library and along the corridor to a set of three rooms. Mary knocked on the middle door, opened it and went in, telling the group to wait outside with Peter. They saw a young woman with short fair hair rise from her desk. She walked with Mary to the door.

"Hello there. Come along in and take a seat. Don't use the back row as there's only twenty-three of you. Thanks you two. See you later."

Peter and Mary went out and she turned to the class. Pippa and Hazel had taken seats right at the front and were asked to hand out little booklets.

"We're going to look at a short poem then I'm going to ask you to write something for me and maybe draw something too if you can."

Pippa stifled a groan. She did not mind the writing but she could not draw. Hazel grinned at her. She was less good at writing than her friend but made up for that by being quite a skilled artist.

The period passed quickly. The teacher, who told them her name was Miss Stevenson, made the poem fun and Pippa spent so long on her own poem that she did not have to draw. Peter came for them and took them through the school, past the foyer where they had come in, along another corridor and upstairs to a corridor from where weird smells emanated. This time they were seated at large tables and a young man showed them an experiment where they put their hands round a sphere and their hair rose on end. When they had all had a turn at this, he dictated an explanation and they wrote it down on pieces of paper which he had given to them.

"In August, you'll be given a science notebook for all your notes," he said.

Next came the interval and they were taken downstairs to an area called The Street where they were allowed to choose a drink and a biscuit from the canteen area. Peter paid for all of them.

Then it was off to Modern Language, with Mary this time. They climbed up to the top floor and were met by a tiny little man, dressed in a pale blue suit. He had almost no hair and wore glasses. One of the girls giggled.

"What is your name, Miss?" the little man demanded.

"Denise, Sir."

The girl's face was crimson.

"Well, Denise. What do you find funny, eh?"

"Nothing, Sir."

He glared at her then told them to come in and sit at any desks. He produced a sheet of pictures of people with French words beneath them. Pippa recognised all of them as they had done some French this year. The period passed very slowly as the teacher laboriously went over each picture and made them repeat the French name. As they went back downstairs to Geography, Hazel said to her friend, "I hope we don't get him. He's so boring and we already knew all that."

The Geography teacher, a middle-aged woman, explained that for one term they would have Geography, then it would be History, then Modern Studies and that in third year they could choose which one they wanted to continue with.

"The fourth term will be RE. What's that?"

Pippa raised her hand.

"What's your name?"

"Pippa Davenport. It's religious education, Miss."

"Good."

She went on to explain what they would be studying in Geography during their first year. Lunch came next and Mary took them down to the canteen where they chose lunch. That done, they were taken to a room near to the library to eat their lunch. Mary explained that the rest of the school would be starting lunch in ten minutes and that they were having an extra fifteen minutes for theirs.

Pippa enjoyed Home Economics, though she decided that Mrs Donaldson would be a strict teacher. She was very nice to them but Pippa could see that she expected good behaviour. Maths was made fun for them by a young male teacher who told them that there would be six maths' classes so he might not see them all again.

"I hope we get him," whispered Hazel to Pippa.

"We might not even be in the same class," Pippa whispered back.

The door opened and Peter came in to take them back to the library where Mrs Martin spoke to them about uniform and homework diaries and about having books and jotters covered. Pippa felt that her head was bursting with all she had learned. Then it was back to the foyer where Mrs Hobson and the other teachers were waiting to escort them back to their primary schools.

They chattered excitedly on the way home, Mrs Hobson only quietening them down to cross the main road safely.

School was over for the day so she let them go off as they came near their houses until only Pippa and Hazel remained. Hazel was always picked up at school because she lived in Newlands which was quite far from the school and Pippa was going with her today as she was having dinner with her friend.

They were so excited they could hardly eat and Hazel's Mum laughed as she cleared away half-eaten plates of mince and potatoes.

Dinner over, they went to Hazel's bedroom and Hazel brought up something which had been troubling her.

"Do you really think we won't be in the same class next year, Pippa?"

"I don't know. It might be alphabetical but it might not. Don't worry. We can still play together at the intervals and lunchtime and we can't talk in class anyway."

With this Hazel had to be content and they spent the rest of the evening going over what had happened that day. Charles came for Pippa at 8pm. She regaled him with what had happened all the way home but when they reached there, she was glad to go to bed as suddenly she was exhausted.

Charles poured himself a whisky and sat back to go over what had happened at work that day.

Penny had returned with the senior women list. It contained many names but quite a lot had been scored out as some of the older women only played during the day and some only played on Saturday afternoons. Anne had told Penny that Monday night was Club night when seniors played with whoever came along and Tuesday night was match practice night. Three courts were for the women and three for the men. Anne had told Penny that the American Tournament had not been well attended. Only sixteen people had turned up.

"Avril Smiley might be able to give you those names as she drew the partners," she had informed Penny.

Fiona had phoned Avril Smiley and had got her in as with four young children, she did not go out to work. It transpired that they had already interviewed all the participants in the tournament. It was the same with the teams, as the senior males had all been seen, as had the intermediates. Of the senior female teams, they had only to see four women, as the last couple in the second team consisted of Samantha McMillan and Henrietta Laird who were intermediates.

"Why do we need to see the ones who come on Tuesday evenings?" queried Fiona.

"Norma's friend said she went to watch then, remember?" Charles reminded her.

He went on.

"I think we'd better see the ones who are regulars at the club and the ones who were there on Tuesday when Norma went to watch. The rest seem to just play during the day and on Saturday afternoon. Avril told Penny that young members were discouraged from going on Saturday afternoons as there were often twenty-four women and that used up all the courts."

Charles recalled all this now as he sat by the fire sipping his drink. There would be more interviews tomorrow and Norma's father and stepfather to be called to the station. Switching on the TV, he decided to give his brain a rest for the remainder of the evening.

CHAPTER 16

Charles and Fiona had left for home by the time the others got back from their investigations and written up their reports. Fiona had been busy with the case of a woman who had gone to a friend for shelter with her five year old daughter after her husband had beaten her up. This had happened on Saturday evening and it had taken all this time for the friend to persuade the woman to report it to the police. Fiona was known for her delicate handling of such cases so she had been requested by the DCI of another department and knowing that there was nothing imminent for her to do with regard to their own case, Davenport had been willing to release her for the afternoon. He himself had been kept busy with a meeting with the chief constable, Grant Knox, who, Davenport always claimed, liked cases solved the day before they happened. He had managed to make the man see reason this time, by telling him all the people involved in a tennis club but he left the office as always, feeling pressurised. Knox was afraid of the press but refused to admit this. He liked to face cameras but always came across as blustering and he repeatedly claimed that he was misquoted by the newspapermen who interviewed him.

Thus it was that when they met on Wednesday morning, all but Fiona had something new to tell the others.

Davenport was waiting in the Incident Room and urged them all to be seated. He began by telling them about his meeting with the chief constable.

"As always, he's champing at the bit for results. He's going to meet the press today. I just hope he handles them tactfully."

His colleagues nodded their heads, sympathetically. During one of the station's recent cases, Knox had lost his temper with one of the more persistent journalists who had, in retaliation, published a report, condemning him for mishandling the investigation. Knox had in turn blamed the DCI in charge of proceedings.

"However, enough about that. Penny, Fiona told me that you saw Anne Scott."

"She gave me the names of the women in the two teams. Avril, the coach and Anne herself play at first couple, then Georgina Laird and Pat Harper are second couple and Jane Green and Sheila Ferguson are third."

"We've heard of all of them except Jane Green. Sheila Ferguson was the one who partners Donald Kinross in mixed doubles' matches and Penny, you and Salma met Georgina Laird. Fiona and I have met Avril Smiley and Penny's met Anne of course. However, we haven't discussed Norma with any of them."

"Have we heard of or met any of the second team, Penny?" asked Fiona.

"Salma and I have met Samantha McMillan and Henrietta Laird who play at third couple and they knew next to nothing about Norma having a boyfriend. Henrietta said Norma was too young for that."

"And the other four, Penny?" prompted Davenport.

"Two sisters, Jenny and Joanne Caldwell play second couple but Anne says they never come to the club at any other time. They only play in matches and the first couple are two older women, Elizabeth McPherson and Jill Owens who, apart from matches, only play on Saturday afternoons."

"So they all could know Norma?" said Salma.

"Well, Anne didn't think the two older ladies would know her as none of the intermediates or juniors ever go to the club on Saturday afternoons. The senior women take all the courts usually and they have precedence over the younger ones at that time."

"I suppose that Norma could have gone to watch the matches that were at home," said Davenport.

"Unlikely if there were no men there, Sir" said Frank.

"True, Frank." said Davenport. "What did Anne say about the two sisters, Penny?"

"They play on Tuesdays at match practice."

"Don't the first couple of the second team go to match practice?" asked Fiona.

"No they don't and seemingly it causes some unpleasantness as some of the women think they shouldn't be in the team because they don't come to practise with the others."

"Do the men come to practise on the same night, I wonder," mused Davenport.

"I asked that," Penny said proudly. "They do. The men have three courts and the women have the other three."

"Norma went to watch on Tuesdays," Davenport said. "I think that might be important."

"Salma, what happened when you and Frank went to find out about heights?"

"We got the young boys in, Sir. Peter Jenkins is small but sturdy. Neil Smith is five feet six inches and very thin and gangly. He weighs 120 pounds."

"And the seniors?"

"We waited till later and got Stewart Bolton. He's five feet ten but his girlfriend Jane Green was with him and she's a looker, Sir, so why would he bother with a fourteen-year old? We hadn't managed to interview Jane Green so we took the chance to ask her if she'd ever seen Norma with any of the men."

"What did she say?"

"She said she hadn't been at the American Tournament but had heard from someone, she couldn't remember who, that Norma had been acting silly with Don Kinross. She said that Norma often tried to muscle in on the women's conversations too."

"And Mr Jenkins and Mr Collins?" queried Davenport.

"Both over six feet, Sir. Mr Jenkins is a widower and so is Mr Collins."

Davenport had been writing things down in his notebook.

"So we leave Mr Collins and Mr Jenkins on our list and Bentley and Bolton but not the two intermediates."

"I think we've ruled out all the intermediate boys now, Sir," said Fiona.

Davenport wrote again in his notebook. He scribbled some more then summarised what had to be done now.

Firstly, someone had to visit Zoe again. Secondly, the sisters Joanne and Jenny Caldwell would have to be questioned and Avril, Anne, Georgina, Pat, and Sheila would have to be asked if they had noticed Norma with any of the men.

Davenport remembered something.

"Penny, did you ask who was at the American Tournament?

"Yes, only sixteen were there. Anne said it was disappointing."

"Any new names, Penny?"

Penny looked at her notebook.

"All the intermediate boys, except Robin Stevenson and Brian Hewitt were there..."

"We've seen all of them." Davenport interjected.

"...Zoe and Norma and Lucy were there. We've seen them too Sir. Pat Harper, Georgina Laird, Avril Smiley, Anne Scott and Pat Harper were the only senior women there and Donald Kinross, Harry Grey and Lucy Collins' Dad were the only senior men."

"Right, so once we're spoken to the senior women we've already mentioned, we've covered all the American Tournament folk."

"Who's doing what, Sir?" asked Fiona.

"Right..."

"...team," said Frank unthinkingly.

Davenport looked at him and Frank grimaced. Penny and Salma wondered if he had gone too far this time. Davenport however was a good humoured man and chose to see the funny side.

"Want my job as well as my saying, Selby?"

"Sorry, Sir...no Sir," Frank stammered.

"Right, everyone. Here's the plan. I've been in contact with Mr Lawson and Mr Gilbert and they're coming in after work, around 6pm. I'll interview Mr Lawson and Fiona will interview Mr Gilbert. Penny you'll be present at the Lawson interview and Frank you'll be present at the Gilbert one. Salma, I want you and Penny to visit four of the senior women, Fiona and Frank you do the other four. Just ask if they saw Norma talking to any of the men at the tennis club."

"We might not get them all in during the afternoon, Sir," said Fiona.

"I know. Try them anyway and make sure that you're back for the interviews at 6pm.

When they reconvened later in the afternoon, all but four women had been seen and the Caldwell sisters were said by their mother to be on holiday abroad. Due back on Saturday, they had been away last week and as far as their mother knew had not played tennis yet this season. Of the four seen, all remembered seeing Norma talking to a man at the tournament and that man was Donald Kinross with whom she had flirted, according to them all. Jane and Sheila had been out and would need to be seen later, after the interviews of Mr Lawson and Mr Gilbert. Davenport had remembered about Zoe and had gone up to Clarkston to ask if Norma had gone to watch the Tuesday night practice. Zoe said she had gone last week. She had asked Zoe to go with her but Zoe had thought it would be very boring and said so. Norma had not said anything about it and Zoe was sure she would have if she had had a chance to chat up any of the men there.

They had met briefly to give their reports. Now it was the turn of Norma's father and stepfather to be interviewed.

"Personally, they and Donald Kinross are my favourites so far," said Davenport. "There's been no comment from any of the other males in the club except for David Bentley who admitted that Norma tried to chat him up and Mark Laing who admitted to liking her. Both of those seem innocent enough."

"I agree, Sir," said Fiona, "and so many of the senior men are too old for a teenager to fancy and the younger ones have girlfriends or fiancées."

Bob rang from the desk to say that a Mr Lawson and a Mr Gilbert had arrived and Davenport and Fiona went along to greet them. Mrs Gilbert had accompanied her husband and there was an awkward, tense atmosphere in the foyer. Mr Lawson seemed almost pleased to be taken away to Interview Room 1 and Mr Gilbert went away with Fiona Macdonald to Interview Room 2 where Frank was waiting. Salma left to her own devices, sat and pondered about what they had learned.

CHAPTER 17

April Smiley was worried. As captain of the ladies' first team as well as coach to the younger players, she was responsible for choosing who played at which position in the team. Last night Pat Harper had failed to turn up for match practice. It was annoying in itself as that meant that there were only five there. They had persuaded one of the first team men to make up the numbers while waiting for his own practice. No one else ever came on Tuesdays nights, so there were no spare women at the club. Had it been last Tuesday, they could have roped in the dead girl, Norma Lawson because she had, for some reason, come down to watch. However it had also caused some friction among the ladies as Sheila had insisted that she and Jane should be moved up to second couple if Pat could not be bothered to practise. Georgina Laird had been angry at that suggestion and suggested that they first of all find out why Pat had not turned up. She had offered to phone Pat when she got home and then this morning, she had rung Avril to say that she had been unable to reach her partner.

Avril had offered to try the next morning since she, unlike George, did not have work to go to. She too had drawn a blank and she was worried. Pat worked from home and was always defending herself against good-natured bantering about what an easy life she had by telling them how she got up early and worked till late. Avril rang once again and the phone rang on till the 1571 facility clicked in and asked her to leave a message.

She decided that once the eldest children were away to school, she would strap her youngest into his buggy and walk round to Pat's house, a few streets from her own home in Netherlee.

Also very worried was Norma's stepfather, Gavin Gilbert. He was sitting across from a serious-looking Fiona Macdonald. He had met her before but that was in his own home, on his own territory. This was very different. He had seen rooms like this on TV: bare rooms with metal tables and no windows, with a tape recording machine on the table, against the wall. Another policeman was standing at the door almost as if he expected Gavin to make a run for it.

The woman switched on the tape recorder. Leaning towards it she said clearly, "Interview with

Gavin Gilbert, Wednesday 15th April, 6.17pm. Present, DS Fiona Macdonald and PC Frank Selby."

She sat back comfortably in her chair and said gravely, "Mr Gilbert, you are the stepfather of Norma Lawson. Is that right?"

"Yes."

His voice was husky and he cleared his throat and repeated his reply.

"Yes. I am."

"Please tell me how you got on with your stepdaughter."

"I got on fine with her."

"She didn't resent you marrying her Mum?"

"She might have at first but she got used to the idea."

"You now have two sons. Did you spend as much time with Norma as you did with them?"

"Yes...I mean no...the twins are only three. They need more attention than a teenager."

"So Norma might have felt left out?"

"No I'm sure she didn't. I...we...that is her mother and I tried to make it up to her."

"In what way did *you* make it up to her, Mr Gilbert?"

At the emphasis on the 'you', Gilbert looked uneasy.

"I bought her sweets on my pay day."

"Sweets, for a teenager, Mr Gilbert? I imagine you bought them for the boys too."

"Yes."

"So that was not specially for Norma. Did you ever take her out by herself."

"No I did not! What are you suggesting?" The man was sweating now. He wiped his palms down his trousers.

"What might I be suggesting, Sir?" Fiona was looking at him innocently.

"I did nothing wrong to Norma."

"In what way wrong, Sir?"

"I know what these interviews are like. You'll try to put words into my mouth. Well it won't work. I have nothing to hide."

"So you never took Norma out by herself, Sir?"

"No I did not."

"So you didn't really get on very well with her then."

"It's not fair. I can't win. If I took her out then I could have been abusing her but if I didn't take her out, I wasn't treating her well."

"Did I ever mention the word abuse?" asked Fiona quietly.

"No but that's what you're thinking."

Fiona got up and said something to Frank who slipped out of the room. Fiona said nothing and Gavin Gilbert wiped his neck with a handkerchief which he took from his trouser pocket. Frank returned and said something in Fiona's ear.

"Well, Mr Gilbert. It seems that your memory has let you down. According to Norma's father, you did take Norma out a couple of times. She told her father that she hadn't enjoyed either time. Why was that?"

"That man doesn't like me. He's lying."

Fiona sat back again. She inspected her nails.

"Mr Gilbert, I think it's you that is lying."

She paused.

"I want to ask you one more thing. Where were you on Friday evening?"

"I was at home with my wife and the boys."

Fiona got to her feet.

"The interview is over for just now but we'll be talking to you again. Interview finished at 6.39pm."

She switched off the recorder and Frank opened the door and ushered the man out.

Norma's father was not worried but he looked distraught. He rose from his seat when Davenport and Penny came into the interview room and held out his hand to the DCI.

"Hello. Paul Lawson. Have you any idea at all who killed my daughter, Sir?"

"Sit down, Mr Lawson. It's me who'll be asking the questions today but I can assure you that we are doing everything we can to find Norma's murderer."

Penny leaned against the wall facing Mr Lawson. She wanted to see his face.

Davenport switched on the tape-recorder and, having fed it with the relevant information, sat back and surveyed the man in front of him.

"When did you last see your daughter, Sir?"

"She came across to the flat I share with Sue, my girlfriend, about a week ago."

"And she stayed the night I believe."

"Yes she did."

"Did you get her mother's permission for that visit, Sir?"

The man reddened.

"No I didn't. I wasn't given access to Norma because it was me who left them but Norma wanted to come. She..."

"So did you inform her mother?"

"No."

The man looked sullen.

"Where did her mother think Norma was?"

"Staying with a girlfriend."

"Talking about girlfriends, how did yours feel about the visit?"

The man looked shifty.

"She didn't know. She was away."

"So you were alone all evening and all night with Norma?"

"What's wrong with that? I'm her father. Surely you don't think..."

"Don't think what, Sir?"

"That I would harm her in any way. That man Gilbert took her out a few times. She told me. Is that not more suspicious?"

"It's you I'm dealing with right now, Mr Lawson," said Davenport crisply. "How did you contact Norma in the first place?"

"I met her at her school gates one afternoon and I arranged to write to her from time to time."

"So you wrote to her at her home address?"

"Well no... Jan wouldn't have allowed that."

"So?"

"So I sent it to her care of her friend, Mary McGregor."

"Whose mother put a stop to that I believe."

"Yes."

"Then what?"

"I sent a couple to her care of another friend, Zoe Stewart."

"Did you see nothing wrong in what you were doing Sir?"

"She's my daughter, Inspector. I had every right to see her."

"And do you realise that her mother assumed that she was staying with a friend that time and on the night she died?"

"I suppose so."

"You suppose so. Did you see her last Friday night, Sir?"

"No I didn't."

"Have you any proof of that, Sir?"

"Sue came in around 11pm. She was out with some girlfriends. She would tell you that there was no one there."

"But no one who can prove that she wasn't there earlier, that you didn't take her to the tennis club and strangle her."

"I don't know where the tennis club is."

"No but she did."

"Why would she take me there? Why would I kill my own daughter?"

"Maybe she wanted to live with you and you knew that Sue wouldn't agree and Norma said she would tell the authorities that you had been seeing her - alone."

The man put his head in his hands and began to sob. Davenport asked Penny to fetch him a cup of tea and he sat and waited until the man had composed himself again. They sat in silence until Penny returned with the tea. She looked shaken. She had only sat in once before with her boss in an interview and had never seen him so menacing.

The door opened and Frank came in. He whispered a question to Davenport and received an answer. He left again.

Davenport let Lawson drink some tea before returning to his questioning.

"So let's get this straight. You let your daughter deceive her mother and come to your house - which is where Sir?"

"Just off Great Western Road, Ascot Court."

"You let her come to the other side of town and stay the night. You never thought to let her mother know. You were alone with her all night. You did not see her last Friday but she told her mother that she was with the same friend, the same alibi she had used for her visit to you, Sir."

"I'm sorry. It was wrong. I see that now but I just wanted some time with my daughter. I missed her so much and she wasn't happy at home."

"Why not?"

"Her Mum and that man Gilbert spent all their time with the twin boys. She had a poky room and seldom got anything she asked for, though the boys got a lot."

"Did you believe that?"

"Yes I did."

Davenport, after his visit to the little cell of a room and having seen Norma's meagre possessions, believed it too. His manner softened a little.

"Mr Lawson, thank you for your co-operation. Your actions were foolish in the extreme but perhaps understandable under the circumstances. I may need to speak to you again."

Davenport leaned forward and ended the interview.

"Interview ended at 6.46pm."

Penny came over and ushered Mr Lawson out. She lifted the cup from the table and followed him along the corridor and up the stairs to the exit. He looked shaken. The seat where his wife had sat was vacant.

Penny made her way back to her own room where Frank was regaling Salma with what had happened in his interview. Salma got up when she saw Penny's face.

"Come on you two. Let's go for a coffee. I don't imagine we'll be needed until the boss has seen DS Macdonald. They'll have their interviews to compare."

Frank, who had also seen how pale Penny's usually rosy cheeks were, got to his feet too and the three went to the canteen.

It was Bob who took the call from Avril Smiley. He transferred it to Davenport's room and Charles heard how Pat Harper had, most unusually for her, failed to turn up for match practice the night before and that Avril was not able to raise her this morning although she worked from home. Avril had been to the house. One milk bottle was sitting outside the door and Pat's cat had come mewing round Avril's legs, obviously wanting in.

"I'm worried that she might be ill, Inspector and having met you, I decided to call your station.

I did look in the front window and the kitchen window but that's all."

Davenport assured her that he would send someone round and told her that if no one answered the door this time and the milk and cat were still there, the policeman would break in. Avril thanked him.

CHAPTER 18

Frank and Penny were dispatched to Stamperland. Pat Harper's house was one of a series of semi- detached buildings. Penny rang the doorbell but there was no reply. The bottle of milk was still on the doorstep. Frank looked in the front window and while he was doing that, the door of the neighbouring house opened and a tiny old lady in a brown tweed skirt and cream coloured twinset stood there watching them. Penny went to the hedge which separated the two houses at the front. She held out her ID card and the lady took it and peered at it through bottle-top glasses.

"My name's PC Price and that's PC Selby." Penny said loudly, pointing to Frank. "We're worried about your neighbour, Pat Harper. She hasn't been seen for a while and her milk is still out here."

"I've got her cat in here. He often comes in when he can't get in there," the old woman said. "Are you going to break in?" she asked, looking excited. "Can I watch?"

Penny went back to Frank.

"Unusual arrangement here, Penny," he said. "She's had the upstairs' windows double-glazed but not this one."

They walked round to the back of the house and found out that it was the same there. The kitchen window was not double-glazed yet the back upstairs bedroom one was.

"Well, makes it easier for us to get in," said Frank and, picking up a large stone from the rockery, he wrapped his handkerchief round his hand, and hit the kitchen window with it.

"Oh, that's great," said a voice, and turning round they saw that the little old lady had followed them round. "Now what?"

Frank put his hand into the hole and opened the window. He climbed in and soon had the kitchen door open for Penny.

"Much more fun than just using her key," said the frail voice.

Penny smiled at her.

"We don't have her key."

"No but I have," the lady said and held it up.

Penny found herself starting to giggle then remembered why they were there and stifled her humorous feelings.

"Now, Mrs..."

"Mrs Jackson."

"Mrs Jackson. Don't follow me in please. Go back home and we'll come in to see you later."

The old lady looked disappointed but turned to go. Penny went inside. Frank was in the lounge. She joined him there.

"The curtains weren't drawn in here so maybe she went out yesterday and stayed overnight," ventured Frank.

"Let's check upstairs first," said Penny.

There were only three rooms upstairs, the first one being the bathroom which was tiny and empty. The door to the back bedroom was shut. They went into the front, main bedroom. Again the curtains were open and the room empty.

"Well it seems as if she's OK, Frank. She hasn't taken ill and died in bed anyway."

"I'll just check the guest bedroom," Frank said and left the room. Penny heard a gasp and hurried to join him. The curtains were drawn this time but in the dim light Penny could see the inert form on the bed. She switched on the light and they both stared at the figure on the bed. Frank went across and felt the right wrist.

"No pulse, Penny."

The body was scantily dressed, in flimsy panties and a bra and lay on its back, legs together. The hands lay by the side of the body. There was something unnatural about the correctness of the body, almost like a soldier's on parade, thought Penny.

"Don't touch anything, Penny," Frank reminded her.

"Do you think it's a suspicious death then, Frank?" Penny asked.

"Why would she be lying so correctly; in her spare room?"

"Yes, I'd noticed that too. The body looks unnatural."

They peered closely at the body. There were no marks round the neck, no marks on the body that they could see. The bed was rumpled. Taking a clean handkerchief out of her jacket pocket, Penny opened the drawers of the dressing table. The top one was empty, the middle one was full of towels and the bottom one was full of shorts and swimwear. She turned to the small wardrobe. In it, she found coats and jackets. Apart from the bed there was no other furniture in the room.

Frank had taken his mobile out of his pocket and was trying to reach his boss.

"Sir, we've found a body, probably that of Pat Harper."

"Yes Sir, she's dead. There's no pulse. No sign of foul play but what is odd is that she was in her spare bedroom."

He switched off the phone.

"The DCI's coming across. I've to stay here. Maybe you should question the old girl next door. See if she knows anything or heard anything strange."

"Frank. She had a key to the house and watched us breaking in," said Penny.

"The old...besom," said Frank.

Before she left, Penny went back into the main bedroom. She looked in the drawers of the larger dressing table there and the matching wardrobe. She found the drawers full of underwear, nighties and makeup and the wardrobe full of everyday clothes.

"I would think that the main bedroom was the room she used, usually," she told Frank.

On the way out, she went into the kitchen. There was one wine glass on the sink and a half empty bottle of red wine on a work-surface. The cork sat on the draining board.

She had to ring the door and then rattle the letterbox before the old lady answered the door. She looked at Penny with a gleam in her eye.

"Is she dead then?"

"Why do you say that, Mrs Jackson?"

"Well it's not every day the police have to break into a house and I saw Mrs Harper go in on Monday evening and I didn't see her come out again."

"Do you sit at the window all day and night then?" Penny could not help herself asking.

"Yes, except for when I'm eating or going to the toilet or on Tuesday evenings when my niece comes to see me. We play scrabble," Mrs Jackson replied, not seeming a bit put out by the question.

"Did you see anyone else at the door or going in?"

"Yes there was a woman at the door before you came and on Monday night someone came out.

"At what time?"

"At about ten o'clock."

"Did you recognise this person?"

"I'm afraid not." The woman looked disappointed. "It was dark by then."

"Man or woman?"

"Think it was a man but they all wear trousers these days."

"Did Mrs Harper have many visitors?"

"No, not unless they came on Tuesdays."

Penny thanked the old lady, telling her that she wished everyone they interviewed could be so alert. As she went back down the short path, Davenport's car pulled up and her boss got out. She told him what Mrs Jackson had said.

"Thanks, Penny. You'll need to wait for a lift back to the station so come back in with me. I've phoned Martin and SOC so keep an eye out for them please."

Davenport climbed the stairs and met Frank in the second bedroom. Together they looked at the woman's body.

"No sign of her being in pain; no sign of her being murdered either, Sir," said Frank.

"Why on earth would she be lying so rigidly on an unmade bed in her spare room?" Davenport mused out loud. "I take it that this is her spare room."

Penny had come upstairs but she remained outside as the room was small and three would have crowded it. She said, "The larger room, I think, was her bedroom, Sir. She has most of her clothes in there, the ones she would use every day. In the wee room she has spare towels and things like that."

"Anything unusual?"

"Well the top drawer's empty, Sir. I wondered why that was. Most women fill every space available."

Davenport thought back to his wife and agreed with his constable. He went into the front bedroom which was a pretty room, pink and cream in colour. A photograph on the dressing table showed two girls in their early twenties or late teens. The spare room was plainer, the bed sheets plain white and only the pillows being lacy. There were no ornaments or pictures.

"I think I hear a car, Penny. See if it's Martin or SOC please."

Penny went downstairs and was in time to see Martin Jamieson's yellow car squeezing itself in between the police car and Davenport's Audi. Pat

Harper's car was in the narrow, short driveway. It was a red Clio. Martin stepped out. He might well have stepped out of a bandbox rather than a car, Penny thought. He was always immaculately dressed and today was no exception. He wore a pin-striped navy suit with a white shirt and navy tie and his shoes shone.

"Hello, Sir," she said as he walked towards the door.

"Hello, Constable Price. Where is the body then?"

"Upstairs in the small bedroom, Sir."

He bounded up the stairs two at a time and Penny heard Davenport welcome him. Frank came downstairs to give them some space and he and Penny both welcomed the two-man SOC team when they arrived, parking their van across the road in between a motor bike and an elderly Ford Cortina.

"I think you'd better wait downstairs till Mr Jamieson's finished," said Frank. "The body's in quite a small bedroom."

"We've just to get back to the station," he told Penny. "We're not needed here now."

The team were all sitting in the Incident Room discussing this latest development when Davenport returned to tell them that Martin had suspected foul play right away, mainly because of the unnatural way the body was lying. He had turned the body over and discovered recent weals on the back. He would have the body of Pat Harper removed to the city morgue and do forensic tests on it. He had another case in hand but would get onto this one the next day.

"I left SOC fingerprinting in the house," Davenport told them, "but I have the feeling that they won't find anything untoward. I think our murderer had time to clean if he had time to arrange the body."

"Sir, what could have been in the empty drawer? Do you think that's important?" asked Penny eagerly.

"Anything unusual is important."

"Sir, do you think that this murder, if it turns out to be a murder, is connected with the killing of Norma Lawson?" asked Fiona Macdonald.

"Because they were both members of the same tennis club you mean?"

"Yes."

"Maybe. It does seem a bit of a coincidence, I admit."

"Maybe Pat Harper saw something at the American Tournament," said Salma who had been quiet until now.

"Well, no point making guesses till we hear from Martin and SOC, folks," said Davenport. He left the room, followed by his DS. Frank let them get some distance down the corridor before whistling softly, "Speed Bonny Boat."

CHAPTER 19

Thursday was a perfect spring day. Charles looked out of his window while waiting for Pippa and noticed that his daffodils were beginning to bloom. He always thought that snowdrops were such hopeful flowers, pushing their way up even through frost and sometimes snow to herald that winter would end and he felt that daffodils with their trumpets were the messengers of spring. What about the crocus he thought now, looking at where they were clustered beneath a tree. Maybe the signs of death to winter with their purple colour a contrast to the bright yellow of the daffodil. His thoughts were interrupted by his daughter asking him if he had seen her school bag.

"Sorry, no. Where did you have it last?"

"In the car after school yesterday."

"You didn't have any homework last night, just a talk to prepare for next week. Did you maybe leave it in the car?"

Fetching his car keys from the hall table, Charles went out to the car and found the schoolbag. He removed the empty lunch box and, taking it into the kitchen, rinsed it under the tap before filling it again with two rolls and gammon and an apple.

"What do you want to take to drink today, pet?" he asked his daughter.

"Some orange juice please, Dad."

Charles lifted the schoolbag and the keys again and made his way out to the car followed slowly by Pippa who was always slow in the mornings. She got into the car and strapped herself in.

The journey down to Shawlands was done to the background music chosen by Terry Wogan who Charles was fond of saying was the only person who could make him laugh before 9am.

They had reached Merrylee and the car was idling at the traffic lights which led to the new Morrisons when a thought struck Charles and he said aloud, "Where's Norma's sachoolbag?"

"What Dad?" asked Pippa.

"Nothing pet, just something to do with work."

It was the first thing he asked Fiona Macdonald when he reached the station.

"Fiona. Do you remember seeing a schoolbag or briefcase in Norma's bedroom?"

Fiona thought for a minute.

"No can't say I do remember but there might have been one there and I just didn't take it in."

"I don't remember one either but we'd better check. Give Mrs Gilbert a ring...no on second thoughts I have something else to ask her so I'll just pop up to Waterfoot."

"Anything you want me to do or can I take some time today to see that battered mum I told you about the other day?"

"Carry on. Just make sure all the others' reports are up to date, especially Frank's."

Salma, Frank and Penny saw him go and minutes later Fiona came into the room to ask if they all had their interviews written up. They had, so she decided to send them to visit the other neighbours of Pat Harper to see if they had seen anyone or anything strange at her house.

"We don't know yet when she was murdered or even if she was murdered but there's no harm in doing some investigating...team," she said, grinning at Frank who blushed. She and Charles had had a discussion about the 'team' incident the other day and she had told him bluntly that he always said, "Right team." She had noticed that he had called them 'folk' the next time he addressed them and wondered if the rest had noticed too.

Davenport reached the Gilbert house shortly before 11am. He had hoped that Gavin Gilbert would be out at work and he was. The two boys were in the front garden, arguing over who could have the tricycle. He was glad to see that the gate was firmly shut although he wondered if the three year old boys could manage to unlatch it. The door was open. He rang the doorbell and when Jan Gilbert came to the door, he mentioned the gate to her, saying that perhaps it would be better if the two boys played in the back garden.

"I meant to take the bike through there, Inspector. You'll think I'm a bad mother what with letting Norma stay out without checking on where she was and now this."

Davenport could see that she was almost in tears.

"Take the bike through now," he said gently. "And no, I don't think you're a bad mother. These things happen."

She gave him a watery smile and, telling one son to get off the bike, she carried it through the hallway and into the back garden which was walled. She walked across the garden to the gate and turned a key, removing it and putting it into her apron pocket. The boys resumed their argument.

Davenport went into the lounge. He motioned the woman to sit down and sat down himself.

"Mrs Gilbert, I'm sorry to have to ask you but did your husband ever take Norma out by himself?"

If he had felt sorry for her before, he felt even sorrier now. He could almost see the struggle going on in her head and realised that Gavin Gilbert must have asked her to lie for him. He decided to make it easier for her.

"Your ex-husband told me that Norma had told him that Gavin had taken her out a couple of times. Was this true?"

Relieved of the responsibility of admitting something now that she knew that Davenport already knew the truth, Jan Gilbert said, almost gratefully, "Yes. Gavin did take her out twice, once to the pictures and once to Macdonalds. He wanted her to get to know him better."

"Did it work?"

"I think so. We were so busy with the twins that I think she felt neglected so she must have been grateful when he took her out, mustn't she?" She was almost asking him to agree with her, he thought.

"He lied to me about it," Davenport said.

"I know. He told me. When we heard that Norma had been killed, he told me that he was sure that he would be suspected. He said that stepfathers were often in the news for having abused or cruelly treated their stepchildren. He's sorry he lied, Inspector but he was scared."

"Norma didn't tell you anything about Gavin mistreating her?"

"Oh no, Sir. She was happy when she came home both times. Full of the film she'd seen the first time and telling the boys what she'd had to eat the second time."

"Well, tell Gavin to come down to the station again when he gets home and we'll have another talk."

"Yes, Sir."

"Now for the other thing. Did Norma have a schoolbag or a briefcase?"

"She had a briefcase. It caused endless rows because she wanted a modern bag."

"Would you mind seeing if it's in her room?"

Jan Gilbert left the lounge and returned empty-handed.

"No. It's not in her room, Inspector."

"Thank you. I'll leave you now. Remember to tell Gavin I want to see him."

Mrs Gilbert saw Davenport to the door. She was looking as if a weight had been lifted from her shoulders.

CHAPTER 20

When Davenport got back to the station, he found his part of the large police station completely empty and, wondering where all his colleagues had gone to, decided to pay a visit to the canteen. None of them was there so he decided to have lunch. There was one PC from another department in front of him in the queue.

"Hello Sir," the man said. "Are you in a hurry? Do you want to go in front of me?"

Davenport assured him that he was in no rush and asked if he could recommend anything for lunch. The man looked embarrassed.

"It's all a bit stodgy, Sir. If you want something healthy, I'd stick to a jacket potato with a filling."

He chose this himself with a filling of cottage cheese and Davenport took his advice and also chose a baked potato, asking for his to be filled with coronation chicken. Not wanting to spoil the man's free time, he went to a different table. The meal was tasty but Davenport had seen the other choices and agreed with the constable about the stodginess of what was on offer. He made a mental note to have a talk with the kitchen supervisor and, having finished his food, he decided against the canteen coffee and went back to his office where he put on his coffee machine.

Salma and Penny arrived back soon afterwards and he told them to wait for Frank then go out for lunch, giving them a £20 note and telling them to have lunch on him.

"I've just sampled the canteen lunch and I can't recommend it," he laughed.

Thanking him gratefully, they told him that DS Macdonald had asked them to visit Pat Harper's neighbours.

"Tell me about it when you get back," he said, and at that moment they heard the sound of whistling and Frank's footsteps coming up the corridor. Frank was whistling something Davenport did not recognise.

"Makes a change from all his Scottish tunes," he commented. "Does he have Scottish relations?"

Penny and Salma looked at each other then Penny said, trying not to laugh,

"I don't know, Sir."

Frank arrived in the doorway of their room. He stopped whistling when he saw Davenport with the girls. Penny, feeling mischievous, told him, "The DCI wondered if you had Scottish relatives,

Frank as you're always singing or whistling Scottish tunes."

"Oh ma auld Heiland Granny d'you mean?" Frank replied, without turning a hair. "She was always telling me about Bonnie Prince Charlie and Flora Macdonald."

Salma had to turn her nervous giggle into a choking sound. Davenport looked at her. "Are you OK Sergeant?"

"Yes Sir, just a frog in my throat."

Penny thought it wiser to change the subject and she told Frank that Davenport had given them £20 to have lunch outside. Frank was delighted and said so and the three went off down the corridor, promising to be back within an hour.

Fiona arrived back shortly after they had left but she had bought sandwiches which she ate in Davenport's room while telling him the outcome of her morning's work.

"How did you get on with the briefcase or schoolbag?" she asked him when she had finished.

"It wasn't in Norma's room. Neither we nor SOC found it in the clubhouse on Friday night. I wonder where it is. Oh, I asked Jan Gilbert if her husband had taken Norma out. He'd obviously asked her to lie for him because she looked embarrassed. When I told her that her ex-husband had already told me about two trips out, she admitted that it was true."

"Do you think Mr Gilbert was guilty of anything other than trying to be nice to his stepdaughter?"

"No I don't think so. According to Mrs Gilbert, Norma came home quite happy on both occasions. I've asked her to get him to come to the station again tonight and I'll get the truth from his lips."

They heard chatter coming up the corridor and the others came up to Davenport's room.

"Sir, there's a message from the desk. There's just been a call from Avril Smiley. One of the senior women who play on Thursday mornings found a briefcase in the ladies' changing room. She phoned Avril to ask what to do and Avril went over to the clubhouse and looked inside it. She found schoolbooks and some jotters with Norma Lawson's name on them."

Penny was excited. She rushed on, "The murderer must have put it there, Sir. Surely SOC would have found it if it had been there on Saturday."

"Yes, Penny. Calm down. What's happened to the briefcase?"

Salma spoke up.

"Bob asked Mrs Smiley if she would bring it here, trying not to handle it too much."

"Right, let's go into the Incident Room and we'll hear what happened when you spoke to Pat Harper's neighbours."

Frank was first to speak this time.

"I went to the neighbour on Mrs Harper's other side. The woman there has a young baby. She said she was too stressed to notice anything next door but did say that Pat was a very pleasant woman who had given her advice when she was pregnant. She said that Pat had two daughters who went to live with their father when the marriage broke up."

"Any idea why it broke up, Frank?"

"The woman didn't know but surely it must have been her fault if the kids went to stay with their dad."

"Likely but not necessarily true," Fiona said.

"I went back to Mrs Jackson, Sir," reported Penny. "I asked if she knew anything about Pat Harper's background but she had only come to live there about a year ago and Pat was already there."

"I bet she was disappointed," laughed Frank.

"She was. She told me about hearing shouting one evening, coming from Pat's house. Her bedroom is through the wall from Pat's and she listened at the wall but thought that the noise was coming from further away, perhaps from the room we found the body in, Sir."

"Anything else, Penny?"

"There was no one in across the road at number 79."

"Salma?"

"There was someone in at 77, an older man who lives with his son and daughter-in-law. He said he found Pat very pleasant to talk to. Two young women who must be her daughters, come together to visit sometimes and another young woman, occasionally. He couldn't remember seeing any men but he admitted that he was addicted to TV watching in the evenings, Sir."

"There was a teenager weeding in the garden at number 82, two along from Pat Harper," said Frank. He said that he hardly knew her and didn't think his mum knew her either."

Davenport thanked them and thanked Fiona for getting them onto that job. He told them that he had Mr Gilbert coming in and asked Frank to accompany him this time in the Interview Room.

"Wonder where the briefcase was until it was dumped in the changing room," he mused out loud.

"The murderer must have found it in his car, or taken it away from the clubhouse then realised that that was stupid," said Fiona.

"Wonder if they came together or met there."

The phone rang in Davenport's room and he hurried up the corridor to answer it.

They saw him passing their room and soon he was back carrying a brown leather briefcase, using a cloth to avoid leaving fingerprints. Fiona left the room and came back with a pair of latex gloves which she handed to her boss. Davenport put them on and opened the case. Leaving everything where it had been, he inspected the contents.

"One book, "The Merchant of Venice", one science notebook, two jotters, one a bit dog-eared, for Maths and the other new, for English, a pencil case." He opened this gingerly and looked inside. "Two pencils, one pen, a small ruler and half a rubber."

He felt down to the bottom of the briefcase and extracted a crumpled up piece of paper.

"Seems she was like Pippa, forgot to give letters to her parents. Here's one intimating a Parents' Evening last week."

He turned it over and they saw a heart drawn on the back with the letters NL on it. There was a smudgy mark beneath Norma's initials. They all peered at it then stepped back to let Davenport have clearer access to the paper. There was what looked like a V or it could be half a K or even an L on its side.

"Not much help there I'm afraid but we'll leave it all with SOC. Frank, get this over to them please."

Frank went off down the corridor. He thought about whistling something Scottish then thought better of it. Penny and Salma moved to their computers to type up what the neighbours had said. Charles and Fiona went to his room where they compared diaries to see if they could fit in a bridge evening soon. Fiona asked him if Pippa was free to go clothes' shopping on Saturday morning and Charles said she was. Fiona returned to her own room to write up what had happened with the battered mum that day. There being nothing else to do till Mr Gilbert came in, Davenport told Penny and Salma to get along home.

"Sir," said Penny having a sudden thought, "When would be suitable for me to have a day off for moving house?"

"A weekday, Penny?"

"Yes, Salma wanted to give me a hand but I realise that with this murder case it might be impossible."

"How about we say this Tuesday coming? Salma can have the morning to help you. You of course are entitled to the whole day. Is that OK?"

"Thanks, Sir," they chorused.

CHAPTER 21

Lucy Collins and her father were hosting a small party. It was Saturday, just over a week after the discovery of Norma's dead body in the clubhouse and Mr Collins had thought that a party might help to take his daughter's mind off the tragedy.

They lived in a large house on Glasgow Road, with a garden which led down to the river and as it had been a good spell of weather they had planned a BBQ. Henrietta Laird had walked down as she lived not far from them. Sam McMillan, Zoe Stewart and Gregory Browne had come together on the same bus. Mr Stewart had promised to come for them later in the evening. Lucy had not asked Robin Stevenson and Brian Hewitt as she found the former a boring swot and the latter she had not seen this season at tennis. Peter Jenkins, his girlfriend and Neil Smith were still to arrive. Mr Collins had been dismayed at the folk Lucy wanted to invite and had tried to persuade her to ask school friends instead but Lucy had been adamant that she only wanted her tennis friends.

"Dad, we're all upset over Norma, so we all need a party and my school friends wouldn't mix with my tennis ones."

Reluctantly, Mr Collins had conceded defeat. He had invited Peter's father, Brian Jenkins to keep him company. They played together quite often at the tennis club now and had become quite friendly through that and the fact that both were widowers with one child. Brian had come up earlier than his son, knowing that the boy would not want to arrive with his father.

The evening was quite balmy for the time of year and the youngsters were in tee-shirts and casual trousers as were the two men who commented on how different things were now.

"Do you remember when we went to parties and the girls were all dressed up in frocks or skirts?"

"Frocks, Kev? You're showing your age. No one calls them frocks any more."

They laughed as they sat under one of the trees close to the river, sipping beers. In their late thirties, they were a handsome pair, both with wavy dark hair, slim and tall.

"Do you never think of remarrying, Brian?" Kevin Collins asked his friend.

"Me? No. I could have once, about two years ago. Met her at the golf club but Peter didn't take to her and in the end, I started seeing her through his eyes and went off the notion. What about you?"

"I've never really socialised since Dawn died. I'm not a member of anything except the tennis club. Lucy and I get on so well and do a lot of things together."

"But she's what – fourteen? – It won't be long till she's off with a boyfriend and then you'll be a lonely old man."

"Don't remind me. What about Peter? Is he serious about this girl he's with?"

"Hope not. He's only a year older than your Lucy. In fact he fancied the girl who was murdered, Norma Lawson but she wasn't interested in boys."

"She was recently. Did you see the way she flirted with poor Don at the American Tournament?"

"Yes. I saw her giggling up at him once but that's all. What did Don do?"

"He seemed to take it in good part."

"Wouldn't like to be him though, now that she's dead and the police are looking for a murderer."

"Not Don surely!"

"Well I'd heard he had a reputation for being one for the ladies. His name's been linked with Sheila Ferguson recently."

"His doubles partner?"

"Yes."

"Well surely if he's playing away with her, he'd not be likely to start something with Norma and why else would he kill her?"

"Well if it was an older man who killed her it must be because he was scared she'd tell his wife. I mean a young, single guy would have no reason to kill her."

"Only if he'd raped or tried to rape her, I suppose. A young lad might panic then."

"It said in the papers that she was found in the clubhouse but it needn't have been a member of the tennis club. She might have taken someone there, someone from school maybe."

"True. I think it's time I got the food on the go. Will you give me a hand?"

Kevin Collins got to his feet and the two walked over to the BBQ, a large, state of the art affair set up near the house as it had to be in Scotland with the uncertainty of the weather, even in summer and this was only spring.

The youngsters, like the two fathers, had been discussing the murder. They were sitting, some on a bench and the others on the ground, on a tartan rug brought from the house. Lucy, as hostess was holding court. She was squashed on the bench beside Zoe, Sam, Henrietta and Gregory and looking down at Neil and Peter who sat either side of Peter's girlfriend.

"Did any of you ever see Norma with a boy?" she had just asked.

"She was always trying to talk to boys at school," Neil said in disgust. "She fancied the older boys."

"Yes I saw her but anyone in particular?"

"Not really. She always had poor Mary McGregor in tow, looking embarrassed and I think the older boys made fun of them," Peter chipped in.

"She was interested in being with older girls too," said Henrietta. "I saw her at tennis chatting to my sister and her friends. They tried to get rid of her but she didn't seem to see that she wasn't wanted."

"Yes," said Zoe sadly. "She seemed to suddenly grow up."

"She told me her Mum didn't have time for her any more now that she had her new husband and the twin boys," said Lucy. "Maybe she was looking for an older person to take her Dad's' place."

"I think she was interested in someone older from tennis," said Zoe. "She asked me to go to the Tuesday night match practice with her last week but I didn't want to go so she went by herself."

"Who goes to that, from the men I mean?" asked Henrietta. She had come without her glasses tonight and blinked at the ones sitting on the ground.

"The first team's that man Don Kinross, Harry Grey and Stewart Bolton," answered Neil. "Sometimes they ask either me or your Dad, Lucy, to come along as reserves but I didn't go on Tuesday and I don't think your Dad did."

"Maybe she thought you'd be there, Neil," suggested Sam. "I can't see her fancying any of the older men. That Don and Harry must be about forty."

"There's Stewart - he's only about twenty," said Peter.

"He's going out with Jane Green," said Henrietta.

"How do you know that, Henry?" asked Gregory.

"George was out with them last Saturday, her and her new boyfriend."

"I asked Norma out last August when school started back," said Neil grumpily. "She just giggled and said no so it wasn't me she was going to watch on Tuesday."

Peter's girlfriend spoke up.

"Maybe she just said she was going there and was really going off to meet someone else."

"Then why ask me to go with her?" demanded Zoe.

Lucy had been quiet an unusually long time for her and she spoke now.

"Norma met her Dad one day at the school gates. Her Mum didn't know. Did he not send letters to your house, Zoe?"

"He did once but Mum said she couldn't do it again. She'd asked Mary, her friend at school and her Mum wasn't OK about it either. Norma and I had fallen out a bit. The letter stuff and her wearing all that makeup - we fell out over that."

Zoe looked upset and Lucy hurriedly burst in, "What I thought was that maybe her Dad killed her."

"Don't talk nonsense, Lucy!" said Peter. "Why on earth would he kill his daughter?"

Lucy, looking stubborn, said that maybe Norma was making things difficult for him and his new girlfriend but the others were convinced that a father would never kill his daughter under any circumstances.

"But her stepfather might," said Sam. "It's usually wicked stepmothers but he could be a wicked stepfather,"

The group looked excited. Lucy, willing now to abandon her idea, ventured that Mr Gilbert had maybe killed Norma because she wanted her Mum's attention. Neil wondered if he had fancied Norma himself and 'tried it on' and had to silence her when she threatened to tell her mother.

"I wonder if she was...you know..." Lucy flushed.

"What?" asked Gregory.

"You know...raped... before she was killed."

"Lucy!" Zoe's pretty face clouded. "Oh, poor Norma. I hope not."

At that moment Mr Collins called them over for the BBQ. Seeing that Zoe was on the point of tears, he drew Lucy aside and asked her what the matter was.

"It was my fault, Dad," she said, ever honest with her father. "I suggested that maybe Norma had been raped before she was killed."

"Oh, Lucy. I can't believe that you're old enough to know about things like that."

"Dad, I'm fourteen. Of course I know about sex and rape and..."

Lucy ran out of things that she knew about and her Dad gave her a quick hug and apologised. Lucy had been protected from all bad things, except her mother's death. She had wanted for nothing. Kevin Collins thought about the dead girl and hoped that she had not suffered too much before she died. Lucy ran back to her friends and they tucked in to the BBQ, even Zoe forgetting about her dead friend for the time being. Kevin went back to Brian Jenkins and told him what Lucy had just said to him.

As the evening came to an end, Zoe's father turned up. He was persuaded to have one beer with Brian and Kevin then said that it was time for Zoe and Sam and Gregory to come with him. Although it was only a short distance to her house, he insisted on taking Henrietta to her gate. Peter and his girlfriend and Neil waited for another half hour, then they too left, thanking Mr Collins for the BBQ.

"Thanks, Brian. Good night. Maybe the kids talking about Norma was a good thing - get it out of their systems."

Kevin looked hopeful.

"I hope so."

Lucy came across to them having waved the others off at the gate and she prettily thanked Peter's father for coming to be company for her Dad. They walked to the gate with Brian, waved as his car drove away and walked back to the house together, arm in arm.

CHAPTER 22

On Monday morning Charles was in early to type up his second interview with Gavin Gilbert. The man had been very nervous but honest this time. He told Charles that he had taken Norma out twice in an attempt to get to know her better and to tell her that he loved her mother and wanted Norma to stop feeling unwanted in the family. He had taken her to the cinema once to see a Transformers' film that she had wanted to see and had treated her to popcorn and coke. The second time he had taken her for a meal at McDonalds, letting her choose the entire meal. Asked if he thought it had helped relationships, Gavin said that he thought it had. Asked if she had mentioned her father, he said she had not. She had not confided in him about liking any man or boy and had only talked about school and tennis.

"We talked quite a lot at McDonalds," the man had told him. "She talked about Mary, her friend, and about how she and her tennis friend Zoe weren't so close now as Zoe wasn't interested in wearing makeup and wouldn't try it for her, unlike Mary who was willing to experiment with her."

"What did you talk about to her, Sir?" Davenport had asked.

"I tried to tell her that Donald and Rory needed a lot of attention right now and that her Mum could trust her to look after herself. It wasn't that she loved her any less than the boys."

"How did she respond to that?"

"OK I suppose, though she did ask why the boys were always getting new clothes and toys and she never got anything."

"What did you say to that?"

"I tried to make her see that the boys were growing out of their clothes whereas she wasn't and I promised her extra pocket money so that she could buy herself what she wanted if she could save up. I thought I'd made her understand that she was wanted."

Davenport had thanked him for his honesty and warned him that it was not wise to lie to the police. He asked him where he had been on Monday evening and once again, Gilbert said he had been at home with his wife and sons.

"I know it's not much of an alibi for either night but we rarely go out."

The interview typed up, Charles had just poured himself a coffee when the phone rang. It was the head of SOC with the report on Norma's murder. The changing room had been full of fingerprints as was to be expected. They had matched Norma's prints to some on the handle of the clubhouse door, quite clear prints as she had obviously opened the door last, except for Avril Smiley on Saturday before the handle had been checked for prints. There were no fingerprints on the briefcase which had obviously been wiped before being returned to the changing room. The contents had Norma's fingerprints on them and one jotter had another set. Davenport mentioned that one of the tennis club women had looked inside to see whose it was and probably had touched the jotter. He promised to get Avril Smiley to give her fingerprints.

The light switch in the changing room had only one set of fingerprints so would probably have been wiped by the murderer and the prints would belong to the junior girl who had found the body. The inside handle of the outside door was full of smudged prints. A search of two containers by the main doorway had turned up lost clothing among which was a pair of cotton panties which could be traced back to Norma because of a damp patch on the crutch. Forensics could trace almost everything these days, thought Charles. He had asked them about Pat Harper's house but was told that another suspicious death had intervened between Norma's case and Pat Harper's so it might be another day before Charles would hear anything from them.

Charles thanked him and rang off. He found Avril Smiley's phone number in his notes and rang her at home. She sounded harassed and explained that she had invited six mums and toddlers for her son's third birthday and was trying to do some last minute baking while keeping her son entertained at the same time. Charles asked her to come into the station to give her fingerprints.

"My fingerprints! Why?"

Charles reassured her, explaining that they needed to eliminate hers from something in Norma's bag.

"I did take out a jotter Inspector. Just to see whose bag it was. I'm sorry. I'm sure I didn't touch anything else and Jane Green who found it, said she had wondered if it could have belonged to Norma so didn't touch it either and called me."

"No problem," said Charles. "We didn't really expect the murderer to leave his fingerprints for us to find but we have to check just in case."

He rang off and was deep in thought when Fiona arrived, looking smart in a navy suit and crisp white blouse.

"Ah, the poor ear's getting it again," she laughed and, seeing his bewilderment, she told him that when he was thinking or worried he pulled at his left ear lobe.

"First, it's my always saying, 'Right team' and now it's my ear-pulling habit! I must look at you carefully to see if you have any mannerisms."

Saying this, he came towards her from behind his desk and looked searchingly into her eyes. His face softened and he dropped a gentle kiss on her nose then noises from down the corridor told them that the others were arriving and they stepped apart.

Charles told Fiona about the SOC report and his second interview with Gavin Gilbert then went down the corridor to tell the others.

"Do you think he could have murdered Norma?" asked Penny eagerly.

"The wicked stepfather scenario do you mean? He seemed genuine about wanting Norma to feel part of the family but that doesn't rule out him having arranged to meet her away from the house. He would know that she had a key to the clubhouse..."

Davenport stopped suddenly.

"Where's her clubhouse key? Frank, ring SOC and ask if by any chance they found a key in the briefcase."

Frank went to his desk and picked up the receiver. They heard him ask for the head of SOC and a minute later, he hung up and came back to the group.

"No, Sir, no key. He said he'd have mentioned if he'd found one."

"I thought so but had to check."

"So that means either that someone now has two keys or someone has a key they never had before," said Fiona then reddened feeling that she had stated the obvious.

"Exactly," said Davenport. "In either case, the key will have been got rid of or will be soon."

"Could it still be in her room at home, Sir?" asked Salma hesitantly, not wanting to suggest that her bosses could have overlooked something.

"It certainly could, Salma," said Davenport. "We were just looking at her things and hoping to find a diary or something that would give us some information. We didn't search the room and there was no need for SOC to go there as it wasn't the murder scene. Take Penny and go back to the house and have a thorough search."

"What if Norma's Mum has tidied in the room, Sir?" asked Penny.

"Ask first if she has and if she found a key. If not, then search."

Penny and Salma left to get into the car and go up to Waterfoot. Davenport put Frank onto a routine phone call from a woman who had rung in to say that she had found a wallet and then he and Fiona went back to his room.

Salma and Penny returned triumphantly about an hour and a half later, to say that the bedroom had not been tidied up, Mrs Gilbert having told them that she felt she wanted to leave it as it was when Norma was alive and that a search of the small room had unearthed the key from under the bed.

"She must have dropped it and it went just under and no more," said Penny. She held up the key. Davenport took it. No need to be careful with fingerprints as the key was not involved in the murder scene. It was however important as he told his team now.

"Well, we can eliminate non-tennis people from our suspect list."

"Afraid not, Sir," said his DS apologetically. "The door might not have been locked."

"Wonder how likely that is," Davenport mused, pulling his left earlobe again. "Fiona, phone someone - Avril Smiley would be best as she's at home - and ask if the door is ever left open."

Fiona returned with the news that the door was often left open, by juniors she suspected, although if the murderer was in the clubhouse with Norma on Friday evening, that meant that it could have been young ones playing after school or seniors playing in the early evening.

"Probably the former, she said, Sir, as it still gets dark quite early."

"Right, let's sum this up," said Davenport. "Someone with no key goes to the clubhouse with Norma expecting her to have her key. She hasn't but they find the clubhouse door open, or someone with a key goes to the clubhouse with Norma. What do you think, folks?"

"My money's on a member of the tennis club," said Frank who had been silent up till now. "That Don Kinross is my bet."

"I still think it could be her stepfather," volunteered Salma. "He would expect her to have her key."

"Penny?" Davenport enquired.

"Well the stepfather's often the guilty person but I think like Frank that it's been a tennis member but not Don Kinross because he's probably having an affair with one of the women so that leaves another man, intermediate or senior."

It being lunchtime, Davenport and Fiona went out to eat at one of the local pubs leaving the young ones to adjourn to the canteen.

CHAPTER 23

Unfortunately for Penny, her removal day was wet and windy. Salma arrived promptly at 9am and they waited for the removal van which turned up late at 9.20. The girls and Penny's Mum, Margaret and new husband Jack, had spent the evening before packing and labelling boxes so all that was left to do was supervise the loading of the van. Penny was only taking her bedroom furniture. Although she had lived with her Mum all her life, she felt that her Mum had built up the home and the rest of the furniture was hers. Jack had surprised her by saying some months ago that she could have any of his furniture that she liked and she had walked round his flat and chosen some pieces such as his dining room table, four chairs and highboard and a coffee table. Alec was giving her two rooms and she would share the bathroom and kitchen with him so she did not need any white goods.

Most of the boxes contained bedding and clothes and Penny had also taken some towels, crockery and glasses. The majority of the boxes however, contained books, as Penny was a squirrel when it came to her favourite novels. They would have to stay in their boxes until she had decided where they could go. Jack, not being a reader, had not possessed a bookcase and her Mum was also a reader and needed hers.

Penny and Salma followed the removal van from Shawlands to Newlands where Alec had a large flat one floor up, near Pollokshaws East station. He was there to meet them having taken the morning off work. Being a rep, he could choose his own hours. Having had to park some way from the flat, both girls were soaked and breathless when they arrived.

"Put the boxes in the hallway," Alec instructed the removal men. "Over on the right hand side." This left room for the furniture and Penny had the bedroom furniture taken into the smaller room and the dining room furniture taken in to the large room where it was placed by the window, leaving room for the lounge furniture which Penny would buy in the future.

The removal men left, seeming pleased with the tip which Penny gave them, courtesy of her Mum who had given her daughter twenty pounds for this purpose. She and Salma arranged the large pieces of furniture, bed and dressing table and wardrobe in the small room and the dining table and four chairs and highboard in the other room. Alec offered them a coffee. Salma asked for tea instead and they all sat in Alec's lounge and refreshed themselves with a hot drink.

"Come on, Penny. If you want help with unpacking those boxes we'd better get started," said Salma, looking at her watch and remembering that she had to get back to the station by 1pm.

They carried a box each into the bedroom and began putting clothes into the wardrobe and dressing table drawers. Alec took a box labelled 'glasses' into the other room and carefully unwrapped the glasses which went into the top section of the highboard.

At a few minutes before 12.30, Penny sat down on the made-up bed and looked round. Salma, closing the bottom drawer of the dressing table, sat back on her heels and looked at her friend.

"Penny, you're crying. What's the matter?"

"Just realised that I won't be going home again," sniffed Penny.

"Don't be silly. You'll visit your Mum and Jack often and just think of the freedom you'll have, having nobody to check up when you come in at night."

Penny gave a watery smile.

"Thanks Salma, you're a pal. You'd better bring your bag up from the car and get changed."

Salma looked down at her tight denims and red tee-shirt, rumpled from lifting and carrying and said laughingly, "Yes. Don't think the boss would be pleased if I arrived looking like this."

She left the flat and returned with her holdall and another box. She took out her uniform, shook out the skirt then took her white shirt blouse and the skirt into the bathroom and returned looking as trim as she usually did. She shrugged into her jacket then picked up the box and handed it to Penny.

"Your first housewarming present."

Penny, looking delighted, opened the box and withdrew a radio alarm clock in a bright red colour.

"Well you won't have your Mum to wake you up now," Salma laughed, "and I didn't want you doing a Frank and turning up late tomorrow."

Penny gave her a hug then told her she had better get away or she would be the one who was late.

"Phone me tonight, Salma and let me know what's happened today that I've missed." She wrote the number on a piece of paper which she took from her handbag.

"Here's my new number. Would you give it to Bob to put on file and perhaps give it to the DCI too, please?"

Agreeing to do this, Salma gave her another hug and departed. Penny and Alec looked at the remaining box and at each other.

"Lunch first, Penny?"

"Just what I was thinking."

They went to the local cafe which Alex said did good sandwiches, and had a break, Penny wiring into a BLT which was her favourite sandwich and Alex having one with egg mayonnaise. Both had a skinny latte. There being no need to hurry back to the flat, they chatted idly about their plans to have a housewarming party for Penny the following weekend. Alec took a serviette and they wrote down the names of those they wanted to invite.

"What about your Mum and Jack?" Alex asked.

"No. I'll keep the party for our age group and ask them up separately the following week. It's good that we have so many communal friends and you've met Salma and Frank."

"Will you invite your DS and DCI?"

"Oh no, they're more Mum's age group than ours and that would make me nervous. Besides the boss has Pippa, his daughter, to look after."

Luckily the cafe was almost empty and Alec knew the owner from many visits so it was nearly 3pm by the time they made their way back to the flat. As they went in, the phone was ringing.

"I bet that's Mum. I said I'd phone her when I'd settled in," said Penny.

It was indeed Margaret Maclean and Penny apologised for not contacting her. Her mother was only too delighted to hear that nearly all the unpacking had been done. It was a busy day at Dobbies Garden Centre where she worked so she did not stay on the line for long, just long enough to agree to come over a week on Saturday with Jack.

"For a meal, Penny?" she teasingly asked, knowing that her daughter was not a cook.

"Oh Mum, not yet, just for supper, say about 8pm?"

It took a short time to empty the last box which contained towels and spare bedding. Alec opened a large hall cupboard and showed her where he kept his.

"I tend to do washing on Saturday morning. We take turns to use the back green for hanging out washing. I'm the only one who works, the rest being retired luckily, so they're happy for me to have the weekend. We also take turns with old Mrs Smith across the landing to mop the stairs and landing."

Penny, having never lived in a tenement before, listened carefully.

"You and I can take it in turns to do that then it'll only be every third week. Do you have an iron and can I use it?"

"Of course you can. Don't know what we'll do about eating."

"I'm not much of a cook but I can heat things up," laughed Penny.

"That suits me. Why don't we take it in turns to do the meal?"

"Maybe you could do it when I'm going to be late and I could do it other times."

"As long as we agree in the morning who's doing it that day," said Alec.

"If things go wrong we can always have a take-away," said Penny. "What about tonight?"

It turned out that Alec was eating out with his boyfriend in town and going on to the Kings' Theatre. He left to get washed and changed and Penny went into what would eventually be her lounge and sat at the table, looking out at the traffic on the main Kilmarnock Road. It was noisy in spite of the double glazing and she wondered if it would be difficult to get to sleep that night. She looked at the bare half of the room and decided that some of her savings would have to go on a three piece suite.

"That's me away, Penny. Leave you to settle in on your own!" called Alec. She heard the outside door bang shut.

Feeling homesick and a bit unsure of what to do, Penny wandered into the kitchen. She had been in Alec's flat a few times but never in the kitchen so she nosed around familiarising herself with the whereabouts of everything. There was a washing machine, a cooker, a fridge-freezer and a microwave. No dish washer. There was no room for one. Penny noticed the pulley. She and her Mum had not had one of those and had hung clothes on radiators in wet weather. She filled the kettle and switched it on and over a coffee - she was pleased to see that Alec used semi-skimmed milk - thought about what she would do about eating tonight. She had noticed on the hall table some menus from various local restaurants and had just decided to phone for a carry-out Chinese meal when the main door buzzer went. Wondering who this could be, she lifted the door phone. It was her Mum. She pressed the button to open the door and opened the flat door. Her Mum and Jack appeared, laden with dishes.

"Hello love. Hope we're not interfering but I thought you might not have thought about your meal tonight so we brought over a casserole and an apple pie and a flask of my homemade lentil soup. There's enough for Alec too if he's in."

"Oh Mum, bless you and you too, Jack."

Penny gave them both a big hug and stepped back to let them in.

"Alec's out for the evening and you're right. I hadn't thought about a meal and was just about to send out for a take-away one. Have you eaten or will you join me?"

They joined her and after taking a while to unearth place mats which had got in with the towels, they sat down to a delicious three course meal.

It was a tired but happy Penny who went to bed in her new home later that night and not even the noise of frequent buses or the late arrival of her flatmate woke her up.

CHAPTER 24

Davenport had called a meeting with the head of SOC and Martin Jamieson. He made them all coffee.

"I know I've had the main findings from you both but as usual I thought maybe it would be better for me to hear the details from the horses' mouths."

"Nei...gh." The head of SOC, Ben Goodwin was noted for his sense of humour. He had recently moved up from Liverpool and had often brought a note of humour into the dryness of inquests down there, Davenport had heard. He liked Ben. The last head of SOC, Vince Parker, had been a pedantic, serious man whose one thought had been promotion. Ben, at fifty- six, looked older than his years, being grey-haired and having a weather-beaten, wrinkled face caused less by his harrowing job than by the fact that he fished in all weathers. He had asked for a move to Scotland on the death of his wife. They had moved to England, he said, so that she could be near her relatives and now he wanted to be back in Scotland.

"Sorry. To be serious, there were a lot of fingerprints on the inside of the tennis club's outside door and only one on the light switch of the changing room the body was in. The switch in the other changing room was covered in fingerprints. This was to be expected, Davenport, as nobody will clean these as well or as often as they would in a house. The first light switch was obviously wiped by the murderer and the prints will be those of the wee girl who found the body. I don't think we need to put the wee lass through the trauma of giving her prints."

Davenport agreed with this.

"And the panties?"

"I found the pair of panties as I told you over the phone, in a tub at the door, where they obviously put left clothing as there was a pair of tracksuit bottoms and a pair of white socks. The panties were slightly damp in the crotch."

"Did this tell you anything?"

"More Martin Jamieson's field than mine, Sir," he replied.

Asked if there was any evidence of anyone else being present at the scene apart from Norma and the murderer, Ben said it was unlikely but possible that there could have been an accomplice. There were so many fingerprints all over the changing room and toilet.

He went on to talk about the briefcase which had not been there when he was called at first but which had turned up later. Everything inside had Norma's fingerprints on it.

He said he had been sent Avril Smiley's fingerprints late afternoon the day before and they had matched the clearest set on one of the jotters.

Davenport thanked him. The coffee cups were empty so he refilled them.

"Martin. What did the dampness on the panties tell you?"

"The fluid came from her vagina and suggested that she was sexually aroused at some point."

"So it's probable that she came to the clubhouse willingly, that she enjoyed what happened at first but perhaps got scared and tried to run and was dragged back as the scuff marks along the carpet in the hallways showed?"

Both men nodded.

"There were corresponding marks on the backs of her shoes," said Ben.

"And she was choked by the killer pressing on her throat with both hands?"

"Yes," said Martin. "With the fingers of both hands, from behind remember."

"Now let's turn to Pat Harper," said Davenport.

"I've written my report on Patricia Harper," Martin said, handing Davenport a large envelope. "I am sorry that I took longer than usual. There has been much pressure of work."

Charles assured him that it did not matter as they were still no further forward with the first case.

"I think these two killings are probably connected," he said. "It's too much of a coincidence that two members of Greenway Tennis Club should be murdered in the space of just over a week. Thanks for the written report but will you summarise what you found in the second case?

Martin said he would.

"Have you both got time for lunch?" asked Charles.

Martin and Ben saying that they had time, the three adjourned to a nearby hotel where they ordered lunch. Charles, aware that he would be eating with Pippa later in the day, had a plate of prawn sandwiches and Martin who knew that his wife would have prepared dinner, contented himself with a panini with tuna mayonnaise. Ben decided to spare himself making a meal later and chose a chicken curry with chips.

Eating over, they settled back with coffees and Martin brought them up to date with his findings on Pat Harper.

"Mrs Harper was smothered. Her assailant pushed her face down into a pillow, the one her head was lying on when she was found. She had bitten the same pillow."

"Why?" asked Charles.

"I would surmise that prior to her being killed, she had indulged in some masochistic sexual foreplay and had bitten the pillow in pain. She had two large purple weals on her backside."

"Made by what?"

"A leather belt. She was probably tied to the bed by her wrists as I also found lighter weals round her wrists, consistent with her having had softish handcuffs placed round them.

"We found no handcuffs or belts," said Charles.

"Maybe the murderer brought them and took them away," suggested Ben.

"We did find a completely empty drawer which I found strange."

"So that drawer probably kept the weapons used for masochistic sex," said Martin.

"Maybe that was why we found Pat in the spare bedroom. Her main bedroom was through the wall from the main bedroom of her next door neighbour and she and her lover wouldn't want to be heard. I imagine the sex between them was often noisy and Penny or Frank said that only the upstairs windows were double-glazed."

"That seems to confirm the masochistic sex angle." Ben finished his meal and sat back in his chair.

Martin agreed.

"What height and weight was Mrs Harper, Martin?" asked Davenport.

"Five feet, four inches and 123 lbs."

"And what about the unnatural position of the body?" Davenport asked.

"The murderer turned her over once she was dead and must have arranged the body that way."

They had all finished eating now so Davenport paid for their meals, thanked them both and said he would inform the procurator fiscal of their findings. Ben said that he would send round his findings on Pat Harper once he had finished his investigations.

"Sorry I'm not as quick as the young fellow here," he said and Martin laughed.

Back at the station, Davenport informed Salma, recently returned from Penny's, and Frank who had been manning the fort, of the recent discoveries about Pat Harper.

"Sounds as if this murder might have been a sex game gone wrong," said Salma.

"No, I don't think so," volunteered Frank. "If that had been the case, she'd have had more injuries, not just one belt mark. I don't think she was killed by mistake, do you Sir?"

"No, I agree with you, Frank. I think our murderer was known to Pat Harper, lulled her into a false sense of normality by starting to play their usual sex game then smothered her."

"It has to be someone quite strong then, Sir," said Frank. "Pat wasn't small and thin. She was of medium height and..."

"...quite light for her height. 123 lbs., Martin said."

"I wonder what she knew," mused Salma out loud.

"And how the murderer found out that she knew something to point the finger at him," added Davenport.

Fiona had been at the canteen and arrived back at this moment so Davenport repeated what he had told Salma and Frank. Penny would have to be told the next day.

At about 5pm, a call came through from the desk to say that the SOC report had been handed in. Frank was dispatched to bring it to Davenport's office. The report stated that there were no fingerprints on any surface in the spare bedroom and those in the main bedroom were those of Pat Harper. The door handles of the spare bedroom and the inside handle of the front door were wiped clean. The outside handle bore Pat's own fingerprints. A minute strand of pink fluff had been found on the bed.

"Pink, fluffy handcuffs!" exclaimed Frank, then blushed when the others turned to look at him.

"I've seen them advertised in a magazine," he said.

Davenport grinned at him. He looked back down at the report.

"Well that seems to be all from SOC, though they mention that the bedroom carpet had some granules of sand on it. A search of the house found a pair of tennis shoes in the hallway by the front door and those shoes had sand on them, sand which, according to SOC, came from the tennis court, so if sand reached the bedroom it's likely, folks, that the killer's shoes also had sand from the tennis courts on them."

"Another link to tennis and Norma Lawson's death," said Fiona.

"It would seem so."

"Have you had lunch, Salma?" Fiona asked.

"No Ma'am. We were too busy."

"How did the removal go?" asked Frank.

"We got it all done. There were only two rooms to fill."

"Well get down to the canteen and have something now," said Davenport.

Salma went off.

"I'm going to ring Norma's Mum and ask about the funeral," said Davenport.

Fiona and Frank left him to it and he came down the corridor a few minutes later to tell them that the funeral could go ahead on Friday, 2pm at The Linn Crematorium.

CHAPTER 25

The car was in a lay-by at the foot of Ballageich Hill on the Eaglesham Moor Road. The windows were steamed up. It was dark. She was fully clothed apart from her panties; he was fully clothed but his trousers were unzipped. They had climaxed together as they always did and now lay in each other's arms in the confined space of his Mercedes' back seat. Sometimes they just petted heavily but knowing that this was the last time, they had gone the whole way.

"Oh, Don. Must we stop seeing each other?"

"I'm sorry, Sheila but Olive has found out somehow. If you had seen the way she looked at me when the police were there asking about Norma and your name came up!"

"Has she said anything to you about me?"

"No."

"Then maybe she was just guessing. Who could have told her about us? Nobody knows unless you've told someone."

"I certainly haven't said anything but we can't be sure that we haven't been seen."

"But we always meet up here."

"Yes I know but someone could have passed this lay-by and seen both our cars together."

"We didn't start meeting till January and the nights are dark. How could they see our cars if they were passing at speed? You're being silly, Don."

"Look, I admitted to you almost right away that you haven't been the first person I've had an affair with and Olive swore that she'd leave me and take the kids if I ever strayed again."

"But she has no proof, I'm sure."

She stroked him and felt him harden. It was so easy to turn him on. She was no better as she felt herself moisten almost immediately. He groaned.

"No, Sheila. I mean it. Never again."

"Not even outside, over the bonnet?"

She felt his erection rise further and knew that she had won. He opened the door and almost dragged her out of the car and round to the front of it. He felt round the back of her slim figure and finding the skirt button, undid it and pulled down the zip. Her skirt fell to the ground. Although it was dark he knew that she was now bare from the waist down as he had her flimsy panties in his trouser pocket. She tugged at his belt, then his trouser catch and pulled his trousers down. He stepped out of them. Luckily the car was coming from the

Kilmarnock direction and his car hid them both but by now neither of them cared if anyone saw them, in fact it probably added spice to the event which was to come. He tugged down his boxer shorts and pushed her roughly backwards over the long bonnet of his expensive car,

"Yes, Don, yes, yes...don't stop." She felt almost dizzy with the force of her orgasm when it came. Within seconds he too had climaxed and collapsed over her, panting. It was Don who heard a car approaching from Eaglesham. He pulled Sheila upright and half dragged her round the side of the car as a van hurtled past them. Don felt round the side of the car and found his trousers and shorts. He stood up and pulled them on then walked round to retrieve Sheila's skirt. Back in the car, in the front seats, they sat silent for a while then Sheila spoke:

"You never want that again, Don?"

"Of course I do. Olive never wants to have sex with me and she certainly wouldn't do anything adventurous but I couldn't bear to lose my kids."

"On the other hand, Don, you said you thought that the police suspected you of tampering with Norma, maybe even killing her, so surely if they suspect that you and I are having an affair that would help to rule you out for having sex with a teenager? Do you think they noticed Olive looking at you suspiciously when you mentioned my name?"

"Yes I'm sure they did."

"Well then..."

Don was easily persuaded. Sex with Sheila Ferguson had been wonderful, the best he had ever had and he envisaged more adventurous liaisons with her. He had married Olive, his teenage sweetheart when they were both only twenty -one. She had been compliant in bed but had always frozen if he tried anything different. Recently she had become worried that his sons, now twelve and fourteen, would hear or she was too tired. As he sat with Sheila in his car, he began to feel that it was all Olive's fault that he had strayed once again.

"You know, Sheila, you're right. An affair with you will stop the police suspecting me and anyway I have rights to my kids and if Olive leaves me, I'll still get to see them."

He could feel himself beginning to harden again and he knew that Sheila was impressed with his ability to make love often in one night. He stroked her breast through her blouse and felt her nipple peak. She was fantastic; she really was, as insatiable as himself.

"Again darling?" he asked, already knowing the answer.

Their coupling this time was almost frantic.

Half an hour later, Don was pulling up outside his house in Netherlee, rehearsing his excuses for being late and Sheila was in her house in Eaglesham, listening to a message on her answerphone from her husband who told her that he would be back from London at the weekend. His job as a politician ensured that he was at Westminster all week, a handy arrangement for his two-timing wife.

CHAPTER 26

Davenport was perusing the typed up report of his interview with Paul Lawson. He had just reached the part where Lawson had said that he had been at home by himself all evening but his girlfriend Sue had come in about 11pm. Putting the report down, he opened his door and called down the corridor;

"Selby, my room please."

"Ooh, Frank. Are you in trouble?" Penny teased him.

Frank laughed back but he straightened his tie nervously. It was not often that Davenport called him Selby these days and he wondered what he could have done wrong. It was a bit like being summoned to the head-teacher when he was at school but then he had always known what he had done wrong.

He walked quickly up the corridor and knocked on the half-open door.

"Come in, Frank."

Davenport was seated behind his large oak desk. It was a pleasant room, made so by the plants dotted round it and tended, unknown to Frank, by Fiona Macdonald.

"I want you to go across town to - he looked down at a paper on his desk - Ascot Court, number 4, just off Great western Road I believe, and interview a Miss Susan Keith. She's the girlfriend of Norma Lawson's father. He says she came in on the night Norma was killed at 11pm and could vouch for the fact that he was there."

"Will I go now, Sir?" asked Frank, relieved that he had not been sent to be reprimanded for something. He really did have a clear conscience as he was getting in on time, seldom early, but on time and he always took care to see that his uniform, including his shoes, was clean and tidy. He had even begun to keep his hair shorter at the back.

"No. Better phone first and see if she's at home. She probably works. Try again at lunchtime and again around 6pm if you can't raise her before that."

"What if she says she's going out tonight, Sir?"

"Tell her you'll be there before she leaves."

Frank turned to go.

"Oh and Frank, I see that you haven't applied for any promoted posts recently."

"No Sir."

"Why not?"

"Well Sir, I was a bit put off when Salma... Sergeant Din... got the one I'd applied for here and I didn't think you'd give me a good reference."

"Well a few months ago you're correct, I wouldn't have but I've been watching you and apart from the tendency to burst into song at odd intervals and the odd take-off of myself..."

Frank felt his face go red and hot. He had thought that his little habit of mimicking his boss had been a well-kept secret but obviously not!

"...I think you've sharpened up your act, so get on with trying for promotion. We'll make a sergeant of you yet."

"Thank you, Sir and Sir, I'm sorry about the singing and...the other...I'll stop doing that."

"Don't Selby. We all need some light-hearted moments in the kind of work we do."

Frank went back to the room he shared with Penny and Salma.

"Not in trouble, thank goodness but he knows that I impersonate him at times and he mentioned the singing!"

He picked up the phonebook and looked under Lawson. There was no address in Ascot Court so he tried under S. Keith where he found what he was looking for. Paul Lawson must have moved in with his girlfriend. He dialled the number but got only the answering service. No point in leaving a message.

About an hour later it was Salma who heard her name called. Making sure that her uniform skirt was straight, she patted her smooth, glossy hair and hurried up the corridor.

She knocked on the door which Frank had closed.

"Come in."

Davenport was standing at the window and turned as his sergeant came in. As always, he was struck by her beauty and wondered if she would be staying for long in her job as he knew that in her religion, marriages were usually arranged. It could be seen as racist if he asked her, as he would never have dreamed of asking Penny about her marriage prospects, so he just smiled and invited her to sit down, taking a seat across the desk from her.

"Salma, would you have any objections to going to Norma Lawson's funeral tomorrow? I know it might be strange for you but you need to have the experience and I want someone there. Sometimes murderers attend the funeral of the person they've killed and I want to know who goes to it."

Salma was a bit taken aback. She had never, as her boss suspected, gone to a funeral apart from ones from her own faith. She knew however that he was right. In her job she would need to attend one at some time or other.

"There are two different types of funeral in the Christian faith, Sir, aren't there? Which kind is Norma's?"

"It's a cremation. 2 pm tomorrow at Linn Crematorium."

Seeing a look of what could almost be called panic on his sergeant's face, a face which was usually so calm, he took pity on her.

"You and Penny take an early lunch. She can fill you in on what happens and tell you how to get to the crematorium and you can ask her questions. Would that help?"

"Thank you, Sir. I know I do need to know what happens. Don't worry. I won't let you down."

"I know you won't."

Salma went back down the corridor and told Penny that they had been given an early lunch. Knowing that they often shared lunch in the canteen with Frank, she took a minute to explain to him why they were going at this time.

"Serge, you're going to stick out like a sore thumb. Never seen a Pak...a bla..."

He ground to a halt and looked embarrassed.

"It's OK Frank. I know what you're trying to say. That's why Penny's going to help me over lunch."

Penny glared at Frank. It had been some time since he had been clumsy over Salma's different race but Salma drew Penny out of the door and threw a sympathetic look at Frank. He looked relieved. He was fond of Salma now and had never meant to hurt her.

The girls found that there was no queue in the canteen and for once they had a good selection of meals to choose from, being quite early today. Penny chose macaroni and cheese. It was her turn to cook dinner tonight and she didn't want to ruin her appetite. She had made one of her Mum's chicken casseroles for Alec and herself, to be followed by apple crumble which she had made a few times at home. Salma took a yogurt and two biscuits with a small portion of cheese. Her Mum always made a large dinner for her family and Salma wanted to keep her slim figure.

Once they were seated, Penny started by giving her directions from the station to The Linn. It was quite simple to get there from Govanhill.

"When's the funeral?" she asked her friend.

"2 pm."

"Well, don't leave here till 1.40. You don't want to be too early because the funeral before Norma's won't be over and all the cars will still be there and you'd have to park a long way from the chapel..."

"Chapel? I thought chapels were Catholic. Is the family Catholic?"

"No. They're Protestant but the two buildings at the crematorium are called chapels and sometimes Catholics call their chapel a church."

"I see," said Salma, not really seeing at all.

"If there are a lot of cars parked up the driveway, stop before the gates and wait for the hearse - the funeral car - and follow it and the family car up. The car park at the top of the hill can get quite packed but it should empty before the hearse gets to the top. Be careful when you come out, to come down the correct path as they're both one way."

Seeing Salma was looking bewildered, Penny took out her notebook and, tearing out a page, drew her a diagram. Salma took it and carefully folded it up and put it into the breast pocket of her uniform jacket. The talk then turned to what happened next.

"Join the queue and just follow everyone else in. Try to sit near the back and that way you can see who else is there. There are hymn books in the back of the seat in front of you. You'll not be the only one who doesn't know the words or the tune. I go to church so I do but there are always lots of atheists at funerals."

Penny ran out of breath and stopped.

"Do I have to kneel at all?" asked Salma, having seen this happening in churches on TV.

"No and the minister should tell you when to sit and when to stand. You'll probably have to shake hands with Norma's mum and stepfather and maybe her dad too as you're leaving."

"What will I say?"

"Just say you're very sorry. They'll know who you are by your uniform."

"Thanks, Penny. Your macaroni's getting cold. You'd better eat it."

They finished off their lunch and returned to their part of the station. The canteen was filling up now and they passed Frank at the back of the queue. He grinned at them. He was standing with a shapely blonde PC from the department in the floor above them. He would not miss their company today!

CHAPTER 27

It was not till about 5pm that Frank finally managed to speak to Susan Keith on the phone. She was going out at around 8pm but agreed to see him if he came straight over. Penny, overhearing him making the arrangement, waited till he had put the phone down and then asked him if he would like to come to her flat for dinner when he got back. She felt that they had not had any time together recently and he might feel left out that Salma had seen the flat.

"If you feel like risking my cooking, that is," she laughed. "Nothing fancy, just a chicken casserole and apple crumble."

Frank said that he would be delighted. His parents were away for a week, down South visiting his aunt who had been in hospital and he had been making his own meals that week.

"Are you sure that Alec won't mind me coming?" he asked.

"Alec will be going out after the meal. His boyfriend lives across the city and he goes over most nights."

Frank made a face. He had toned down his racism since getting to know Salma but was still homophobic. Penny caught the look.

"Frank Selby. The only thing that matters is that Alec is a nice guy. You'll like him if you don't let his sexuality get in the way."

"Don't worry, Penny Farthing, I won't say anything. I'll be the perfect guest."

So saying, Frank collected his uniform jacket and hat and went out to one of the police cars. It took him about half an hour to get across to Great Western Road but once there he soon found Ascot Court. Number Four was one floor up and there was a lift, a smooth-running affair which was carpeted. The door was answered quickly by a petite brunette wearing denims and a tight navy jumper. Frank estimated her age at around twenty-five.

"Miss Keith?"

"Yes."

"I'm PC Selby"

He showed his warrant card and she read it carefully before handing it back and ushering him inside the flat. There was no one else in the lounge and he wondered where Paul Lawson was.

As if reading his thoughts, the young woman said, "My partner, Paul, thought you might like to speak to me alone. He's gone on to the pub where we're meeting our friends. Please sit down."

Frank took a seat on one of the black leather chairs and the woman sat in the middle of the matching settee. The room was tastefully furnished with a large digital television in one corner and a cabinet full of crystal glasses in the other.

"Nice room. Is it your flat, Miss Keith?"

"Yes. Mummy bought it for me last year when I left home to live with Paul. He doesn't have much money left after alimony to his wife and maintenance for Norma...I hate to sound mercenary but that'll stop now, won't it?"

"I suppose so. Does he contribute at all?" Frank asked, thinking that this young woman certainly had the whip hand in this relationship. How could Paul Lawson have brought Norma to live with him here?

"Not much but anyway what has this to do with you?"

"Sorry. Did Paul ever see his daughter?" Frank wondered how much the man had told his girlfriend.

"He saw her twice. He went to the school to speak to her and he invited her over to the flat one night."

"Did he ask your permission to bring her here?"

The girl looked peeved.

"No he didn't and I only found out last night when he told me about it. I wanted him to forget his past life and it suited me that his wife didn't want him to see Norma. I'm only twenty-four and I didn't want a teenager about the place."

"Did you know that he wrote to her?" asked Frank.

"No I didn't!"

The look on her face boded no good for Paul Lawson when they met up, Frank thought. Then the expression on her face changed to one of suspicion.

"Why are you asking me all these things? Surely you don't think Paul killed his daughter."

"In a murder investigation all avenues are explored, Miss Keith. Just one more thing. What time did you come home a week last Friday, in the evening?"

"I came home just after 11 o'clock and Paul was here when I got home."

Paul had obviously warned her about this question, Frank realised.

"Wasn't it unusual for you to be out without him on a Friday night?"

"We're not joined at the hip. We're not married. I like to go clubbing with my friends on Fridays."

"Surely 11 o'clock was very early to come home?"

"I had a headache. I get migraines sometimes and one started …the strobe lights I think."

"What was Paul doing when you got home?"

"Watching television,as usual."

Frank wrote in his notebook to remember to find out what the man had been watching, earlier in the evening, if he had indeed been in all the time.

"One last question, Miss Keith. Where was Paul on Monday evening of this week?"

The girl thought for a moment.

"Visiting his mother."

"Where does she live?"

"Somewhere in Shawlands. I don't know exactly where. The old bat doesn't like me. Thinks I split up his marriage."

"When did he get home?"

"About 10.30."

Frank rose to leave and the girl got to her feet, looking relieved that the questioning was over. Frank took the stairs two at a time and was soon on his way back across Glasgow. The roads were quieter now and in twenty minutes, he was outside Penny's new home. He was just about to press the buzzer when he realised that, as this was his first visit, he should really take Penny a present. He looked round. Across the road was a small Tesco. He went over. Knowing that he was not being very original, he picked up a bottle of white wine. He was just about to scan the bottle when he had second thoughts and going back to the drinks' section, he exchanged it for a bottle of quite expensive champagne.

Back across the road, he pressed the buzzer. A male voice answered and when Frank said who he was, he was told to come up. Alec welcomed him in.

"She's in the kitchen, all hot and frazzled," he laughed. "Don't think the words 'domestic' and 'goddess' describe our Penny."

Frank felt himself bridling at the 'our Penny' then remembered that Alec had known Penny for a lot longer than he had and grinned at the man. He shrugged off his jacket and removed his hat. Alec led him into a room with a dining table and chairs at one end and a brown corduroy suite at the other. It looked very like his parents' lounge suite and he wondered if Alec had been given his parents' cast-off furniture. This feeling was confirmed when he put the bottle on the table and saw the signs of wear and tear on the teak surface.

"We're eating in here as Penny hasn't got lounge furniture yet," Alec explained.

As he said this, Penny came in looking hot and wearing a bright PVC apron. She gave Frank a peck on the cheek.

"Dinner's almost ready," she said. "I asked Gordon too but he's had to cancel. A doggy patient had a relapse. Maybe just as well as I've burned some of the meal so there's less of it."

Frank picked up the bottle from the table and handed it to her.

"Oh, champagne! Can I keep it till I ask you up for a better meal, Frank? I've got a bottle of cheap plonk in the fridge."

Frank readily agreed. He wasn't a connoisseur of wine and actually preferred cheaper stuff if he couldn't have a beer.

"Beer instead if you'd rather, Frank," said Alec and Frank, apologising to Penny, said that would suit him better.

Penny left to bring in the meal and they all sat down. As she had said, there was not a lot but what there was tasted fine and the apple crumble was delicious. Alec turned out to be a humorous fellow and the evening was a jolly one, all of them cramming into the small kitchen to clean up.

Alec left soon afterwards as Penny had said he would. At 11pm, Frank looked at his watch. "Work tomorrow," he said. "I'd better go."

He gave Penny a big hug and left.

CHAPTER 28

F rank and Penny were telling Salma about their meal the night before when DS Macdonald came into their room to tell them that Davenport had been summoned to see the chief constable again. She had a copy of The Herald with her and she showed them the front page with its large headline:

DOUBLE SOUTHSIDE MURDER

"Grant Knox is quoted as saying that the police are following some important leads," Fiona told them. "So the DCI will be on the carpet for not having any."

Fiona really felt for Charles but could not, out of loyalty to the chief constable, run him down to a sergeant and two PCs. Penny looked thunderous and rushed to the defence of her boss.

"The first murder only took place about two weeks ago and the second one not even a week ago. What does the man expect with so many people involved?"

Salma, always reasonable, tried to point out that Knox had the press hounding him and had to be seen to be pushing for results.

"Is there anything we can do, ma'am?" asked Frank, the 'ma'am' coming easily and naturally now.

"Well, I'm going off to visit Sheila Ferguson to see if she is indeed having an affair with Donald Kinross. If she is then it's less likely that he would have been trying it on with Norma. I rang her early this morning and she had some flexi-time due to her so will see me this morning."

"What about us?"

Penny, in her eagerness, forgot to give Fiona her title and always fair, Fiona said, gently, "Ma'am or DS Macdonald, Penny," as it would not be fair to let Penny off with something she had been strict with Frank about. Penny's already rosy cheeks, reddened further.

"Sorry, Ma'am. What about us? Can we do anything?"

"I remember someone saying a young woman visited Pat on Tuesday evenings. I wonder if that would be one of the women who played tennis on Tuesday evenings. They would have to stop quite early because of the light..."

"They have floodlights, ma'am," said Penny. "I noticed that last week when we passed the club."

"OK but even if it continued in the dark, maybe one of them went to Pat's for supper and might be more than just a tennis friend. She might know more about Pat's life. Salma, you check with Avril who doesn't work. See if you can get a name for us."

Salma went to her desk to phone Avril Smiley and returned with a name.

"Georgina Laird, her partner, sometimes went off with her after the practice, ma'am."

"Right, get Georgina's phone number from our lists. I think you and Penny said they were well-off so maybe Mum doesn't work and can tell us when her daughter will be home."

Salma went off again. She returned to say that Mrs Laird had informed her that her elder daughter was at college but that on Thursday afternoons she had no classes and would probably come home. She had offered to contact 'George' on her mobile and make sure that she was at home. Salma had thanked her and asked her to do that.

"Right, Salma. You and Penny get up to Waterfoot and see what information on Pat you can get from Georgina Laird."

Penny and Salma got their jackets and hats and went off.

"And me, ma'am?" asked Frank.

"Get your interview with Paul Lawson's girlfriend written up. What did she tell you Frank?"

"She corroborated his story about him being in on the Friday evening when she came home but I felt that they had discussed this so ..."

"...not a good alibi then. Anything else?"

"She hadn't known that Norma had been in the house, her house by the way, until last night. Don't think Paul contributes much and the girlfriend, Susan Keith, is, I think, the boss of the outfit. She didn't know that Paul had been writing to Norma either."

"Did you ask her about Monday night?"

"She said he had been visiting his mother in Shawlands. He got home around 10.30. She couldn't give me the address. Not that it's relevant, ma'am but I don't think that partnership will last very long. They seem to lead separate lives."

"So he could have got across to Stamperland, killed Norma and been back before Susan arrived home and on Monday he could have been in Pat Harper's house before or after visiting his mother. Frank, ring Mr Lawson and get his mother's address, then pay her a visit."

When Davenport returned from his visit to Grant Knox, he found no one waiting for him but there was a note from Fiona on his desk, telling him that his team were busy with regards to the two cases and would be back in the early afternoon. Still smarting from his superior's scathing comments about his handling of the case so far, Charles made himself a coffee and thought how lucky he was to have Fiona in his private and working life.

Fiona was first to return, bringing with her some news and some sandwiches for herself and Charles. She sat down across from him at the desk, took the coffee he had poured for her and unwrapping two packets of sandwiches, gave him a cheese and tomato one and one with prawn Marie rose.

"How did it go, Charles?"

"Not good. As usual he handled the press badly and now wants results to give them. Did you get anywhere with Donald Kinross's other woman?"

"She admitted to having an affair. Said she and Kinross went off together after the match practices sometimes. I asked her about Monday evening and she said they were together that night as he and Olive were going to a parents' evening this Tuesday after match practice and she was already annoyed that he had insisted on going to tennis and would be late."

"Where were he and Sheila on Monday evening?"

"In a car on the moor road."

"So no witnesses?"

"No, so she could be lying for him?"

"We'll need to ask him where he was before she gets a chance to speak to him."

"With mobile phones, Charles?"

"I guess so. She'll have spoken to him already."

Frank arrived back next. Paul Lawson's mother confirmed that he had been with her for a couple of hours. He had brought her flowers which were sitting on her dining room table. He had left at about ten o'clock.

"That ties up with the time he arrived home. Just need to confirm when he left work. Frank, ring Mr Lawson on his mobile and find out where he works and get there this afternoon."

Frank loped off down the corridor and a few minutes later they heard him go off towards the outside door.

Penny and Salma arrived about twenty minutes later. They too carried wrapped sandwiches and a can of coke each. Mrs Laird had given them coffee while they waited for Georgina to come home. Georgina had verified that she had often gone to Pat's house after match practice on Tuesdays. Pat had given her supper and they had chatted, usually about their forthcoming tennis match.

"We both wanted to be first couple and I'm afraid we bitched a bit about Avril and Anne," she had told Penny and Salma.

Asked about Pat's family, Georgina told them that her husband had divorced her when he had found out that she was having an affair. That had been about five years ago and her two daughters had gone to live with their father. As they had got older, they had got back in touch with their mother and came to visit her, occasionally.

"I asked her if Pat had any other friends, male or female, Sir and she said that Pat was a friendly person who had kept up with people from her last job," said Salma.

"She said that Pat had a boyfriend she had mentioned a couple of times but she had never divulged his name, Sir," added Penny.

Davenport thanked them. He told them to eat their lunch and then get their interview typed up and they went to their own room where Frank found them on his return. He took off his hat and went up the corridor to the boss's room to tell him that Paul Lawson had left work at around 7pm, possibly a bit later. He worked overtime as often as possible, his boss had told Frank.

Davenport thanked Frank and asked him to tell the girls the news that they could probably remove Paul Lawson from their suspect list.

CHAPTER 29

Salma sat nervously in her car outside the gates of Linn Crematorium. She had driven through the gates and looked at the board which told visitors which chapel to go to, then reversed quickly through the gates to wait, as Penny had recommended, for the funeral cars. She inspected her hair in the car mirror and straightened her hat. In the mirror, she saw a black car approaching. It passed her slowly and she saw the coffin with two wreaths of white flowers on top. Another car followed it and she saw, in the back seat, a man and a woman. She followed the little procession up the hill and waited some way behind it until another black car moved off in the other direction and cars came out of the car-park. Silently thanking Penny for her helpful instructions, she waited until she could get into the car-park. This took some time and by the time she got out of the car, the queue of mourners was moving off. She joined them and for the first time in her life walked into a crematorium. The seats right at the back were all occupied so she slid into an end seat in the middle.

They were all asked to stand and four men came down the aisle carrying a wooden coffin. They placed it at the front and covered it. Two men went back out and the two remaining bowed towards the coffin.

The minister, an elderly man, gave out the number of the first hymn and Salma copied the man beside her and picked up a booklet from in front of her. Any fears she had about not knowing the hymn were allayed when she realised that the man next to her was not singing either. It was quite a stirring hymn and she liked the words.

A prayer followed the hymn, then a talk about Norma. It sounded quite impersonal as if the man did not know the girl he was talking about. Salma felt sad. The committal came next, the minister asking them to stand for it. Salma watched the coffin, covered by a dark red cloth, sinking downwards, leaving the cloth lying flat. Norma's stepfather put his arm round his wife.

During the last hymn, Salma remembered to look round. There were some youngsters with parents, probably school and tennis friends. Salma recognised Avril Smiley from her visit to the police station and she was standing beside another woman about the same age.

The minister thanked them all for coming and asked them to join the family at The Redhurst Hotel. He walked to where Norma's mother was sitting and shook her hand then led the front row out of the room. Everyone stood and the rows left one by one, everyone lining up to shake the hands of Mr & Mrs Gilbert. Salma stood at the back and waited until everyone else had passed. This gave her the chance to listen to what was being said. Avril Smiley said she was from the tennis club and the other woman said the same. A man and a young girl said they were from the tennis club and the youngster said, "I'm Lucy," then hurried out as her tears started. A man in a dark suit said he was the head teacher of Norma's school and he introduced a girl called Mary who was there with her mother.

Salma shook hands and said how sorry she was and that DCI Davenport also sent his condolences. Mrs Gilbert asked her to come back to the hotel and Salma, wishing herself anywhere else, went back, knowing that her boss always did this. She sat at a table with Avril Smiley who introduced her to Anne Scott, "our membership secretary."

Salma asked if anyone else from the tennis club was there and Avril told her that the only other members were Lucy and her father.

"I thought Zoe might come and Henry Laird," she said. "Maybe their parents didn't think it was a good idea."

A man came over and asked how the murder investigations were going.

"I'm Norma's Dad," he said, "not just a curious member of the public."

Salma said that everything was being done that could be done. It sounded lame to her but he seemed satisfied and thanked her.

Feeling that she had found out all she could, Salma finished her tea and left, thanking Norma's mother for her hospitality. It was with a sense of relief that she got back into her car and made her way back to the station. Only Davenport and DS Macdonald were there, in the boss's room. She heard them laughing as she went up the corridor and promised herself that she would tell Frank that the two were getting on well. It did not take long to tell them who had attended the funeral.

"Well, I don't think the murderer turned up this time, unless it's Mr Collins," said Davenport.

"Could be, Sir," said Fiona. "No other parent, except Mary's mum, brought their child. Why did Mr Collins bring Lucy?"

"Knowing that young lady, she would insist on going," her boss replied.

He thanked Salma, asking her how she had liked her first visit to a crematorium. She told him that it had been quite impersonal but that she had liked the hymns.

"A pity you had to attend one where the family were obviously not churchgoers," Fiona said. "It can be quite moving if the minister knows the dead person. I suppose too with it being a violent death, there wasn't anything comforting for him to say."

Davenport thanked Salma again and told her to get off home.

When she had gone, he put on his jacket and escorted Fiona to her room where she got her coat and the two of them walked out to their cars together. They were playing bridge that night, at Fiona's this time and would be seeing each other in about an hour's time so she had asked him to come for a meal and he had arranged for Pippa to have her dinner with Hazel. Hazel lived in Newlands and her mum had invited Pippa to have a sleep-over. This suited their arrangements for Saturday as Fiona was taking Pippa into Glasgow to look for some holiday clothes and it would save her driving up to Newton Mearns. Charles had packed a small suitcase for his daughter with her night things and casual clothes, Pippa having refused to go into town in her school uniform.

Having had a few makeshift meals at Charles's house, Fiona did not feel ashamed to be giving him something similar and they sat down to a lasagne with oven chips, followed by ice cream and peaches from a tin.

CHAPTER 30

Charles and Fiona had changed their twice monthly bridge game to a Friday night when Fiona's friend Kim had moved to live in Stirling. Friday, except in times of extreme pressure at work, was a good night for them and it suited John as his weekend started then. Jean Hope who had made up the foursome from time to time had been delighted to be asked to play on a regular basis. She lived very near Fiona and on the nights when the game was played at Charles's house or John's, Fiona gave her a lift.

Jean had inherited her cat, Esmeralda, from a friend now dead and was fond of saying that she was glad that it had not been a dog as she would have felt really foolish shouting, "Esmeralda, come here, girl!" At first when she had left her alone, Esmeralda had set up a terrible racket but when she asked the neighbour across the landing to see if the noise continued, he had said that it had stopped almost as soon as she reached the foot of the stairs. Now the cat seemed to have settled down with her, so there was no more noise when she left the house.

She looked at her watch. It was just after seven and she had to be at Fiona's in fifteen minutes. They had decided almost from the start, when Kim left, not to bring something for each other and never ever to provide home baking as the others would feel obliged to do the same so she was empty-handed when she left the house, carrying only her reading glasses in her hand.

Watching from Fiona's top flat window, Charles saw her coming and went to greet her when she buzzed on the intercom. She was puffing when she reached the door.

"These stairs! It's OK for you young things."

This was borne out by John arriving right behind her. He had caught the downstairs' door before it shut and wanted to save someone having to come to the flat door twice. He grabbed Jean round the waist and lifted her off her feet.

"How's my favourite partner tonight? Are you ready for some grand slams?"

Laughing, he put her back on terra firma and she made a mock swipe at him. He knew that she hated going for a game contract, never mind a slam but she knew him well enough now to realise that he played carefully but never took the score seriously.

Fiona came out of the kitchen and joined them in the front room. She kissed them both and asked after Esmeralda.

Having decided to do all their talking at supper time, around 10pm when they had finished playing, they sat down and Fiona cut for dealer. It was Jean who had the highest card. She dealt carefully. Charles had already poured them all drinks. He would only have one whisky as would John since both were driving home. Jean and Fiona were the lucky ones tonight. Fiona would have a couple of gins and tonic and Jean two sherries.

Nothing exciting happened in the first hour. Nobody went to game and nobody went down. Charles dealt and managed to lose a card so they all had to count. It was Fiona, his partner, who had fourteen cards instead of thirteen. She spread her cards face down and he chose one. He looked at his hand and counted. Twenty-one points.

"Two hearts," he said. John on his left passed. Fiona was delighted. She replied,

"Stop, four diamonds." Jean made a face and passed, leaving Charles to ask for aces and then kings and make the first grand slam of the night.

With much laughter - none of them took the game very seriously - the evening passed quickly. Soon it was 10.10 and the last hand had been played. Fiona got up to get the supper and Jean went into the kitchen cum sitting room at the back of the house, to help her. This was the room where Fiona sat when she was alone and her paperback book was lying on the carpet by her favourite chair.

"Monday Mourning?" Jean commented. "What's it about?"

"It's most unusual. Kathy Reichs is a bit like… I've forgotten her name but she writes about Kay Scarpetta. They're both forensic scientists. A bit too detailed on the bodies being sawn to bits. I prefer an ordinary murder mystery."

The words were just out when she remembered that she was talking to Jean whose good friend Arthur had been murdered some months ago.

"Oh, Jean, I'm sorry. That was thoughtless of me."

Jean patted her arm.

"Don't be daft. You didn't mean anything by it. Come on. Will I take the tray with the mugs and teapot?"

Suiting her action to her words, she lifted the tray and, followed by Fiona with a plate of chocolate biscuits and a plate of sliced Madeira cake, went into the front room where Charles and John were adding up the score and discussing the running total. They had decided early on to pretend that they were playing for a pound a point and see where they got to at the end of a year. They also put a pound into a little box that Fiona kept and this was going to pay for a meal out quite soon.

"Well, Charles?" asked Jean. "How much do we owe you now?"

"Only £3,050," was his reply. "but things can change suddenly and we still have about six months to go."

Over supper, the talk ranged over many things. They discussed the holiday that Charles, Fiona and Pippa were going on in the summer to Penang in Malaysia, and then went onto John's love life. He never went out with the same girl for more than a few months and Jean was fond of asking him what was wrong with him.

"What's wrong with me? I'll have you know I'm perfect. Trouble is Jean, I'm looking for someone like you. Will you marry me?"

They all laughed and Jean thought, as she often did, that it would be a lucky woman who eventually won this young man's heart.

There was a sudden loud noise which startled them all.

"Thunder!" said Charles and just then they heard the sound of very heavy rain. Jean shivered. She was scared of lightning and hoped she could stay at Fiona's until the storm died down. Then she thought of her cat which was even more scared than she was and would be securely under her bed by now.

"More tea, anyone?" asked Fiona. Everyone declined. Jean knew that at her age - she would be seventy next birthday - she would have to get up to the toilet if she had two mugs of tea at this time of night.

The rain had abated a little though the thunder and lightning were still going on. Fiona had seen the look on Jean's face so she instigated another topic of conversation, John's new job, which lasted some time. Neither John nor Jean ever mentioned the work which Fiona and Charles did as they knew that both relished being away from work on their bridge evenings. John waxed eloquently on his new office and especially on his new secretary whom Jean suspected would be his next conquest.

The last peal of thunder had rolled away faintly into the distance and no lightning followed, so Jean rose to go, hoping to reach the safety of her own house before it returned, if it did. Charles brought all the coats from the bedroom and John helped Jean into hers. He always walked his partner to her close before getting into his car and driving off home so they left together, arm-in-arm.

Charles stayed briefly to kiss Fiona gently on the mouth and tell her that he would repay anything spent on Pippa the next day in town.

"She needs nearly everything, I'm afraid. Nothing she wore last summer will still fit her. Let her spend up to a hundred pounds but don't tell her that at the start."

Fiona laughed.

"Anything I can get for you?" she asked.

Charles, who hated shopping above anything else, looked delighted.

"If you're serious, could you get me a couple of sports' shirts to go with black shorts and beige shorts? I like ones with collars, not tee-shirts."

"Polo shirts, d'you mean?"

"Yes. Thanks Fiona. You're a pal."

As he walked down the stairs he thought about what he had just said and realised that that was what was so special about their relationship. They were pals and good workmates and hopefully soon they would be more than that. He whistled happily.

CHAPTER 31

Saturday morning was, unfortunately, very wet so Fiona took two umbrellas with her when she went to collect Pippa at her friend Hazel's house in Newlands. Pippa was still in the middle of breakfast so Fiona was invited in by Hazel's mother, Sally. Charles, Pippa and Fiona had been invited to the Ewings' Christmas party in December so they knew each other and Fiona took the chance to ask after Diana Ewing, Sally's niece. She was pleased to hear that the girl seemed to have settled down at her new school and had made some good friends there. She had hated her private school up North.

"I'm ready, Fiona," said Pippa, coming into the hall and pulling down her jacket. "I'm glad Dad's not coming. He gets so bad-tempered in town."

She picked up a holdall and school bag and stood looking bright-eyed and as her father would say, "bushy-tailed". Fiona thanked Sally for taking care of her last night and then she took the holdall from Pippa and the two walked out to the car which

Fiona had parked on the road. By this time Hazel had reached the front door, and she shouted, "Cheerio Pippa! See you on Monday!"

They reached town at about 11am and Fiona parked in the St Enoch Centre car park. She asked Pippa to help her remember which floor she had parked on and put the car park ticket safely in her wallet. They took the lift down to the bottom floor and Fiona asked her young companion which shop she wanted to go to first.

"Can we just walk and see what comes up, please?" Pippa said.

Fiona looked aghast at the first shop window Pippa stopped at but let herself be dragged in. The music was deafening. Soon Pippa was excitedly looking through the racks of tee-shirts in gaudy colours with strange messages on them. Fiona wondered what Charles would think of these clothes and whether they would go down well in a five star hotel. Then her mind was made up for her when Pippa held up a fluorescent pink shirt with: "Practise Safe Sex. F*** Yourself" on it and asked, "Fiona what does this mean?"

"It's a very rude, adult saying Pippa. Your Dad would not allow you to wear it and anyway these will all be too big for you."

Luckily, as Pippa was looking a bit mutinous, Fiona spotted the stairs leading down to 'children's and teens' fashions' and steered her young charge in that direction. Fortunately, downstairs held younger versions of the gaudy tee-shirts without the messages on them and Pippa went into raptures over an electric blue one with a white pattern on it and a sunny yellow with red flowers over the front. She did not want shorts but settled for two pairs of cropped trousers in white and pale blue cotton. The shop also stocked swimwear, including bikinis for young girls with no bust and Pippa chose two of them, one with a white bottom and a red top and one with white and yellow stripes. There was just enough money left over for some underwear and Fiona hoped that she had covered everything. She had never shopped with a young girl before.

Finding out that Pippa was thirsty now, they went over to Marks and Spencers and went downstairs to their cafeteria where Fiona had a latte and Pippa had orange juice along with a large muffin which they decided to share.

When they had finished and had queued up to use the toilet, Fiona told Pippa that it was her turn now and they went up to the ground floor where Fiona chose four tee-shirts in various colours and two pairs of shorts. Pippa tried to get her to buy some cropped trousers but Fiona resisted, feeling that that style was for teenagers and young women with slim legs. She did let herself be persuaded to buy two bikinis instead of one piece bathing suits but made sure that the bottoms were not too brief.

Next it was up to the first floor to get Charles two polo shirts to match his shorts. Pippa was scathing about the polo shirts in self- colours and wanted her Dad to have something more modern but Fiona could tell her that that was what her Dad had asked for. She took a chance and bought him two pairs of swim-shorts - he could always ask her to return them- as she had the feeling that he probably had not bought these for some time and would have the skimpy variety which was mostly worn now by elderly men.

She asked Pippa if there was anything else she wanted to see or anywhere else she wanted to go and Pippa expressed a desire to see the Walt Disney shop in the St Enoch Arcade. Hazel had told her about this shop and she wanted to see it for herself. They crossed the road again and walked through, between John Smiths and Debenhams, to the entrance to the arcade.

Once inside the Walt Disney Shop, Pippa was entranced. Her childish self came to the fore and she oohd and aahd over the Lion King and Jungle Book clothes. She stood deep in thought and Fiona realised that she was probably toying with the idea of asking if she could return the other tops and get two of these instead. She took pity on her.

"Pippa, pet. I want to buy you something for your holiday. Would you like to choose two of these tops?"

It had been worth it to see the delight on Pippa's face.

"Oh, Fiona. Are you sure? Oh thank you."

They spent some time holding up the various colours and various animals from Pippa's two favourite shows and eventually chose a red one, picturing Balloo the bear from Jungle Book and a green one with the Lion King himself.

Discovering that they were now both quite hungry, they went to Princes Square and found a place which sold burgers and chips, amongst other things. They dumped all their bags round the base of the table. Pippa chose a cheese burger and coke and Fiona had a panini with tuna mayonnaise and salad and a small glass of white wine.

Pippa talked about her visit to the big school and her hope that she and Hazel would be in the same class, though she said that they could always meet at playtime and lunchtime. Fiona did not want to point out that they both might make other friends if they were in different classes. This had happened to her in secondary school. There was time enough to discuss this if it happened. She went on to talk about Diana who often joined them at Hazel's, if they were there at the weekend. Pippa said that Diana was more fun now that she went to a normal school.

"What do you mean by *normal* Pippa?" Fiona asked, with interest.

"You know, not a posh one where you stay all week and only come home at weekends."

"Did you not want to go to a boarding school once?" asked Fiona.

"Yes but only if it was the Chalet School and it's not real," replied Pippa.

The talk turned to their summer holiday. Pippa had been on a plane before but not a jumbo jet and she had not been on such a long journey. Fiona told her that she would have her own TV screen and could choose what pictures she wanted to see from the booklet given to her. Pippa was delighted but said that she had also bought three new Agatha Christie books and the next Chalet School book.

"Which Chalet School book have you reached now, Pippa?"

"Peggy of the Chalet School."

"Is that Bride Bettany's young sister?" asked Fiona who had the whole set of the books except for two which she could not find.

"I think it's her older sister. Her name's Peggy Bettany anyway. It says so on the back of the book."

"What about the Agatha Christie books? What are they?"

"Death on the Nile", Murder on The Orient Express" and something about a Christmas pudding. I'm keeping two for the holiday. The Christmas pudding one made me think of the murder at Hazel's Christmas party, last year."

She blushed and Fiona knew that she was thinking about the fact that she had eavesdropped on her Dad and Fiona discussing the case and shared her knowledge with Hazel, much to her Dad's annoyance.

Fiona changed the subject quickly.

"Do you mind me sharing a room with you and your Dad on holiday?"

"Oh no, Fiona. Dad explained that it was awfully expensive to get a single room and we'll not be in the room much anyway."

Fiona had been a bit unsure herself as her relationship with Charles had altered a bit recently but she knew that it did make sense and with Pippa there with them, that would lay out the rules of their behaviour towards each other.

She asked for the bill and paid it and they went back out into the rain. Up went the two umbrellas again and they hurried over to the St Enoch Centre. Pippa had remembered the floor number for the car and Fiona extracted the parking ticket, put it into the machine and paid the four pounds asked for. She hated getting out of these car parks with their spiralling ramps which were a tight fit for even the smallest of cars and Pippa, seeing her frown, kept quiet until she sensed her companion relaxing when they were once again out on the street.

"Thanks, Fiona. That was good fun. Are you staying after you run me home?"

"I don't know love. I'll see what your Dad says when we get you home."

It took them about forty minutes to reach Newton Mearns. Pippa's fair hair was coming out of its pony tail and Fiona felt untidy and hot. Charles, having heard the car, came out to meet them and laughed at their dishevelled appearance.

"I think you could both do with a shower. Pippa, in you go first. Put out fresh clothes first, remember."

He turned to his friend and colleague.

"Thanks, Fiona. Do you want to come in and freshen up and stay for the evening or have you had enough of the Davenports for one day?"

"I'll take you up on that shower, though I'll have to go back into the same clothes, I'm afraid. I want to show you what I bought for you and I want to see your reaction to Pippa's clothes. They're a real mixture of teenager and child. Oh, I bought you some swimwear too but I'll take back anything that you don't want and I *will* stay for the evening, thank you."

It did not take Pippa long to freshen up and by the time Fiona arrived back downstairs, she was showing her Dad her spoils.

"What was that tee-shirt you said was too adult for me, Fiona?"

"I forget," said Fiona.

"Something like, 'Have safe sex'. Dad, what does F and three stars mean?"

"Sorry pet, I have no idea," replied her father, trying not to laugh.

When she had shown off all her new clothes, she went upstairs to put them away, promising not to wear them before her holiday and Charles agreed with Fiona about the dichotomy in the styles she had bought.

"A child still in many ways, yet becoming a teenager a bit early too," he said quite sadly.

"I know. I was still climbing trees at sixteen," said Fiona. "They grow up so quickly these days. Her choice of books for the holiday shows the same thing - adult books and a child's books.

"Child's books, DS Macdonald! I thought you had a collection of them!"

"You can talk. Who still plays with trains then?"

They were still laughing when Pippa returned and the talk turned to what they had eaten in town and how they would not want much for their evening meal.

"That's lucky as I haven't made anything," said Charles. "I'll be hungry so I'll go out for a fish supper and if you too have any appetite you might want to share one between you."

They agreed to this and they spent the next few minutes looking at what Fiona had bought Charles. He was delighted and went off upstairs to put away his new clothes. He went out soon after for his fish supper and the other two agreed to share a sausage supper. Fiona had left her purchases in the boot of her car but described what she had bought.

It was a happy evening and when Fiona left for home, about 11 pm, she was tired but contented.

CHAPTER 32

Sunday morning saw the team assembled in the Incident Room. Davenport had agreed to Saturday off but knew that they could not afford two free days. He had set up the flip chart and had headed a new page, "Possible Suspects." He was writing the first name, 'Gavin Gilbert', as they sat down. Salma was pleased, as he was the one she thought most likely to be the guilty party. Next, he wrote underneath, 'Donald Kinross'. Penny started to speak, "But Sir, he…"

"Later, Penny. I'm just putting down any possible suspects and it is just possible that he could be our man."

Other names followed until the list read:

1. Gavin Gilbert
2. Donald Kinross
3. Kevin Collins
4. Brian Jenkins
5. Stewart Bolton

6. David Bentley

7. Pat's boyfriend

"I've left Paul Lawson off the suspect list now that he has an alibi for Pat's murder and I really can't see him murdering Norma just because she might have wanted to stay with him and his girlfriend. Agreed?"

"Yes, Sir," they chorused.

"Now," he said, "give me your comments on any of these."

Penny raised her hand.

"I think Donald Kinross is too wrapped up in Sheila Ferguson to be bothered trying it on with a teenager, Sir."

"Possibly. I want you, Frank, to see Mr Kinross today if possible and ask him where he was on Monday evening. He'll have been warned by Sheila no doubt, but ask him something specific and we'll check with her."

Frank was next.

"Why would Pat Harper's boyfriend, whoever he is, have met with Norma Lawson? Surely Georgina Laird would know him if he was a tennis player."

"Probably, but maybe not. Fiona will you go to Pat's house and look for a diary or address book, please."

"OK, Sir. I think that Pat Harper was too well built and muscular for the younger boys, Peter, Mark and Neil to be able to keep her face down in a pillow long enough to smother her," said Fiona. "And she must have known her murderer. They had obviously had sex before for her to let whoever it was tie her up face down on the bed."

"Yes, Sir, I agree with DS Macdonald," said Frank. "I can't see three young boys getting into kinky sex games with an older woman."

"I know what you mean, Frank but it's not impossible. However they've got alibis which is why I haven't put them on the list."

Fiona and Frank looked a bit foolish and Fiona apologised.

"Sorry, Sir. I forgot they'd been ruled out."

"Me too, Sir," said Frank.

"No problem. No harm in going over things twice. Anyone else got anything to add?" he asked.

"Kevin Collins and Brian Jenkins are single men now. Either of them could have started an affair with Pat Harper and then tried something on with Norma Lawson," said Penny.

There were mutters of agreement.

"A final thing on the young boys. My own opinion is that the young lads are too young, both physically and mentally for these murders. If one of them had tried to have sex with Norma, I think she might well have agreed or if she hadn't she would simply have said no. I think we have to narrow it down to someone who feared that anyone would find out that he had forced Norma to have sex," added Davenport.

He hesitated.

"That leaves, in my view, Donald Kinross whom nearly everyone saw Norma flirt with. She would be flattered if he responded then probably frightened when things went too far. It also leaves Gavin Gilbert who might have lured his stepdaughter to the tennis club. She might have felt she was paying her Mum back by having sex with Gavin then changed her mind too late. He would be scared that she would tell his wife. It could be one of the widowed fathers. Norma seemed to be flirting at school and tennis club with anyone older so she might have tried it on with one of them, then as with Gavin Gilbert, she panicked at the last moment."

"And any one of them except perhaps Gavin Gilbert could have been having an affair with Pat Harper," said Fiona. "I mean Gilbert didn't go to tennis so wouldn't have met her."

"Sir," said Penny, "you've not said anything about Stewart Bolton."

"Neither I have, Penny, nor about David Bentley. Thanks."

No one had anything to add about these two.

"OK, tea…eh…folks, get on with what you have to do. Fiona and Frank, you have your instructions. Penny I want you to ask Brian Jenkins, Peter's father, where he was on the two evenings in question and if anyone can witness to where he was. Salma, you do the same with Kevin Collins please."

"What about you, Sir?" asked Fiona.

"I'm leaving out Bolton and Bentley for now as they have alibis of a sort. I'll go to see Anne Scott and Avril Smiley. See if they have any idea who Pat Harper could have been seeing and I also want to see Gavin Gilbert about an alibi for Monday night."

Davenport went first to Waterfoot where he found Gavin in the living room, watching TV with his twin sons. Jan Gilbert was grocery shopping at Asda in Newton Mearns. Asked where he had been last Monday evening, Gavin said that he had been at home with his wife. She was a soap addict and they had both watched two episodes of Coronation Street and one of Eastenders. No one had phoned or called round. Avril Smiley was also at home. She knew nothing of any boyfriend but said that she was not particularly friendly with Pat Harper who along with Georgina Laird, wanted first position in the team, the position which Avril and Anne had. She knew that Pat was divorced, nothing more.

Anne Scott was not at home but her husband said she would call the station when she came home from church.

Fiona went to Pat's house. She ran the gauntlet of old Mrs Jackson and her inquisitive questions and hurried inside, leaving the old lady unsatisfied. They had not searched the downstairs room and kitchen although SOC would have done so, looking for fingerprints. In an old bureau, scratched round the drawers and pull-down flap, she found an address book and in a black handbag, also well worn, she found a diary. Looking through the diary, she saw where Pat had recorded her tennis practices and other games and where on Tuesday evenings she had noted Georgina's visits. Other appointments written down were two, one in February and one in March, when she had seen what were presumably her daughters, as the names Debbie and Joan were written there and various doctor, dentist and hospital appointments. There was no sign of a boyfriend being slotted in but if he was married she might not have written his name, Fiona thought.

The address book was quite empty of names. She had her ex-husband's address and some addresses in England, one in Australia and two in USA and the addresses of two tennis club members, Georgina Laird and Anne Scott. Once again it was possible that she had not written the address of a new boyfriend because he was married and she would not be writing to him.

Fiona put both small books in her pockets and looked carefully for any letters. There were none. Electricity, gas and telephone bills were docketed in the pigeonholes of the desk and there were bank statements there too. Fiona left these items where she found them.

Frank, arriving at Donald Kinross's house at around ten thirty, found Donald alone at home. He was invited in. Kinross, looking relieved, told him that his wife, Olive, and his two children had just left for church and Sunday school.

"You'll have had time to speak with Mrs Ferguson, Sir so you'll know that she has given you an alibi for Monday night but I want some details that we can verify."

Kinross looked embarrassed but Frank could not know that he was thinking how much worse it would have been if he was being asked about a few nights ago.

"Such as?"

"In whose car, hers or yours?"

"Mine."

"Details please, Sir. Tell me something she might not have mentioned but which only she would know about."

Kinross, feeling bad but knowing that refusal could make him look guilty of murder that same night, said that they had just petted heavily.

"Dressed or undressed, front or back seat?"

"Sheila was completely undressed, I was dressed that night. I liked her with no clothes on. In the back seat, constable."

Frank thanked him for his honesty, instructed him not to contact Sheila and left. Once in his car, he rang Davenport to ask if he wanted him to see Sheila next, telling him that maybe she would prefer to speak to a female PC as what Kinross had told him was very personal.

"It's a murder enquiry, Frank. We can't afford to pander to peoples' sensibilities. She did whatever it was so she can just tell you."

It took Frank only about ten minutes to reach Sheila's house, having asked his boss for the address. A man answered the door. Frank explained who he was and asked to speak with Sheila. He was invited in.

"Sheila's just been telling me about the two murders. I'm MP for this district, only arrived home yesterday afternoon."

Sheila looked aghast when she saw the police constable in her living room. Frank was in a quandary. He did not know if his boss would ask the questions he was going to ask under these circumstances but he remembered Davenport saying to a suspect once that nothing was secret in a murder enquiry.

"Mrs Ferguson. Will you give me some details of what you did on Monday night, the night of the second murder?"

"Look Sheila, I'll give you some space. I've got a lot of paper work to do," said her husband and picking up some folders, he left the room.

Sheila looked extremely relieved.

"What do you want to know, constable?"

"Did you have penetrative sex with Mr Kinross that night?"

"No."

"Whose car did you meet in?"

"His car."

"Front or back seat?"

"Back."

"Describe your state of undress please."

Sheila blushed.

"Donald always likes me to have no clothes on but he stayed dressed that night."

"Thank you, Mrs Ferguson," Frank said. "That's all for now."

Like Donald, Sheila was feeling relieved about which night she had been asked to describe.

Sunday was obviously a good day for finding people at home, Penny thought, when Brian Jenkins opened the door. Peter, however, was out. "At BB Bible class," Brian told Penny.

Penny explained that she wanted to know where he had been on Monday evening.

"Why, constable?"

"Did you not read your Saturday paper, Sir?"

"You surely don't think I murdered Pat Harper!"

"I'm afraid every senior male within reason is a suspect for Norma's murder, Sir and we think the two murders are connected so if you would just answer my question please."

"Peter came home from BB at around 9.40 and we went for a Chinese Meal at The Moon Garden."

"Before that, Sir?"

"I was at home catching up on the newspaper."

Salma had been interviewing Kevin Collins who was not taking kindly to being viewed as a possible double murderer. He spoke like someone used to taking charge and Salma was finding it difficult to take control of the conversation.

"This is ridiculous. The police are harassing me. This is the second time I've been questioned."

"Well, Sir, there's been a second murder."

"Are you being impertinent? I can count, sergeant!"

"Please, Sir, I'd be grateful if you would just answer the question. Where were you on Monday evening?"

"This is preposterous. I read about Pat Harper's death in yesterday's paper. Why on earth would I want to kill her, sergeant?"

"All older boys and younger men are possible suspects for Norma's murder, Sir and we suspect that the murderer was the same in both cases. You have nothing to fear if you are innocent."

"Fear? I'm not afraid, sergeant. I'm angry, very angry."

"If you're not prepared to answer my question, Sir, I'm afraid I'll have to ask you to accompany me to the station."

Salma stood her ground.

"Oh, very well. I took Lucy to the pictures at East Kilbride to see that film about Benjamin Button, the guy who was born old and got younger. We went to the 7 o'clock showing and got home about 10ish. We stopped off at McDonald's for burgers and chips on the way home. How's that!"

"Thank you, Sir."

Salma was very tempted to say, "That was quite painless, wasn't it!" but that would have been impertinent.

Davenport's little team had all returned by lunchtime so, it being the weekend, he decided to treat them all to a Chinese or Indian carry-out. Frank was dispatched to get a chicken curry for himself and a prawn one for Fiona while Penny went off to get lemon chicken for Salma, king prawn and tomato for her boss and sweet and sour chicken for herself.

During their meal, Anne Scott rang. Like Avril, she knew nothing about Pat's current boyfriend but confirmed that Pat's marriage had split up a few years ago because Pat had had an affair. She could give them no details about this affair, not being very friendly with Pat.

"Let's eat first and talk later," said Davenport.

CHAPTER 33

Jane and Georgina always met on Sundays for lunch after Jane went to church. She kept trying to get her friend to come with her but, unlike Jane whose family had a history of church-going, none of Georgina's family ever went and she was a confirmed atheist. This Sunday, Jane was later than usual, as this month she helped with the after-service teas and coffees. It was a large congregation so there were lots of cups and saucers to wash up afterwards and this week there had been fewer helpers than usual.

"Sorry, George," Jane sounded breathless on her mobile. "I'll be outside your gate in about ten minutes."

"No problem, Jane. See you then."

Georgina strolled out to the gate just as Jane pulled up in her old red Renault Clio. She got in and, smiling at her friend, asked what had kept her.

"Oh, only me and one other person washing up today."

It took them less than ten minutes to reach The Wishing Well in one of Eaglesham's main streets. Jane parked down the hill and they walked up. The tearoom was busy but they found a table in the little annexe and ordered lunch, Jane having her usual sandwiches of cheese and pickle and Georgina choosing soup: carrot and coriander this week.

"That was awful about Pat, wasn't it?" said Georgina. "Who on earth would want to kill her?"

"Do you think she knew something about Norma Lawson's murder and the murderer found out?" asked Jane.

"That's all I could think of too," agreed Georgina. "But what could she have known?"

"Maybe Norma spoke to her about a man or older boy. Remember, she kept pestering you to get two men to make up a foursome some evening. She seemed determined to fraternise with the older members, men and women. Maybe she met Pat somewhere and told her who the person was."

"But how would the murderer know that Pat knew?"

"I guess she must have told him."

"Pretty stupid don't you think?"

"Yes but folk do things like that. Did Norma ever talk to you?"

"No, she tried to get friendly but I wasn't having any of it. We tried to put her off nicely but she couldn't seem to take the hint. Poor Don. He got landed with her at the American Tournament and did you see the way she flirted with him?"

"Do you think he killed her?" asked Jane.

"Why?"

"Well, maybe he was flattered at her attention and tried it on with her and she panicked and said she would tell her parents."

"I suppose so but I thought he was having a fling with Sheila so why would he take on someone else?"

"Well, who do you think did it?"

"I wondered about her stepfather. I heard that she had one and maybe he abused her."

Their lunch arrived along with a pot of tea for two. They never suggested that their boyfriends came up here with them as they were sure they would find it too old- fashioned, yet Jane noticed that there were quite a few men here today.

"Think we should ask Stewart and Barry up here some time, George?"

"No. It's the only time the two of us get to have a girly chat and I'm sure the boys prefer a pint in the pub."

"Right enough. Stewart was going to ask Barry to join him and his friend Joe in The Swan today. Do you know if he was going to go?"

"Yes, he said he was. He seemed disappointed that we wouldn't be there too."

"Oh, smitten is he?" her friend laughed. "Will he last longer than usual, George?"

"I seem to go off them more quickly than you," Georgina made a rueful face. "How long have you been going out with Stewart now?"

"Almost six months."

"Have you...you know..."

"Had sex with him do you mean? No I haven't and I think he's getting fed up with me saying no."

"Why don't you?"

"I suppose it's being a Christian."

Jane flushed a little. She felt almost ashamed of saying this and felt guilty about that.

"You mean you want to wait till you're engaged?"

"No. Worse, I'm afraid. I want to wait till I'm married."

"Have you told Stewart that?"

"No way! That would surely scare him off, using the 'm' word. What about you George?"

"A couple of times only. I really like Barry, so maybe with him too. I don't have your religious scruples, Jane."

Across The Orry, in The Swan Inn, Stewart and Barry were having a similar conversation. Joe had not yet turned up and Stewart had taken the chance of being alone with Barry to bring up the question of sex. Joe was a homosexual and could not be expected to understand about women. They were sitting in the snug, surrounded by mostly male, Sunday drinkers and it was noisy enough for them not to be overheard.

"Barry, how long would you go out with a girl before you suggested you had sex together?" Stewart asked.

"Well, I've only had one serious relationship and she agreed after about three months."

"So what ended it?"

"She went to uni and we ended up with different friends and drifted apart. Why do you want to know?"

"Well, Jane and I've been seeing each other for nearly six months now and she won't even allow heavy petting."

"Is she frigid, do you think?"

"I don't know. She lets me kiss her and seems to enjoy that but as soon as I touch her boobs, she draws away from me."

"Have you asked her about it?" asked Barry.

"No."

"Why not?"

"I really like her Barry and don't know what I'd do if she said she wanted to wait for marriage. I'm not ready for marrying anyone yet. She goes to church. It might be her religion that stops her."

"So what now?"

"I'll wait a bit, I suppose. Thing is I get really horny and I know I could get some action elsewhere. There's a girl at work who seems to fancy me."

At this point they were joined by Joe and the conversation turned to football so Barry had no chance to ask Stewart if he thought he would have any success with Jane's friend. When Joe went to the toilet, he did manage to ask if Georgina went to church too and Stewart told him that she did not.

At about three o'clock, Jane and Georgina joined them, Georgina having a glass of white wine and Jane a coke as she was driving and refused to touch a drop of alcohol if she had the car. The talk turned again to the double murder of tennis club members and Barry laughingly said, maybe he should not join after all. Joe had not heard about the second murder so Stewart told him about Pat Harper being found dead in her house, at the beginning of the week.

"Any of you girls know any more details?" Stewart asked.

Georgina knew only that she had been worried when Pat had not turned up for match practice and that Avril had gone round the next day and found milk on the doorstep. She had contacted the police who had found the body. Jane knew only the same, having been told by Georgina.

"We think that Pat must have known or found out something about the first murder of the teenage girl," volunteered Jane.

"Certainly seems a bit of a coincidence that two tennis members have been killed," said Barry. "I can't imagine a serial tennis hater going about trying to get rid of all players."

They laughed and the talk turned to what they would do that night.

CHAPTER 34

Also meeting this Sunday afternoon, were Brian Jenkins and Kevin Collins. Peter always played tennis on Sunday afternoons if there was a court free. It was senior time but not all six courts were often used. He had rung Neil Smith who had agreed to meet him at the courts and Brian had given him a lift there. Lucy was visiting her grandmother, her dad's mother, in Shawlands. Kevin had dropped her off there before going up to the Eglinton Arms to meet Brian.

Brian arrived first, right on time and he had to wait a while for his friend. He declined a drink, telling the barman that he was waiting for a friend and went to sit at a vacant table. Kevin apologised when he arrived.

"Sorry, Brian. I went into my mother's and got caught with some things she wanted me to do for her. She never could change a light bulb and several had gone out since I was last there."

"My mother was the same. She's in a nursing home now but there were always chores for me when I visited when she was in her own house."

"Is your father still alive? Sorry to ask but we never get time for chit chat on the courts."

"No. Dad died some years ago. He took a stroke on the bowling green. What about your Dad?"

"He left home when I was twelve. I saw him regularly, every week, till I married, then only spasmodically. He went to live in Sussex a few years ago."

They ordered two beers and changed seats to sit in an alcove as one became empty just as their drinks arrived. They had only started meeting on Sundays a few weeks ago and had found in each other kindred spirits, both being keen on football, golf and of course tennis and both being single parents with one child. The talk turned to the most recent murder.

"I never spoke much to Pat Harper. I don't think I warranted any attention with only being third couple with you," said Brian. "She took her tennis very seriously, I think."

"Yes, I know what you mean. She didn't give me a second glance either, though she was always laughing and chatting to Don and Harry," replied Kevin. "She and Georgina Laird are kindred spirits."

"I wonder who killed her," mused Brian.

"Yes and why."

"It must be connected to the death of that girl, Norma, surely. It's too much of a coincidence to think that there are two murderers going around the district."

"So you think that the person who murdered Norma suspected that Pat knew something about it and got rid of her too?" questioned Kevin.

"Well, why else would anyone want rid of Pat?"

"I feel sorry for Don. Norma was his partner at the American Tournament. She flirted with him and the police have been questioning him, so he told me last week when I met him in Clarkston."

"The police came to see me too."

"Yes and me but I think it was just routine, trying to find out where we'd been on the nights of the murders. 'Fraid I got a bit stroppy with the sergeant who came to see me. Another drink, Brian?"

"Yes please Kev, then that'll be my last with having the car. I wasn't any too pleased either but thank goodness, I had an alibi this time. I didn't have one for Norma's death."

"Me neither but like you, I had an alibi for Pat's."

Kevin went to the bar and returned carrying two pints of beer. The talk turned to their two children. Kevin told Brian about how well his daughter was doing at school and how proud he was of her and Brian spoke of Peter being in the school under- sixteen football team.

"He's not interested in academic things - yet - but I hope he'll get his act together when he goes into fourth year and has important exams to sit. Has Lucy got any hobbies, apart from tennis?"

"Not really. I wish she had something to do in the winter months but at the moment she seems perfectly happy to stay in with her old Dad and watch TV and do homework."

"Does she know what she wants to be?"

"A vet she says, but that's a hard job for a girl to get into and I don't know if she could face the sad side of the job. What about Peter?"

"Still young enough to hope he'll be a footballer, I'm afraid. I keep telling him that even if he was lucky enough to make football his career, he should have another job to fall back on but he doesn't listen."

They drained their glasses and rose to leave. Brian reached his car first as he had parked it on the main road.

"OK Kev, see you at match practice on Tuesday."

"I wonder who'll take Pat's place on the ladies' team, Brian."

"Maybe Jane or Sheila will move up to partner Georgina Laird."

"Or maybe someone else will be roped in and Georgina will move down to third couple."

"That won't please Georgina. I heard that she and Pat were hoping to be moved up to first couple."

Brian slid into the driving seat and adjusted his rear-view mirror and Kevin gave him a wave and went off round the back of the hotel to get his own car.

CHAPTER 35

It was lunchtime at the local secondary school and Mary McGregor was lonely. The trouble with having one particular friend was that when that friend left, or as in Norma's case, died, there were no other friends to turn to. She and Norma, mainly because of Norma's sudden liking for older boys, had tended to spend intervals and lunchtimes on the other side of 'The Market 'which was the name given to the area indoors at school where there were seats, tables and food outlets. The second years congregated at the tables near the food and drinks' machine, the third years by those near the water dispenser.

Mary had ventured over to her fellow second years the Monday after Norma's death. She found antagonism in some groups who turned away from her as if to say that she need not look for friendship from them. Other groups wanted to quiz her about the murder which was worse. She had taken to going outside, even in bad weather when she sheltered under the trees on the main road.

Today she was there as usual when she saw someone coming towards her. From a distance she could only make out that it was a boy then as he came nearer, she saw that it was one of the third year boys, one whom she thought had quite liked Norma though she had not responded to him for some reason, preferring some of the older, trendier, ones. This one was immaculate in his uniform and Mary had quite taken to him herself.

"Hi, Mary. Is this where you've been hiding?"

"It's better on my own. I haven't got any friends in my class. There was only Norma and now she's..."

"...dead. I know. Do you mind if I stay and chat to you?"

"Sorry, I can't remember your name."

Mary felt silly saying this but the boy smiled.

"I'm Neil Smith, the one Norma *didn't* fancy."

He made a rueful face and Mary felt herself warm towards him even more. He was honest it seemed, as well as smart-looking. She smiled back, not realising how the smile transformed her rather plain face.

"Don't think you were old enough for her. She suddenly seemed to like older boys and even men. She talked about a guy at tennis and he was a lot older, I think."

"That'd be Don Kinross I expect. I played in the American Tournament a few weeks ago and she was his partner at that. I know she was your friend, Mary but I have to say she made a real fool of herself flirting with him. I was playing with Anne Scott who's the membership secretary and we played against Norma and Don and she kept smiling up at him all the time."

Neil's face was sulky as he remembered and Mary wondered if he really had fancied Norma himself. She was startled to find herself minding about this. She changed the subject slightly.

"I think maybe Norma was looking for a father-figure. Did you know that she lived with her mum and stepfather?"

"No, I didn't. What happened to her father? Did he die?"

"No. He left her mum for another woman and her mum wouldn't let him see Norma."

"Poor Norma."

"Yes but she did see him. He came to the school gates one day a few weeks ago and she arranged to go over to where he lived. He wrote to her at her tennis friend's house. My Mum wouldn't let him write to her at our house."

The bell rang, startling them both. Side by side, they hurried back to the school building.

"Where's your next class?" Neil asked.

"Maths."

"I'm going that way. I'm the floor above - English with Mr Gordon. Look Mary, will you meet me after school? Which bus do you get?"

"I get the 44 to Eaglesham, well Waterfoot now that they've changed the boundary lines!"

"I go the other way, down to Stamperland but we'll have time to meet, at the same trees. Yes?"

"OK."

They had reached the Maths' corridor so there was time for no more. Mary gave him another shy smile and he smiled back.

School over, they met at the trees. Not wanting to draw attention to themselves, they stood apart as the queues formed on either side of the road, shepherded by two members of staff on the busy side. Only one boy and two other girls waited at the bus stop on Mary's side.

"No time to chat more, Mary," said Neil. "How about you come to the tennis club tomorrow night? I turn up at 6.30 in case they're short of anyone for match practice. You could come a bit later and sit upstairs in the lounge if I'm needed and we could go for a coke afterwards. If I'm not needed, I'll wait for you and we can have that drink earlier."

Mary felt herself blushing and reminded herself that Neil was probably only doing this so that he could talk about Norma. He must have sensed her doubt.

"I'd like to get to know you, Mary. I promise not to talk about Norma. Look, here's my bus coming. Have to go. How about it?"

"Yes. OK. I'll have to ask Mum first but I'm sure it'll be alright."

Neil grinned at her and loped off across the road in time to jump on the bus as it was about to drive off. He got a glare from the teacher in charge.

Mary walked back to her bus stop, feeling happier than she had since Norma died. She had only a few minutes to wait for her bus. She arrived home and her grandfather was in the front garden, looking up the road for her coming. She loved him dearly but wished that he would not treat her as if she was still a child.

"Hi, Gramps! What are you doing out in the cold? Come on in and I'll make us a cup of tea. Did Mum leave any instructions about dinner?"

She grabbed his arm and pulled him indoors.

"Your Mum's going to be home soon so don't worry about the meal. I've done the potatoes for her," said the old man.

Mary waited till after dinner and she was helping her Mum with the washing up, before she broached the subject of her date with Neil. She was delighted when her mother seemed pleased instead of anxious.

"Of course you can go, silly. A third-year boy, you say? Just be sure to take your mobile phone with you in case you need a lift home or I want to get in touch with you."

Mrs McGregor was relieved to see Mary so cheerful and hoped that this new friendship would fill the space left by the death of Norma Lawson.

CHAPTER 36

Mary dressed carefully for her date with Neil. She had been given new denims for her birthday recently and teamed them up with a turquoise blouse which made her hair look fairer. She would have liked to have had highlights put in but knew that her mother would never agree. The style these days was for long hair but in spite of being quite shy, Mary bucked the trend and having never liked her hair long, had a neat bob. She slipped on her black pumps and, picking up her black bag, made her way downstairs.

Her Mum and grandfather were in the lounge, watching TV. Her Mum smiled at her and told her not to be later than 9.30 as she had school the next day. Her grandfather put his hand into his trouser pocket and produced a ten pound note which he gave to her.

"Just in case you have to get a taxi home, love."

"Thanks, Gramps. I'll give it back if I don't need it."

"Bless you love. It's yours whatever happens."

It took Mary about half an hour to get to the tennis club. She looked over the hedge as she walked from the bus stop and saw that Neil was indeed on one of the courts. She went round the corner and down the path to the clubhouse, hoping that it would be open. It was. She went in and climbed the stairs to the lounge as she had been told to do. It was empty and she chose a chair near the window from which she could see the courts. Neil was playing with three older men, probably in their thirties, on one of the courts near to the clubhouse and she could see women playing on courts further away.

It was about 7.40 when she saw one of the women coming across the courts. She waited until it was safe to cross behind the men playing and came towards the clubhouse. Mary heard footsteps on the stairs and then a young woman came in. She looked surprised to see Mary who explained why she was there.

"I'm meeting Neil after his game. I'm...I was... a friend of Norma Lawson," Mary said. "She used to talk about someone from here, someone she fancied."

She stopped suddenly, feeling that she was gabbling on but the woman sat down and appeared to be interested.

"Who was that?" she asked.

Mary told her and the woman looked a bit shocked.

"I'd never have believed it," she said. "Have you told the police about this?"

"Do you think I should? It was only a schoolgirl crush. I don't want to get him into trouble. I'm sure he never encouraged her. The older boys at school didn't. The police came to see me but I didn't think to tell them then."

As Mary looked down at the courts, she saw Neil and his partner coming off.

"Here's Neil coming now."

She got to her feet.

"I think I would tell them," the woman said. "He is a nice guy. That's him over there practising. I'm sure he's not a murderer but the police need to know."

She pointed through the window.

"The one on the right hand side facing us on the middle court."

Mary was about to thank her but the woman was leaving and Neil was arriving.

"Mary! So glad you came. Let's get off to the cafe. I don't imagine your mother wants you to be late on a school night."

Thinking how thoughtful he was, Mary went with him downstairs and together they walked down to the nearby cafe. Most of the time there, they talked about school and their teachers. Norma was mentioned but only briefly. Mary told Neil that she had always felt inferior to her friend and Neil was at pains to show her that he preferred her although he admitted to liking Norma at first, before she made such a play for the older boys.

All too soon it was 8.50 and Mary thought that she should make for the bus stop. Neil escorted her there. The bus was due in about ten minutes and when the rain started, Mary told Neil to get off home as there was no point in both of them getting wet. He was reluctant at first but as the rain got heavier he agreed, and kissing Mary gently on one cheek, he said he would see her under the trees outside school the next day. They waved to each other until Neil turned the corner and went out of sight. The first bus to arrive was the 66 which was going to East Kilbride and the only other person at the bus stop got on board.

Mary looked at her watch and as she did so, a car pulled up and a friendly voice shouted, "Hi! Get in. I'm going your way."

Mrs McGregor looked at the clock. It was 9.40. She wondered if she should phone her daughter on her mobile but did not want to embarrass the girl, by being an anxious mother on her first date. Her father had retired to bed early as he always did these days. She decided to give it ten more minutes. At 9.50 she dialled Mary's number and got the voice telling her to leave a message. She did this, getting annoyed with her daughter for switching her mobile off, her annoyance changing to anxiety as the clock hands moved towards 10.15. She dialled again, with the same result. She wished that she had thought to ask Mary for Neil's address and phone number.

She paced the floor for another half hour, then got out her car and drove to the tennis club which was in darkness then she drove to the cafe and went in but Mary was not there either. Her daughter was a sensible girl who would not frighten her mother in this way and Mrs McGregor was getting really scared by now. She knew no one who was a member of the tennis club so she phoned the police. The man who answered told her it was too early to be concerned yet. He had daughters of his own and they had often stayed out later than they had been told they could. He advised her to go home in case Mary had arrived there and to call again if the girl had not arrived home by midnight.

Mrs McGregor drove home quickly. Mary was not there and was still not there at midnight. The policeman this time took details and promised that there would be someone at the house shortly. Unfortunately, the call to the main police station at Govanhill was not taken by Bob who usually manned the desk and who would probably have alerted Davenport to another case in the Clarkston/Eaglesham area. The policeman who arrived took a photo of Mary and tried to reassure her mother.

Mrs McGregor spent an anxious night. Not wanting to worry her father-in-law, she let him sleep on and did not tell him what had happened until he got up around 8am.

"I gave her money for a taxi. Why didn't she take one?" he fretted.

When the doorbell rang at about 8.40, Mrs McGregor ran to answer it but the policeman at the door had no news. He wanted to know if she had any details about whom Mary had been with last night and where she had been.

"I told the policeman last night all this. At Greenway Tennis Club in Stamperland. She was meeting a young boy there. His name's Neil Smith."

"Do you have his address or phone number?"

"No I don't. It was the first time they'd gone out together."

"Have you tried ringing her?"

"Of course I have. Many times."

Then Mrs McGregor had an idea.

"Do you know DCI Davenport, constable?"

"Yes. Why?"

"He's dealing with a murder at the same tennis club. He'll have contact numbers surely."

Mrs McGregor heard herself saying the word 'murder' and shivered.

"Not my daughter. Please let Mary be safe," she thought fervently.

The PC went outside and rang the station, asking to be put in touch with Davenport's office. Davenport was there and listened carefully to what the man had to say.

"Mary McGregor was a friend of the teenager whose murder we're investigating. I want the search stepped up, constable. I'll send some of my own team up there to help the men already searching. They'll meet you outside Clarkston Clinic. Tell me where she was last night and with whom."

He told the constable that he had an address for Neil Smith and would go there himself.

Davenport hung up and shouted down the corridor for his staff who came immediately.

"Another possible murder up around Stamperland. Norma's school friend, Mary McGregor has gone missing. She was out last night with young Neil Smith and didn't get home. I'm going to his house now. No, wait. He'll be at school. I'll go there."

"What do you want us to do, Sir?" asked Fiona.

"I want Salma, Frank and Penny to give a hand with the search. The PC in charge will meet you outside Clarkston Clinic and detail you to an area for searching. DS Macdonald, I want you to stay here and man the phones."

It took Charles about half an hour to reach the school. He went to the office and asked to speak to Neil Smith who came to the office area about ten minutes later.

"Neil Smith?"

"Yes."

The boy smiled at him.

Davenport showed him his warrant card and the boy's face paled.

"What's wrong? Is it Mum? Has my Mum had an accident?"

"Calm down,son. Your Mum's fine but Mary McGregor's gone missing."

"Mary! Missing? But I was with her last night."

"I know that and that's why I'm here. Where was she when you last saw her?"

"Waiting at the bus stop just down from the cafe at Stamperland."

Neil looked distressed.

"It started to rain quite heavily. There's no shelter there and Mary told me to get off home as there was no point in both of us getting wet and my bus was coming the opposite way. I should have stayed, Sir and made sure she got on the bus."

"It's not your fault, Neil. These things happen. Did you happen to notice anyone from the tennis club while you were on your way home? Where is home by the way?"

"Muirend, Sir. That's not the direction of the tennis club. It's the other way, nearer Clarkston."

"Did Mary know anyone at the club? Apart from yourself?"

"Don't think so, Sir. She never came with Norma, I'm pretty sure of that. Norma came with Zoe usually, up until recently when she came alone."

"Were there many members at the club last night, Neil?"

"Yes, Sir. It was match practice so all the courts were full. I go in case I'm needed to make up a four and I was last night as Harry called off."

"So the two ladies' and gents' teams, apart from Harry were there?"

"Yes."

Davenport thanked the boy and the woman in the office and left the school. Back at the station, he and Fiona looked at their lists of members and Davenport retrieved the report which noted the team members. He looked at the gents' list.

"Donald Kinross but not Harry, Neil, Stewart Bolton, David Bentley, Brian Jenkins and Kevin Collins. Did we ever get the intermediate boys' team list?"

"Don't think so, Charles."

Fiona hardly ever called her boss by his Christian name when at work but all the rest were out searching so she felt it was safe to do so now. He smiled at her and kissed her on the nose, gently.

"There are only six of them, I think," she continued, "so they are probably the team."

Charles asked her to phone Avril Smiley and confirm the names of the intermediate boys who had been practising last night.

"She'd be there, I imagine and she's the only one likely to be at home right now," he pointed out.

Fiona rang Avril from her own room and came back to her boss's room to tell him that the boys there last night were Peter Jenkins, Gregory Browne, Robin Stevenson and three promising junior boys, one of them being Norma Lawson's young cousin.

"She said they had had to contact one of the youngest when Neil was needed to stand in for Harry Grey," Fiona informed him "as two of the intermediates had let them down by not appearing. I asked her if any strangers came last night and she said she was playing on the far away courts and wouldn't have seen who was coming and going but no strangers had ever turned up on a Tuesday night before. People wanting to join, usually came along at the weekends."

"Good girl. I was wondering, if to make our job easy, Gavin Gilbert had turned up for some reason. Do you think we can rule him out now, if Mary doesn't turn up alive and well, that is?"

"Yes. I think if Mary has been harmed or worse then it's definitely a tennis club member who's been responsible. The coincidence of three people, attached in some way to the club, being attacked by someone from outside it, seems unlikely."

The police men and women searching the lanes and minor roads between Stamperland and Mary's house in Waterfoot, drew a blank and when darkness fell, they returned to the station. Davenport had rung his sister Linda to ask if she would collect Pippa from school and take her home with her for dinner. He had contacted Salma by mobile phone and told her that they would all be working late as they had people to interview as soon as possible. He had already sent Fiona off to visit the three intermediate boys as they were likely to be home from school and he wanted the others to see the five senior males. He told Salma that he would visit Donald Kinross in Netherlee, if she and Penny would go to Waterfoot and interview David Bentley and Kevin Collins. Frank should go to see Stewart Bolton and Brian Jenkins.

It was nearly nine o'clock by the time, Frank, who was last, arrived back at the station. The others were in the Incident Room, drinking coffee supplied by the DCI. He was looking at the names on the flip chart and was talking about Donald Kinross as Frank came in:

"He went straight home after match practice, stopping, he said, for a bag of chips on the way. His wife said he arrived home at about 8.30. If we can believe her, that would mean he was safely home before Neil left Mary at the bus stop. I went into the chip shop but the man said he was busy last night and couldn't remember anyone in particular. What about you Fiona?"

"Gregory and Robin went home together after match practice and anyway I don't see Norma fancying either of them. They're too young and if neither killed Norma why would one of them kill Mary? That is assuming that Mary is dead and that she has been murdered."

"Yes, she might well turn up all in one piece," agreed her boss. "What about Peter Jenkins? He's more presentable."

"He went straight home, before his father." Fiona looked at Frank who nodded, "Yes Sir, Mr Jenkins confirmed that when I saw him. Peter was in when he arrived home."

"And your other man, Frank, Stewart Bolton?"

"No alibi, Sir. He went home alone and there was no one in when he got there."

"Salma, what about your two, Bentley and Collins?"

"David Bentley rushed off to meet his fiancée, Nancy. They were viewing a flat in Shawlands and had agreed to meet there at around eight o'clock and he was five minutes late. I asked for Nancy's address and went up there and checked and she confirmed that. We could check with the estate agent, Sir but I think they were telling the truth and they know we can check."

"I agree, Salma. I think we can rule out David Bentley."

"Mr Collins said he got home about eight o'clock. His daughter was out at a friend's house doing homework and she got in just after nine and she said her father was sitting watching TV when she arrived home..."

"...so we can't rule him out, Sir. He could have met Mary between when Neil left her and his daughter arrived home," said Penny excitedly.

"Well not much of a margin for error. Lucy could have got home early and found him still out but you're right. It's possible."

"So, Sir," said Fiona, "Donald Kinross could have got his wife to lie for him, Kevin Collins could have had time to meet with Mary and Stewart Bolton has no alibi at all. Is that a fair summing up?"

"Yes, DS Macdonald, that's about it. Anyone else got anything to add?"

No one had, not even Penny who was looking tired, as was Salma. Davenport told them all to get off home.

"Hopefully we'll have good news in the morning, folks."

CHAPTER 37

The news next morning was not good. Davenport arrived early at the station, going up the steps immediately behind a burly individual. The man went to the desk and told Bob on duty there that he had been told to come in.

"My name's Fraser, Ronnie Fraser. I rang you about half an hour ago and was told to come in and see someone called DCI Davenport."

"That's me, Sir," Davenport said. "What's the problem?"

"This gentleman found a young girl's body early this morning, Sir," Bob informed him.

Davenport told the man to come along to his room where he heard the story. Ronnie Fraser was a local farmer. He had gone out to one of his fields and noticed a group of cows surrounding something on the ground. He had walked over and, on pushing through the herd, had discovered the body of a young girl, lying huddled on the ground. He had felt for a pulse but found nothing.

She was lying on her front and he had not wanted to disturb her body but had hurried home, having not taken his mobile phone with him.

"Not one for these new-fangled gadgets. The wife bought me one but I leave it at home most days," he admitted. "I rang the station and the man told me to come straight here and see you. He said you would be on your way."

"Where is this field?"

"In Waterfoot. If you go up Floors Road which leads off the main Glasgow Road, past the houses and round the sharp corner, the field is on your left. There's a wall and the body is lying over that wall."

The man was looking rather pale and was not a young man. Davenport asked if he would like a cup of tea and when the man looked grateful, he switched on his kettle. He was a coffee person himself but sweet tea was, he thought, the order of the day.

Leaving Mr Fraser sipping his hot reviving drink, Davenport went out of his room and met Fiona Macdonald arriving so he told her what had happened.

"Get in touch with Martin Jamieson and Ben Goodwin. Arrange for them to meet us there as soon as possible."

"Mary McGregor, Charles?"

"I'm afraid so. I won't contact her mother yet but I think the chances of this being another young girl are slim."

Davenport went back into his room. Ronnie Fraser was looking better and agreed to drive ahead of them, to show them the way. Davenport and Fiona followed him out, Davenport having left word with Bob for the others when they arrived. There was no need for them to come to the scene.

The cows had congregated once more at the wall and were all looking down at the girl's body. The three adults climbed over the wall. Fraser chased the cows away and Davenport and Fiona looked down. The girl was wearing denims which were mud-splattered and a short denim jacket. She had one shoe on, a black one and her tights were ripped and torn.

A car's engine was heard coming up the road and soon Martin Jamieson was climbing over the wall looking out of place in his immaculate dark-grey suit and lemon coloured shirt with dark grey and lemon striped tie. He seemed not to notice the damage the mud was doing to his beautiful Italian shoes. He bent down and felt for a pulse, then pulled latex gloves from his bag and put them on. He rolled the body over and Davenport saw once again the purple skin and protruding tongue of the strangled victim. Under the denim jacket, the girl was wearing a turquoise blouse which was sodden from the wet ground. Having issued his team with a description of Mary McGregor and the clothes she was wearing, he knew without a shadow of a doubt that this was indeed Mary.

"Good morning, Charles. Do you know who this is?" Martin stood up.

"'Fraid so. Her name's Mary McGregor, a school friend of the other dead girl, Norma Lawson. She went missing last night. We've been searching for her since then. Mr Fraser here found the body this morning. Being in close to the wall, it wasn't visible from the road."

The sound of another car pulling to a halt was heard and another man climbed the wall, much less agilely than Martin had climbed it. Ben Goodwin was fatter and older than Martin Jamieson and was rather breathless when he joined them. He was followed by two other members of the SOC team, younger men carrying all the equipment they would need. It took only minutes for them to erect a tent over the body and clamber into their white overalls.

"No need to tell you how she died, Charles. Any layman could tell you that but I' shall need to examine the injuries more closely to give you any details. The mortuary van should be here soon and I shall get the body taken away as soon as Ben tells me it is OK to do so."

Thanking his lucky stars for two men who got on well and cooperated with each other, Charles thanked them both and he and Fiona clambered back over the wall.

"Sir, here's her other shoe."

Fiona picked up a black shoe from the grass verge. She threw it over the wall to Ben.

"There aren't many houses here, Fiona. Let's strike while the iron's hot and see if anyone heard anything last night."

All the houses seemed to be occupied by retired people. Some were still in bed, others had noticed the activity in the field and were agog with curiosity but none had heard anything unusual.

"We often get courting couples in the late evenings, Inspector," said one elderly man.

"It's a through road from Mearns to Waterfoot,"said another, "so in spite of being a narrow road it's quite a busy one."

"Jessie - the dog - made a lot of noise last night," said another and when asked at what time, the woman said it must have been about nine o'clock as the news was just starting on TV. She lived at the end house, the nearest one to the field. Fiona asked her if she had noticed anything and she said that she had not looked out of the window and had just told the dog to be quiet.

"It might just have been a car. She barks at everything. Sorry."

"The dog probably heard the car with Mary in it," Davenport commented when Fiona told him the time it had barked. "I don't imagine that Mary walked up to the field with her murderer."

"Why on earth would she get into a car with a strange man from the tennis club? Young folk these days are well - warned not to get into a car with someone they don't know," said Fiona.

"Maybe she'd met the person at the tennis club while waiting for Neil."

"What danger could she possibly be to the murderer?" asked Fiona.

"Norma must have told her something and somehow the murderer found out," Davenport answered.

"Let's get back to the station. The others will want to hear what has happened and I want to speak to Neil again. See if he knows whether or not Mary spoke to anyone at the club last night. It's a slim chance but you never know. We'll need to get Mrs McGregor down to the morgue, poor woman, to identify the body but we'll wait for Martin's say-so before we get in touch with her."

They reached the station to find Salma, Penny and Frank waiting in the Incident Room and told them what had happened. Davenport left Fiona to give them the details and he went off to phone Neil Smith's home. He reckoned that the young man would not have gone to school that day and he was correct. He told Neil that someone would be over to question him further about the evening before, saying nothing about the discovery of the body as no one could be told until Mary's mother identified it as being that of her daughter.

Frank was sent to Muirend and came back to say that Mary had spoken to Georgina Laird at the club but Neil did not know what about as they had obviously finished their conversation when he had come into the club house. He had passed Georgina on the stairs and assumed that she had spoken to Mary.

Late in the afternoon, Martin Jamieson rang to say that he had cleaned up the body and it was ready for inspection, though not very pleasant so Fiona drove up to the McGregor home in Waterfoot and escorted Mary's mother and grandfather to the mortuary. Mr McGregor volunteered to look at the body but he was so frail that Fiona was glad when Mrs McGregor said no, she would do it herself. Martin pulled back the white sheet and the woman moaned and turned away from the sight of her daughter's distorted face. She left the room and, sinking down on the bench where her father-in-law sat, told him brokenly that it was Mary. The old man put his arm round her and nodded to DS Macdonald. Fiona left them for a few minutes before suggesting that they let her drive them home. They sat together in the back seat of the car, clinging to each other, Mary's Mum saying over and over, "Oh Mary, why?"

Once inside their house, Fiona went to the kitchen to make tea for them. She returned to the living room in time to hear the old man saying, "I gave her money for a taxi. Why didn't she take one?" and his daughter once more saying, "Why did she get into the car of a strange man? We'd warned her so often, Dad."

They took the tea. Fiona left, telling them that someone would be up later to talk to them. They should get their doctor up to see them both.

"I am a doctor. I'll see to my father-in-law," said Mrs McGregor.

Back at the station, she found the rest discussing the case in the Incident Room. Penny and Salma were to go up to Waterfoot to interview Georgina Laird to see if she had indeed spoken to Mary the previous evening but she would not be home from college yet. Charles would wait till they got back but he told Fiona and Frank that they could go home.

Three murders. He was not looking forward to meeting the chief constable but it would have to be done tomorrow.

CHAPTER 38

For the second time, Salma and Penny made their way down the impressive driveway to the Laird house. It was raining heavily by this time and the trees lining the drive were dripping water all round them. Bushes fringed the route the women were taking and the whole atmosphere was oppressive, unlike the last time when they had noticed the signs of approaching spring.

This time it was Georgina herself who opened the door. She looked surprised to see them and they had to ask if they could come in.

"Of course. Sorry. I was expecting my boyfriend, Barry. I didn't mean to be rude."

She led them this time into a large drawing room. The ceiling was high and paintings adorned every wall. Penny sat down on the edge of the cream-coloured leather settee but Salma, feeling awed, remained standing. It was she who spoke first.

"Miss Laird, I'm sorry to bring bad news. Another young girl was found murdered this morning and we have reason to believe she was killed because of her link to Greenway Tennis Club."

"Another murder! Who is it this time? Another intermediate girl?"

At this moment the door opened and her sister came in. She saw the police women and started to back out but Penny got up and went over to her and led her back in.

"Henrietta. We're here to tell you and your sister that another girl has been murdered. You might as well stay in case you can help in any way."

"Another tennis girl?" The young girl echoed her sister's question.

Salma spoke again to Georgina.

"Miss Laird, it wasn't a member who was killed this time. It was a friend of Norma's from school, a girl called Mary McGregor. You met her last night at the tennis club according to Neil Smith. You know him I think?"

"*I* met her?"

"Yes, he said you went into the clubhouse just before him and you were coming out as he went in. Mary was waiting for him and he thought you might have spoken to her."

"Oh, wait a minute. I did speak to a teenager. I didn't get her name I'm afraid but she did say something about a man whom Norma had talked to her about. I told her she should tell the police. She said she would."

Henrietta spoke up.

"I remember that Norma had a school friend she had tried to get to join the tennis club but the girl wasn't sporty and didn't join."

"Miss Laird, what name did Mary give you?" Salma tried to keep the excitement from her voice.

"I can't believe he would every hurt anyone, never mind kill them, Inspector. He's going out with my friend Jane Green and he's such a nice guy."

"His name, Miss Laird," Penny interjected.

"Stewart. Stewart Bolton. I pointed him out to her. He was playing on one of the courts near the clubhouse but surely Norma could have mentioned a lot of the tennis club males. She flirted with Don at the American Tournament."

"Yes, we know that. Thank you Miss Laird. Henrietta, can you remember Norma ever mentioning Stewart?"

"No. She talked about some older boys at school but never gave any names that I can remember and Stewart wouldn't have anything to do with someone her age. Would he, George?"

"No, he wouldn't. He's going out with Jane. Why would he want to chat up a young girl Norma's age?"

Thanking them both for their time, Salma and Penny left.

Salma, knowing that her boss would be waiting for them to come back and knowing that they now had a name to go on, decided to phone him.

"Sir, Sergeant Din here. Georgina Laird did speak to Mary at the club last night. Mary told her that Norma had spoken about Stewart Bolton."

Try as she might, Penny could not keep from smugly smiling as she listened. She had favoured that young man all along. Salma listened, then she spoke again:

"Georgina said she told Mary to tell us and Mary said she would."

Salma's face fell. She rang off.

"What is it, Salma?" asked her friend.

"The DCI said how would Stewart Bolton know that Mary had spoken to Georgina? How did he know she was going to give us his name? We've to go back to the house and ask if Georgina told him."

The two policewomen retraced their steps. Henrietta answered the door this time and took them into the kitchen where her sister was making coffee. The kitchen was full of the latest gadgets and Penny thought what a contrast it was to her own kitchen at Alec's flat.

"Miss Laird, sorry to be annoying you again but did you mention Mary to Stewart Bolton?"

Georgina looked embarrassed. She put down the coffee mug she was holding.

"I'm afraid I did, constable. I thought it was such a joke, the idea of him fancying a teenager. He's one of my best friends and he's going out with one of my girlfriends."

"Why didn't you tell us this?"

"I foolishly hoped you wouldn't need to know."

"Was anyone else nearby when you told him?" asked Salma.

"Most of the guys were in the same room, upstairs in the clubhouse. We were having a chat after the practice as we often do. I wasn't in a hurry. No Pat to go off with this week. This is a nightmare. Pat dead and Norma and now another youngster."

Georgina looked tearful and her young sister patted her on the shoulder.

"Thanks, Miss Laird. You were foolish not to tell us in the first instance," said Salma.

She and Penny left for a second time and this time made their way back to the station where Davenport was waiting for them. He poured them both a coffee in his room and listened while Salma told him what had happened when they went back.

"So anyone could have overheard Georgina Laird talking to Stewart Bolton."

"But why on earth would someone kill Mary for saying it was Stewart? It would let the other man off the hook surely," said Penny puzzled.

"Not if we questioned Bolton and he said other folk had heard her and he could prove his innocence," her boss reasoned.

"Which we are going to do - question Bolton I mean," said Salma. "So it wasn't necessary to kill

Mary. He surely must have reasoned that Georgina would tell us what had happened."

"Only if someone knew Georgina had met Mary last night otherwise he might just have hoped that Georgina wouldn't mention it. I guess the murderer panicked and didn't reason things out before taking action. Murdered Mary to make sure we couldn't question her. If it was someone else, Mary would have told us this if questioned," Davenport said.

"But Sir, if Mary thought Norma had mentioned Stewart she wasn't going to suddenly change her mind and mention someone else." Penny sounded confused.

"Who can get into the mind of a murderer Penny? Who knows why they kill in the first place but we've found out quite often that once someone has killed, they seem to be able to do it again more readily."

"What now, Sir? Do we interview Stewart Bolton?"

Salma was curious to know the next step.

"Of course, sergeant but I'll do that. My sister is going to take Pippa home and get her into bed for me so I'll do this myself. Get off home both of you and I'll see you in the morning."

Penny looked disappointed but Salma got up and nudged her to her feet. She knew that Penny was curious as was she but Davenport would have asked them to accompany him if he had wanted them there and he obviously did not.

Charles drove up to Clarkston. Stewart Bolton lived in a large house in Eastwoodmains Road and Charles wondered why he was not a member of Clarkston Tennis Club which was nearer for him than Greenway in Stamperland. This was the first thing he asked the young man when he was seated in the lounge.

"Why did you not join Clarkston, Mr Bolton?"

"I did join it but members came with their own foursome and I wasn't getting many games so I left and joined Greenway as I'd heard it was friendlier. However, Inspector, I'm sure you didn't come here to ask me that."

"No I didn't, Sir. I came up to ask you if Norma Lawson fancied you."

"If Norma said that, she was telling lies to make herself look good. I certainly didn't fancy her. I've got a girlfriend, Jane Green. You can ask her."

"I know Jane Green is your girlfriend, Sir but that doesn't count out you trying to get a bit of action with a younger girl. Maybe, to put it bluntly, you weren't getting enough sex with Jane."

Davenport thought that the young man paled slightly and looked slightly less arrogant and when he spoke, it was to tell him that Jane was not the kind of girl to have sex out with marriage but that did not mean that he was sex-starved. He knew plenty of girls who would willingly sleep with him. Davenport was glad that Penny was not there and could understand why she did not like him. He was far too confident and aware of his own good looks and his attraction to the opposite sex.

"I also want to know where you were on Monday evening, Sir."

"No alibi for Pat Harper's murder, I'm afraid, Inspector. I was here by myself that night."

His cool, confident attitude had returned.

Thanking him for his honesty, Davenport asked Bolton if he lived in this house on his own.

"My parents are away on a cruise, Inspector. That's why I have no alibi for the murder of Pat Harper."

"And last night, Sir? Where did you go after tennis practice?"

"I came home after a bit of a chat with the others in the clubhouse. Why, Inspector?"

"Mary McGregor, Norma's friend, was found murdered this morning and we have Georgina Laird's word that you knew that Mary had pointed you out."

The young man's face had drained of all colour and his brash confidence seemed to have deserted him, as this time he said nothing.

Davenport left.

CHAPTER 39

Davenport was a bit later getting into the station the next day. After the late night, he had let Pippa sleep in a bit longer and dropped her off a few minutes before nine o'clock. His colleagues were standing talking in the corridor, outside DS Macdonald's room. Fiona was standing in her doorway and she was the first to speak.

"Glad to see you, Sir. Mr Knox wants to see you as soon as possible.

Charles grimaced.

"Well he can just wait a few minutes while I tell you what happened with Stewart Bolton last night. Come into the Incident Room."

When they were all seated, he asked if Penny and Salma had told the others about Mary mentioning Stewart Bolton as being someone Norma had talked about. Fiona said they had. Glancing at his watch, then pulling at his ear lobe, he proceeded to tell them about his interview with Stewart Bolton.

"He has a flimsy alibi for the night of Norma's murder as his girlfriend might have been persuaded to bend the truth about him being with her. He might have been with her nearly all evening and he's asked her to say all evening. He has no alibi for the night of Pat Harper's murder and again he was at home alone on Tuesday evening when Mary was killed."

"Well, Sir. Donald Kinross has an alibi for the Monday night of Pat's death and his recounting of what happened on the moor road tallies with Sheila's account and I rang his wife yesterday evening and he definitely arrived home when he said he did," said Fiona.

"And Mr Collins and Mr Jenkins were out with their children," said Frank.

"Just David Bentley, Gavin Gilbert and Donald Kinross to check up on from our last list then," said Davenport. "See if they have an alibi for Tuesday evening."

"And a possible boyfriend of Pat's," added Penny.

"That reminds me," said Fiona. "Georgina Laird rang after you left yesterday to say that Pat Harper's funeral is to be on Friday, 11 o'clock at The Linn. Who do you want to attend that one boss?"

"Think I'll go myself; see if I can find out from the family if there was a boyfriend. The marriage split up over some affair, I think. However, right now I've got the chief constable to see. Who hasn't seen Gavin Gilbert yet?"

Penny and Salma raised their hands. The DCI and DS had seen him on the first occasion they had visited Norma's house and Frank had sat in on the interview at the station.

"Right Salma, you go over to the Gilbert House in Waterfoot and find out from Gavin Gilbert where he was on Tuesday night. He was at home on the other two murder nights and I suppose Jan Gilbert might have covered for him though I don't think so as it was her daughter who was murdered on one of those nights. Ring the house and find out when he'll be in from work. Frank, you get to David Bentley's house. Find out where he was on Tuesday night. Fiona would you do Brian Jenkins and Kevin Collins? They do have alibis but again it's a member of the family who is vouching for them. Penny you visit Kinross and ask where he was on Tuesday evening. Ring them first folks and save yourselves wasted journeys."

Charles's spirits were low as he took the elevator to the floor where Grant Knox had his office. He felt that they had narrowed the field down to Stewart Bolton, David Bentley, Gavin Gilbert, Kevin Collins and Brian Jenkins and Pat Harper's possible boyfriend but he could not honestly say that he favoured any one of these people.

He came out of the lift and almost bumped into Solomon Fairchild.

"Sorry, Sir."

"Oh it's you, Charles. Well met. The chief constable has had to leave suddenly and he said you were on your way to see him."

Fairchild looked at his watch.

"That would be about forty minutes ago." His eyes crinkled humorously. "I see you bust a gut to get here."

Davenport started to apologise.

"I only heard about it when I got in just after nine o'clock, Sir and I had my team to..."

"...only joking, Charles. I know you're a busy man. Come along to my office. I've to interview you instead."

Seated in Fairchild's office, Charles accepted the offer of a cup of tea and a biscuit and felt himself relaxing.

"Right, Charles. How much further forward are you with the first two murders?"

Charles told him about narrowing the field down to seven people, some of whom had alibis of a kind. He told the assistant chief inspector about his interview with the rather arrogant Stewart Bolton who had no alibi for the last two murders and a shaky one for the first.

"But your gut's telling you it's not him, Charles?"

The man must be a thought-reader. Charles was indeed feeling this but he could never have told this to Grant Knox who did not go along with such airy-fairy things as gut reactions.

"Well, Sir, he seems the kind of arrogant bastard who would trifle with a youngster's affection and maybe even lead her on but on the other hand he seems to be respecting his girlfriend's wish to have no sex until marriage, so raping a fourteen-year old doesn't match up somehow."

"And what about the other six men?"

"Checking five alibis tonight, Sir, though they all have alibis of a sort for one or other of the first two murders and the murders must surely be connected. We still don't know if the woman murdered second had a current boyfriend but even so he would seem unlikely to have murdered the first youngster unless he's a member of the tennis club."

"So I'll tell Grant that you're on top of things, will I? It was family business he had to rush off to. One of his sons has been in an accident. He lives outside London and Grant and Eileen are driving there tonight so I think you might have a few days' grace to find out more."

It was difficult to imagine the irascible Knox with a family somehow, thought Davenport, as he made his way back down to his own office but he had been given some breathing space and was mightily relieved.

CHAPTER 40

Martin Jamieson's report arrived on Davenport's desk mid- morning on the Thursday after Mary's body had been found. He confirmed that Mary had been strangled, not by hands this time. Something else had been wound round the girl's neck and pulled tightly. Martin had examined the whole body and there were bruises to the arms just below the shoulders. Mary was a slight girl weighing only 117 pounds and with a height of exactly five feet. There was no sexual interference this time.

"I would suggest that the girl was man-handled out of a vehicle and then strangled," he wrote.

"Or got out willingly and then was man-handled."

Davenport rang Ben Goodwin who told him that his report was being typed up as they spoke. On being asked what was in the report, he said that there were scuffle marks on the road side of the wall and a flattened section of grass suggesting that a body had lain there, briefly.

"I think the lassie was killed on the road side of the wall then tipped over the wall. She looked small and of light weight but Jamieson will give you those details."

Davenport thanked him and rang off. He went into Fiona's room and gave her the news.

"Time for another update, I think. I gave the others time to write up the reports of their recent interviews but they should have them finished by now, even Selby!"

They walked down the corridor towards the Incident Room, pausing only for Davenport to stick his head round the door of the main room and tell Salma, Frank and Penny to join them there.

"Did you all manage to see the folk you were given to interview?"

"Yes, Sir," they chorused, taking their seats in front of him and the DS who remained standing.

"First of all, Mary was strangled by someone who maybe dragged her out of their car or persuaded her to get out, killed her, then shoved her body over the wall into the field where she was found."

He motioned to Frank.

"Right, Frank you go first. You spoke to David Bentley?"

"I got him at home after work. His fiancée was there having a meal with David and his parents. They've been seeing houses and on Tuesday night they were out at two after the match practice. His fiancée, Nancy, says she was to have met David in Shawlands but decided instead to meet him at the tennis club and was waiting outside the club in her car. She drove them to the houses. I asked her if she saw anyone else leaving and she saw a young couple walking in the direction of the cafe. David said he left first because he knew that Nancy was waiting for him. Donald Kinross was, he said, right behind him."

"Salma?"

"Gavin Gilbert was in by himself, baby-sitting his two boys while his wife went to visit her mother, Norma's gran. Mrs Gilbert came home around 9 o'clock. Surely he wouldn't have left his two sons alone, Sir."

"Probably not, Sergeant. Penny?"

"Donald Kinross has a rock-solid alibi, Sir. His wife was at the school for a parents' night. It started at 7 o'clock and Donald joined her there at about 8 and they were there till nearly 10. One of their boys has been in trouble and they spent a long time with his Guidance teacher."

"We can check that by phone. See to that Penny, please."

"Yes, Sir."

Penny sped off.

"Now, Fiona, what about Brian Jenkins and Kevin Collins?"

"They said they remained at the club, chatting to some of the others for quite a time, and then

Collins gave Jenkins a lift home. He had picked him up as he passes close to his house."

"It's beginning to look a bit bleak for Bolton," Davenport commented, putting a large cross against Stewart's name on the flip chart.

"Yes but either Jenkins or Collins could have gone out again, Sir," said Salma.

"Did any of your folk mention a time when they left the clubhouse? Bolton and those two must have been the only ones left talking..."

"...and the intermediates who were practising, Sir," said Frank. He reddened and apologised for interrupting.

"Quite right, Frank. I'd forgotten about the youngsters. They could hardly have hefted Mary's body over a wall but they might be able to give the three men alibis if they stayed to chat too. Would you get onto that after school? Forget the juniors and concentrate on Peter Jenkins, Gregory Browne and Robin Stevenson."

"Peter Jenkins is a tall lad, Sir," said Fiona. "He might have managed it."

"Yes but we've ruled him out of having an affair with Pat Harper and killing Norma and these three murders have to be connected and I can't see Peter murdering Mary for his dad, though..." he hesitated... "funnier things have happened."

Penny returned at this point with the information that Mr Kinross had indeed turned up at parents' evening and had joined his wife. The Guidance teacher, brought to the phone, had confirmed that both parents had stayed with her for quite a long time between 8.30 and 9.00.

Davenport asked if they had all completed their reports of the most recent interviews and was told that they had. He dismissed them all, apologising for eating into their lunch time and telling them to take time off now. The canteen would be quite bare of food by now so he suggested that they all eat out and they all repaired to one of the local pubs.

Frank left before the rest, to catch the younger boys as they arrived home from school and he returned about an hour and a half later to tell his boss that Gregory Browne and Robin Stevenson had remained behind for about an hour with Stewart Bolton, Brian Jenkins and Kevin Collins who had been giving them tips for their next match. Bolton had left first, then the other two had left together.

"Did Peter Jenkins go away with his father and Collins?" asked Davenport.

"No, the boys said he seemed to get fed up with the conversation and he left earlier, Sir. When I spoke to Peter he said he had walked home and gone into the local garage for a can of irn bru and some chocolate. He had been home for about half an hour before his dad arrived home. They had watched TV together for the rest of the evening."

"So it seems unlikely that Jenkins went back out."

At this point, Fiona joined them and Charles filled her in with what Frank had been saying.

"Fiona, did you think to ask Collins what he did when he got home?"

"Yes, Sir. He said that Lucy was doing homework at a friend's house and that he went to collect her at about 9.30 so he could have driven back down to Stamperland."

"But Sir, why would Jenkins kill Mary for saying that Norma spoke about Bolton?" asked Frank, puzzled.

"I know. It's unlikely. Unless he had chatted her up too and was just worried that Mary might have heard about him too and had mentioned him or would mention him at a later date. It's thin, I know."

Davenport called to Salma and Penny and they all congregated once more in the Incident Room.

Davenport went to the flip board and scored out Donald Kinross's name, Brian Jenkins' name and that of David Bentley. His hand hovered over that of Kevin Collins but moved on to that of Gavin Gilbert.

"What do you think, folks?" he asked the others.

"Leave it on, Sir. His wife might just not believe that he could have murdered Norma and backed his story about being at home with her. He might have given her a good reason for being out of the house for a short time. If he was desperate, he could have left his young boys for a short time on Tuesday night."

Salma was reluctant to give up her suspect. Penny agreed with her friend. Davenport summarised what Frank had found out, for Penny and Salma.

"So, we're left now with four possible candidates."

They all looked at the list.

"Gavin Gilbert, Kevin Collins, Stewart Bolton and Pat's boyfriend," intoned Davenport. "Leaving out the first three, let's concentrate on the last one, Pat's boyfriend. Are we agreed that if he is the murderer, he has to have some connection with the tennis club?"

"Yes, Sir," said Fiona. "It's too much of a coincidence that this mystery man would know Pat and Norma out with the club and that the same man would overhear Mary talk about Norma liking Bolton and feel threatened again."

"Agreed everyone?"

They nodded.

"So this mystery man can only be one of the other three left on the list," said Penny eagerly.

"Yes, Penny. Let's take them one at a time. Gavin Gilbert."

"With a wife and two young boys, would he start an affair with someone else, and then start something with Norma?" asked Fiona.

"If his wife was frigid, ma'am," said Frank, "or too tired to have sex with two young boys to look after all day."

"Kevin Collins?" asked Davenport.

"Could have met Pat at tennis and started an affair, then wanted some new blood and started on Norma," Frank again supplied the reason.

The women were silent.

"Stewart Bolton?"

"If his girlfriend won't give him sex," volunteered Penny, "he might have started something with an older woman and then moved on to Norma."

"So we've really boiled it down to three. Agreed?"

"Agreed," they chorused.

"Right. The funeral of Pat Harper is tomorrow. I'm going myself this time. I still want to ask the family if there is anyone they know of with whom Pat might have been having an affair and I want to find out the name of the person who caused the break- up of her marriage. It might be the same person with any luck. On Saturday, I'm going to call in the three suspects for further interview. Saturday should be a good day to find them free."

CHAPTER 41

Every time Charles Davenport went to Linn Crematorium, he wondered who had designed it. He never knew whether to drive straight up to the car park or wait at the gates for the hearse and following cars. Today was no exception. There were lots of cars lining the pathways inside the gate so he decided to wait outside and follow the hearse and hopefully the car park would have emptied by then. Admittedly, when the place was planned, there would not have been so many cars, he thought now. The first time he has come here, it was for his father George's funeral in the late 1970s when he was about nine years old. His father had been a popular man and had died young, at 51 so there had been many mourners but not so many cars.

He looked in his rear-view mirror and saw the hearse approaching, one large black car following it. As it passed him, he saw the figures of two young girls in the back seat. He followed slowly and was relieved to see cars coming from the car park. He found a space, got out and joined the other mourners in the queue forming round the side of the building. He got a smile of recognition from Avril Smiley who was with a woman he presumed would be her tennis partner, Anne Scott and he noticed another young woman nearer the front of the queue and presumed that this would be Georgina Laird, Pat's tennis friend and partner.

When he got into the crematorium he was surprised at how few people were in attendance but had no time to reflect on this before two young girls in their early twenties were ushered into the front seat and as the coffin was carried in, he realised that Pat's ex-husband had chosen not to appear.

The service was brief, the minister obviously not knowing Pat well, if at all, and soon he was in the short line of people waiting to shake hands with Pat's two daughters. Both were dry-eyed and coping very well with what could have been their first experience of a funeral. Charles shook hands with each of them, saying nothing about who he was, as he had decided to leave this till they were back at The Redhurst Hotel.

Avril and Anne were joined by two men, rather older than themselves and they were introduced as two former members of the tennis club. Charles commented on how few tennis people had attended and Avril explained that Pat had not been very popular with the men who had found her abrasive and critical when they had partnered her at any time.

"The younger men especially steered well clear of her, I'm afraid, Inspector. She tended to treat them like schoolchildren and was always telling them where to stand and what to do."

"What about the women? Did they like her?" asked Davenport.

Avril threw a look at her friend before replying.

"Not really. She tended to ignore us. She and Georgina Laird thought they should be first couple. She was scathing about Sheila Ferguson's flirtation with Don Kinross and only spoke to Jane Green because she was friendly with Georgina."

"She was a bit of a loner, Inspector. I always wondered why she ever joined a club."

The black limousine carrying Pat's two daughters was moving off, so, saying that he would see them at The Redhurst, Davenport went for his car.

It was a journey of about twenty minutes to the hotel on Eastwoodmains Road and he was pleased to find a car space, the reason for this being made clear when he entered the room reserved for them. There were only about ten people there.

He went across to the table where Georgina Laird was sitting by herself and asked if he could sit with her. She looked a bit put out but said yes and a few minutes later they were joined by Avril and Anne and the two older men.

The elder of Pat's daughters made a stilted short speech thanking them for coming and it was not till after eating some sausage rolls and some sandwiches, that Davenport went across to their table to talk to them.

"Hello, g...ladies. I'm Charles Davenport the DCI in charge of your mother's case. It was a lovely service."

The older girl asked him to sit down.

"Who would want to kill my mother, Inspector?"

"That's what we'll find out soon. Did she have any enemies that you know of?"

"Apart from dad you mean!" said the younger girl, bitterly.

"Joan!" The elder girl reproached her. "Dad's over it all. You know he is. He didn't hate mum any more."

She turned back to Davenport.

"Sorry Inspector. It's just that dad was gutted when he found out that mum was having an affair. He got custody of us because the judge said she wasn't a fit mother. She'd left us alone a few times to sneak out of the house you see."

"What age were you, Miss Harper, when your parents split up?"

"Debbie, Inspector. Please don't call me Miss Harper, it sounds so formal. I was fourteen and Joan was eleven."

"Your mum didn't stay with the person she left your dad for then?"

"No. She went back to living on her own about three years ago and that's when I decided to visit her …"

"…And dragged me along every time too," the younger girl muttered.

"I'm sorry to have to ask you but did your mum take up with another man after the first one left her?"

"Not as far as I know. There was no sign of anyone else living in her house."

At this point Georgina Laird came across to thank them and say that she was leaving.

"I'll miss your mother," she said stiffly. "She and I were tennis partners and friends."

The girls stood up and shook hands, thanking her for coming and Georgina left.

Davenport thanked the girls and gave them his card, telling them to get in touch at any time, then he too left, after having said goodbye to Avril and Anne and thanking them for their company.

He caught up with Georgina in the car park.

"Miss Laird. Pat's daughters didn't know of any boyfriend. How do you know she had one? I think it was you who mentioned it before."

"Well she's not likely to tell her daughters, is she Inspector? She probably told me because I was her best friend at tennis."

"You can't give me his name?"

"Pat never told me his name. I wondered if it was someone I knew, maybe someone at the tennis club. She didn't go out to work so it couldn't have been a workmate."

"One of the older men at the funeral today perhaps?" asked Davenport.

"Definitely not them." Georgina laughed. "One was her mixed doubles' partner a few years ago and the other is his brother who was also a member. Pat made fun of them both. Called them two sweetie wives. They live together in what was their parents' house. They've never been married as far as I know and they're certainly not the types to have affairs! Now if you'll excuse me, I have to get back to college."

"Does Jane go to college too?"

"No, she's a brainbox. She goes to Glasgow Uni. She's going to be a doctor."

Georgina got into her car, winding her long legs in gracefully and Davenport stood back. Avril and Anne were coming out. He went up to them and asked if Anne could remember Jane Green's address.

"Yes, Inspector. Jane lives in Muirend, number 10 Corrie Grove."

Taking a chance, Davenport called in at Corrie Grove on his way back to the station. It didn't take him far out of his way. An elderly woman answered the door.

"Sorry to bother you, Mrs..."

"Green. Who are you?"

Davenport took out his ID card and the woman took it suspiciously and peered at it.

"DCI Davenport. I'm one of the team investigating the murders at your granddaughter's tennis club."

"My *daughter's* club, Inspector."

The woman glared at him. Jane, he realised, had been a very late baby.

"Sorry, Mrs Green. I wonder when I'll get her at home."

"She should be home soon. She should be home already in fact."

She looked at her watch.

"She has a half day at university today and she's taking me shopping."

She made no move to invite him in.

Davenport thanked her and turned to leave. Just then a car pulled up outside and a young woman got out.

"Jane Green?" Davenport asked.

"Yes," Jane looked flustered. She shouted over his shoulder to the woman standing in the doorway:

"Mum, sorry I'm late. The traffic was dreadful on the bridge. I'll be with you in a minute."

The woman gave what sounded like a snort and turned back into the house.

"I'm DCI Davenport, in charge of the investigations into the two murders connected to Greenway Tennis Club. I won't keep you long. I just wanted to ask you one thing. Did you ever go with Georgina Laird to Pat Harper's house?"

"No, Inspector. George is my friend but Pat never invited me after tennis practice. I found it odd but I think that George was her only friend and she didn't want to share her. It didn't bother me. I see George most weekends and anyway, I usually went for a coffee with Stewart, my boyfriend."

"But not last Tuesday?"

"No, Mum wanted me to set her hair for her. She and Dad were going out that night."

It was obvious that the elderly Mrs Green expected her young daughter to jump when she called.

"One more thing, Miss Green. Did you ever have sex with Stewart?"

Jane went red.

"I don't see that that's any of your business, Inspector."

"I'm afraid in a murder investigation everything's my business. The two murders had sexual connotations and Mr Bolton is, like the other males at Greenway, under suspicion until shown to be innocent."

"I've been brought up a Christian, Inspector and I don't believe in sex before marriage. Stewart respects that."

"Thank you. I'll let you get to your mother now."

Davenport was thoughtful as he drove to Govanhill. Jane had confirmed what Stewart Bolton had told him. Either he was a considerate lad who was prepared to forego sex or he was finding action elsewhere, maybe with Pat Harper and, he had hoped, with Norma Lawson.

CHAPTER 42

The front courts at Greenway Tennis Club were all full. It was a beautiful, spring day. Coaching was over for the day and Avril Smiley should have been enjoying her tennis but she had just had a row with Georgina Laird over the first team pairings. Avril had decided to put Jane and Sheila up to second couple and had asked Georgina to choose one of the second team women to partner her at third couple, hoping that by giving her this choice, she might be more amenable to going down a position. She had been out of luck. Georgina was furious.

"Why should I go down? Why can't I partner Jane or even Sheila?"

"They're used to each other now. I don't want to have two couples unused to playing with each other. One's enough. You must see that!"

"And who would you have me choose? Elizabeth and June are glued together. They've played together for years, since I was a junior and as far as I can see haven't got any better at tennis in that time. Jenny and Joanne don't take their tennis seriously and never come to match practice. Or perhaps you'd like me to play with my kid sister or her little friend Sam!"

Georgina had worked herself up into a temper and Avril had seen red.

"Well, don't play at all then! I'll move Elizabeth and June up to the first team and get Zoe and Lucy Collins to play at third in the second."

Avril had then stomped off to where Anne was waiting for her on court to play a set against the Caldwell twins. Jane and Sheila were already well into their first game against Henry Laird and Samantha McMillan, the two youngsters throwing themselves enthusiastically round the court in an effort to take even one game off the senior women and Elizabeth and June were spinning on the middle court to see who was going to serve between them and their opponents, Zoe Stewart and Lucy Collins.

Georgina had always played with Pat on Saturdays as well as on Tuesdays evenings and she realised that by doing this, she had never played with any of the other women, for some time. She went upstairs to the clubhouse lounge and threw herself moodily into one of the chairs. She was still there, contemplating going home, when Stewart Bolton arrived.

"Hi, George! Glad to get a chance to talk to you. I've just been at the police station, in the interview room, the kind of thing you see on TV, only this was real. The police have got the idea now that that girl Norma Lawson fancied me and I've got no alibi for the night Pat was killed and now seemingly another girl's been murdered and I've got no alibi for that night either."

Georgina had never seen the confident, suave Stewart in such a state.

"I'm sorry, Stu. I gave the police your name. I had to. I mean yours was the name that girl gave me. I didn't tell them that you knew about it but they came back and asked me if I'd told you and I had to tell the truth."

"It's not your fault, George, but thanks to that girl, I'm in real trouble."

"And she's dead now. "

"Who's killing all these folk and why?"

"Goodness knows."

They sat in silence for a while then Stewart seemed to cheer up.

"At least I've got an alibi for the first murder. I was with Jane."

"I'm sure that will convince them that you're innocent. I mean surely the other murders are connected and they can't imagine that you and Jane are in it together!"

They even managed to laugh at the thought of the moral, respectable, church-going Jane being involved in three murders.

Georgina turned the conversation to tennis.

"That bitch Avril has put me down to third couple."

"With whom?"

"Exactly! She is graciously letting me choose from the second team."

"D'you know what, George, your wee sister is getting really good. Why don't you choose her and get yourselves known as the Laird Sisters. You could practise a lot with her on your court at home and force Avril to put you back up. I know Jane wouldn't mind staying at third couple and Sheila's thoughts are...elsewhere."

"Do you think she and Don are having an affair?" Georgina was curious.

"I'm sure of it. Have you not seen the looks they give each other?"

"Can't say I have. At least if he is and the police find out, it'll stop them thinking he's the murderer. I don't imagine he'd be having an affair with Sheila and trying it on with a youngster."

Stewart looked worried again.

"I had to tell then that I wasn't having any sex with Jane so that'll give them more fodder for suspecting me."

They heard footsteps coming up the stair and Avril and Anne came into the lounge.

Georgina smiled at Avril.

"Sorry, Avril. I shouldn't have bitten your head off. If it's OK with Henry, I'll partner her at third couple."

"Thanks, Georgina. Speak to your sister and let me know as soon as possible."

Avril looked relieved. She smiled at Stewart.

"That's a court free now, Stewart. Pity about the back courts being out of commission for a week but they had to be treated. Who are you playing with?"

"Don's coming down, hopefully."

At that moment Henrietta Laird and Sam arrived and Georgina asked her sister if she would play at third couple with her in the first team. Henrietta was ecstatic.

"Play with *you*, George! In the first! Wow! Yes please. We can practise at home."

She saw her friend Sam looking despondent and, being a nice child, was instantly apologetic.

"Oh, Sam. Do you mind?"

Sam grinned at her.

"Go for it, partner! Who will I have now, Avril?"

"Well you choose. Lucy or Zoe."

"What do you think, George?" Henrietta asked her sister.

"Lucy's a bit erratic but she has some lovely strokes and Zoe is steadier but less exciting. You choose, Sam. Sorry to be taking your partner away."

"OK. I'll have Lucy, though I feel sorry for Zoe because she's already lost Norma."

"Don't worry about Zoe. There's a promising wee junior who can partner her. She's the oldest junior so won't be too much younger than Zoe."

Avril was delighted that it was all working out. She smiled round at the others and then she and Anne went off to have their usual Saturday afternoon coffee in Clarkston.

Georgina patted Stewart's arm and sent him an encouraging smile before suggesting to her sister that they go home and get started on their practising.

CHAPTER 43

Davenport and Fiona were alone in their section of the police station. Three interviews had been arranged for today and they had agreed to cover these to give the others Saturday off.

First to arrive was Gavin Gilbert. He had been before and knew what to expect but he did not look any happier for knowing. This time his wife did not accompany him. Bob took him down to Interview Room1 and then rang for Davenport who went down with Fiona. Davenport asked Mr Gilbert to take a seat, then he and Fiona sat down across the table from him. After the usual ritual with the tape recorder, Charles told the man that none of his alibis so far were watertight, wives having been known to lie for husbands.

"And as for the third murder, you could have left the twins sleeping."

"I'd never do that!" Gilbert looked astounded that anyone would consider this. "Who was killed that night anyway?"

"Norma's school friend, Mary McGregor," Fiona told him.

"I wouldn't know her and why would I want to kill her?"

"Norma might have told her something about you, about something you did to her," Fiona sounded harsh.

"Did to Norma? This is crazy. I'm no paedophile."

"What would you say if I said someone had seen you out the night Mary was murdered?" Davenport gazed intently at the man as he said this but the man's face was blank.

"Saw me? How could anyone have seen me when I didn't go out? This is a nightmare!"

Gilbert put his head in his hands.

"Look up, Sir, please," said Davenport. "Did you know the murdered woman, Pat Harper?"

"No but I don't expect you to believe that either."

"A man called at her house quite often. If I took you to her neighbours are you sure they wouldn't recognise you?"

Gavin Gilbert looked up and his expression was now one of relief.

"Yes please, take me. I never went to this Harper woman's house so they won't recognise me."

Switching the recorder off, Davenport told the man he could leave. When he had gone back upstairs, Fiona said that she thought he was innocent.

"The look of relief on his face, Charles when you offered to parade him in front of the neighbours, seemed so genuine."

"I agree with you. Come on, there's time for a coffee before we see the next one."

Penny had decided to host a last minute party. Salma and Frank were free, Gordon had a day off, Alec said his friend Phil could come and he had also rung some of their church friends and most were available or were prepared to cancel former arrangements. They counted twelve people and that would be enough for their small flat. Penny was now at Morrisons getting in provisions. Hurrying down the aisles, she put cans of beer and a few bottles of wine into her trolley which was already quite full with French loaves, various cheeses, cold meats, a couple of pizzas, sausages rolls, tomatoes and two frozen desserts. She was a bit anxious about how Salma would get on, knowing that she seldom socialised with any but her own Muslim friends but Salma had appeared to be delighted to be asked and Penny hoped that at least Frank would talk to her, until she got to know anyone else. Her church friends were a friendly bunch and she knew she could rely on them to leave nobody standing alone.

Penny was going home from Morrisons at just about the same time as Stewart Bolton was entering the police station. He was wearing formal clothes, the kind he wore to work, feeling that the occasion was too serious for denims and a tee shirt. He heard his voice wobble as he asked the police constable at the desk where he should go for his interview. He was taken downstairs to a small cell-like room with minimum furniture and felt sweat form under his armpits as he sat and waited for what was to happen next. Whether by accident or on purpose, he was kept waiting for some time and by the time Fiona and Davenport arrived, he was a nervous wreck. Nerves made him rise from his seat and say, angrily, "What am I here for, Inspector?"

"*I'll* be asking the questions, Sir," Davenport replied. "Please sit back down."

Fiona spoke into the tape recording device, giving date and time and Stewart's name.

"DS Macdonald and DCI Davenport in attendance," she finished.

This time it was Fiona who began.

"Mr Bolton, you are in serious trouble here. You have a flimsy alibi for the night of Norma Lawson's murder as you could have got your girlfriend to lie for you. You have no alibi whatsoever for the second and third murders. Can you give us any reason to believe that you are innocent of three murders?"

Stewart's face, already pale, drained of all colour. He took out a handkerchief and wiped the palms of his hands, then his neck.

"I want a lawyer."

"Certainly, Mr Bolton. Do you have your own lawyer or do you want us to find you one?"

"I have a friend who's a lawyer. Can I call her now?"

Given permission, he took out his mobile phone.

"Sarah, Stewart here. Look I'm in a spot of bother. Well more than that. I'm being almost accused of three murders. Will you come and help me?"

He listened for a few seconds.

"Shawbank Police Station. Thanks Sarah. What?"

He put his phone back in his pocket.

"I've not to speak to you until she arrives."

"That's OK, son," said Davenport. "We'll leave you in peace. I'll have coffee sent to you unless you'd rather have tea."

"No, coffee's fine."

Davenport and Fiona left the room and went back upstairs. They had another coffee themselves and were talking about their coming holiday, when Bob rang from the desk to say that a Miss Cox had arrived.

Sarah Cox looked like a schoolgirl. She had obviously dressed for the occasion in a smart black suit and white blouse but on her it looked like a school uniform. She put out her hand to Davenport.

"Sarah Cox, Inspector, Stewart's lawyer."

The three made their way downstairs. Stewart looked pathetically grateful to see his friend.

"Stewart. Say nothing unless I tell you it's OK. Got that?"

"Yes, Sarah. Thanks for coming."

Fiona went through the routine with the tape recorder, saying that Stewart's lawyer, Sarah Cox, had entered the room, and then she continued her interview.

"Mr Bolton. You have no alibi for the last two murders, that of Pat Harper and Mary McGregor and a flimsy one for the murder of Norma Lawson. Have you anything to say?"

Stewart looked at his lawyer who nodded at him.

"I had no reason to kill any of the three people. Surely if I had been guilty, I would have provided myself with alibis."

He had obviously had time to think of this and came out with it almost triumphantly.

"Not necessarily, Mr Bolton. Some murderers don't plan ahead," said Fiona.

"I put it to you that you had sex with Norma against her will, in the tennis clubhouse on April the 10th and when she said she was going to tell her parents, you killed her."

"Are you accusing my client of rape and murder sergeant?"

"Yes."

The lawyer shook her head at Stewart and he remained silent.

"I put it to you that you tied up Pat Harper after sex with her on the 13th of April and smothered her with her pillow."

Silence.

"And that on the 21st of April you drove Mary McGregor to Floors Road and strangled her."

Another silence.

"Very well Mr Bolton. You will remain in custody for the time being. Miss Cox, I'll leave you with your client for a few minutes before a police constable takes him to the cells."

Fiona switched off the recorder and she and Davenport left the room.

Back up in his room, the DCI congratulated Fiona on her handling of the interview.

"Not much else you could do, faced with the refusal to speak, Fiona."

"I know. I sometime think lawyers make things worse."

Davenport looked at his watch. Even with waiting for the lawyer to arrive, that interview had taken less time than he had allowed for and they weren't seeing Kevin Collins till the afternoon so he suggested that they go for lunch in one of their favourite pubs near to the station.

Over a pint of beer for him and a diet coke for her, they waited for their ploughman's' lunches to arrive. The pub was busy and they had been fortunate to get a table in a quiet place.

"Penny's having a housewarming party tonight, Charles. I overheard Salma and Frank talking about it yesterday. I'm glad she didn't invite us. I'm past parties."

"It would only cramp their style, having their two bosses there, Fiona."

Their lunch arrived and they were silent as they tucked in.

Back at the station, they saw Kevin Collins seated in the vestibule and asked him to follow them to the interview room downstairs. Collins looked quite calm until he saw the bareness of the room, the metal table and four basic chairs. He attempted a joke, saying with a laugh, "Should I be calling my lawyer?"

"That's up to you, Sir." Davenport was formal.

"Only joking, Inspector. I'm not guilty of anything so why should I need a lawyer?"

Realising that this was a rhetorical question, Davenport motioned the man to sit down and he and Fiona sat down across from him. This time it was the DCI who conducted the interview.

"Mr Collins. Your alibi for Pat Harper's death is not a strong one. You could have gone to her house late at night after Lucy was in bed. You were at home alone on the night of Norma Lawson's death and on the night in which Mary McGregor was murdered, you had no alibi at all. You didn't collect your daughter till about 9.30 you said, so you could have driven Mary McGregor to Floors Road and killed her."

"Why would I want to kill this Mary girl?"

"She could have known you were involved with her friend, Norma."

"Look Inspector, I didn't even know this Mary McGregor. Surely she wouldn't go with a man she didn't know, especially one she suspected of killing her friend."

Davenport questioned him further but the man remained quite calm and adamant that he was innocent of any of the murders. Davenport told him he could leave but cautioned him not to leave the city.

Back up in his room, the DCI remarked on what he had said.

"He's right, Fiona. Why on earth would Mary McGregor get into a car with a person she suspected of killing her friend?"

"That goes for Stewart Bolton too, Charles and we know that it was Stewart she had mentioned to Georgina Laird so she would surely never go off with him."

"People do stupid things at times. That guy Collins is a cool customer. He never once lost his relaxed attitude."

"He's either a good actor or an innocent man. What now?"

"We leave Stewart Bolton cooling his heels till Monday morning then see him again and hope that his lawyer lets him speak to us. We'll have to let him go then, anyway but he maybe doesn't realise that and she hasn't had much of a chance to tell him.

On a lighter note, I didn't tell you that it's Pippa's birthday next Tuesday and I'm having Hazel and a wee girl who lives near us who's quite friendly with Pippa, and Hazel's cousin Diana over for a buffet lunch tomorrow. Would you come and keep me company? I meant to ask you ages ago but with all the pressure at work, it went right out of my head. Do say you can come!"

"I can come. Can I bring anything? A dessert maybe. I make a mean trifle, remember."

"That would be great. Pippa enjoyed your trifle at Christmas time. I suggested party games but that met with a look of disgust so I'll just leave them in the lounge with the CD player, DVD player and some DVDs. I've got another DVD player in the sitting room and we can watch something if you'd like to. I've got quite a selection of DVDs you can choose from."

Saying that that would be fine, Fiona got up and put on her jacket. Charles had picked her up that morning, so he drove her home then left to go home to his daughter who had been spending time with the girl who lived along the road with whom she had become friendly recently. She and Davenport had helped rescue her cat when it had got stuck up a tree some weeks ago and the two girls had got friendly after that, going out together on their bikes a couple of times. Kathy's mother had invited Pippa for lunch today which had suited Charles perfectly and gave his sister Linda a break from looking after her niece.

The two girls were on their bikes when he parked the car in the driveway and Pippa was pleased to hear that Fiona was coming up the next day.

"That'll keep Dad busy while we enjoy ourselves," she told Kathy.

CHAPTER 44

Charles pulled back his bedroom curtains; cream coloured with black and white swirls, and saw what Glaswegians would call a 'dreich' day. Glad that he had not to get formally dressed for work, he slipped into his en-suite shower. He found himself singing and wondered at his happy mood when he was still no further forward with a murderer, then realised that it was because he was seeing Fiona later, at the party. He dressed himself in beige chinos with a brown polo shirt, then thought that a bit drab and knew his daughter would not approve so changed the top for a red shirt. Looking in the mirror, he stroked the brown sideburns which were turning grey and wondered if he should buy more Grecian 2000 which Pippa had found for him in the supermarket about a year ago. Fiona was lucky, as being fair haired, her grey hairs would not show so well.

He put his head round Pippa's bedroom door. She was hidden under her duvet so he left her sleeping and went downstairs.

He had bought three large pizzas and, opening the freezer, he took one out and wrote down the timings on his kitchen notepad. Next he checked the timing on the packet of sausage rolls and wrote that down too. Chocolate biscuits had been bought and a frozen lemon meringue pie which he took out in case he forgot nearer the time. With Fiona's trifle, that should be enough for four young girls, he thought, then wondered what he and Fiona would have. Maybe they should just have a Chinese take-away to save trying to cater for adult tastes as well. He knew Fiona was easy to please with food.

Next he looked through his DVDs and pulled out a couple that he thought might suit both of them, deciding to ask Pippa what she might like. He should have done this a few days earlier but he could easily slip out to Newton Mearns shopping centre and get a couple in Asda.

In the event, this is what he did, as he realised after Pippa got up that he had forgotten crisps, though he had plenty of soft drinks. The two of them went up to the centre and Charles left Pippa to choose two DVDs while he went for nibbles and a lemon for Fiona's gin and tonic. He collected his daughter, with her selection of films, and they went to the self -service check out where Pippa read out the instructions and he followed them, the queues being too long when they only had a few items. Pippa enjoyed scanning the items and the only problem turned up when she put her purse down and they were told by the mechanical voice that there was a 'foreign body in the baggage area'.

Laughing, they walked down the centre to Costa Coffee where Charles had a skinny latte and Pippa had a coke. They shared a double chocolate chip muffin and laughed again about Charles having the healthy latte and a fattening cake. Back at home, Pippa tidied up the lounge and put cushions on the floor, knowing that no one would want to sit on the settee and chairs and Charles tidied up the living room and picked out three DVDs for Fiona to choose from. They were all films he had seen already but would not mind seeing again. They had a light lunch of yoghurt, toffee flavoured for Pippa and mango for Charles, followed by crackers and cheese, cheddar for Pippa and a fat- reduced cottage cheese for Charles who was half trying to lose some weight before their holiday. He was not fat but had gained some pounds over the winter months.

Pippa went off to phone Hazel as she had not spoken to her for twenty four hours and Charles took a beer into the living room and sat down with his Guardian newspaper. He had glanced at the news while waiting for his daughter to wake up, so now turned his attention to the small crossword. That took him only five minutes then he went on to the Sudoku which he had developed a liking for recently after Fiona had shown him how to do it. It was a medium one but he made a mistake half way through, discovering two nines on the same line and being unable to sort it, he disgustedly scored through it and turned to the cryptic crossword which was as usual by Araucaria on Saturday. He liked this setter and was glad it was not one of the new compilers whose crosswords he found harder to do. He had bought Pippa an easy crossword book some weeks ago and was delighted that she had taken to this hobby as he knew how much pleasure it gave him. Fiona did The Herald and he would like to introduce her to some of his favourite Guardian crossword people. They shared a love of golf but pressure of work recently had meant that they had not managed a round for some time. Pippa was not very sporty, unlike her friend Hazel who wanted her dad to teach her golf and went for tennis lessons early on Saturday mornings at Newlands Tennis Club, a prestigious club which had many members and quite a few senior teams unlike Greenway which only had two female teams and one male one.

Thinking of this, made Charles's mind drift to the murders and he considered his three suspects. His gut reaction was that Gavin Gilbert was innocent, as he was sure that Jan Gilbert would not give her husband an alibi that was not true, for the murder of her daughter and he did not really think he would leave his twin toddlers alone in the house. Kevin Collins was a cool customer but somehow, although this was not logical, he could not see the father of the bubbly, straightforward Lucy being a triple murderer. Stewart Bolton was the type of brash young man who might 'try it on' with a young girl, basking in the knowledge that she was flattered by his attentions. It could have all gone wrong in the clubhouse that evening and he could have killed, to save himself being prosecuted for underage sex. Charles could equate all this with Bolton and the other murders - well, he could easily have had an affair with the older woman, a woman flattered also by the attention of a young virile man. She might have realised that he was the one who had been seeing Norma and threatened to tell the police. He could have convinced her that he was innocent, started their S&M sex and decided to make sure she kept quiet about her suspicions by pushing her face into her pillow and holding her there. When Georgina had told him that Norma had named him to her friend, Mary, he had killed again to remain safe. The only snag was that Charles could not see Mary happily getting into the car of a man who might have murdered her friend.

"Dad, it's four o'clock. I'm going for a bath. When is Fiona coming over? Did you ask her to come early? I hope so. I want to talk to her about the holiday."

Charles looked up.

"What love?"

"Did you ask Fiona to come early? I want to talk about the holiday."

"No, I didn't. I asked her to come at seven o'clock like the others but I'll give her a ring and see if she can come earlier than that. In fact I'll go and collect her, then she can have a drink and stay the night. The spare room's not been used recently because Hazel slept in your room the last time she stayed over, didn't she?"

"Yes. You go and phone Fiona now."

Charles did as he was told. Fiona had just got back from shopping for a birthday present for Pippa and said she would be delighted to stay the night. He went over at about 5.30. Some residents of Grantley Street must have been away shopping, as he got a parking space for once, almost outside Fiona's close. She had been keeping a look out for him and came downstairs, meeting him as he was about to press the entry buzzer. He held the car door open for her and put her parcel and overnight bag on the back seat. She held the trifle carefully as she got in. Charles got into the driver's seat and gave her a kiss before buckling his seat belt.

"I got Pippa a handbag, a large white one for going on holiday with," Fiona told him once they were on their way. "I know I like the one I have. It takes my book and all the other things I need for the journey. Do you think she'll like it?"

"I'm sure she will. I don't think she's ever had a proper handbag."

On the way up to Newton Mearns, he told her what he had been thinking about the three murders and Fiona told him she agreed with him, unfortunately, as that meant that they did not think they had found the right suspect.

"Well, let's not talk about it anymore this evening, love," said Charles, "otherwise we'll have a gloomy time."

Pippa, dressed for her party, in red leggings and a long white top with flat white pumps, came out to meet them and was given her present which she opened once back inside. She was, as her father had predicted, delighted with her adult gift and dragged Fiona off to show her the list she had written already of what she was going to pack. This led to a discussion of what books she was taking and Fiona promised to bring the next two Chalet School books. Pippa had already persuaded her dad to buy her two more Agatha Christies so she now had seven books to take and she asked Fiona what books she was taking. Fiona told her that she had not planned that far ahead but that she would probably be taking some Anne Perry books as she had discovered this author a while ago and had bought a couple which she had not found time to read so far.

"What about your Dad, Pippa? What will he take to read? Does he like to read?"

"Dad doesn't read much, just the paper but he'll probably take a Sudoku book and maybe a crossword book. Fiona, will we need any injections for the holiday? My friend Kathy said she and her family went to Thailand last year and they needed some."

Fiona told her that she and her father should see the nurse at their doctor's and she would tell them what they needed.

"Anything else you want to know, Pippa?"

"Can I phone Hazel from Penang?"

"Well you could but if you use your Dad's mobile phone it's very expensive, so is using the phone in our room, I expect but maybe your Dad will let you text Hazel a few times."

At that moment Charles came up the stairs to ask if they were ever going to come down and join him and they laughed at each other and went down into the living room.

"What are you going to watch tonight?" said Pippa, picking up the three DVDs that Charles had left out by the DVD player. She read out the titles:

" 'Pretty Woman', 'Presumed Innocent', 'Atonement'. I've never heard of any of them. Which one are you having, Fiona?"

"Well, I saw 'Pretty Woman' on the plane two years ago when I went to America. I love it, so maybe I'll choose that again. I saw 'Atonement' when it came out and it's quite a serious film so maybe not. Charles, what's' Presumed Innocent' about? I can't remember if I ever saw that one. Which one do you fancy?"

"Well, to be honest I think 'Pretty Woman' is more a woman's film than a man's but I'm happy to watch it if that's the one you choose. I agree about 'Atonement' and if you've forgotten 'Presumed Innocent' then I don't think you can have seen it."

"Let's have that one then."

The bell rang. It was Hazel with her Dad. He carried her overnight bag and came in for a few words with Charles and Fiona before going back off home for what he called, a "daughter-free evening" with his wife Sally. Pippa and Hazel went up to Pippa's room but came back down when the doorbell rang again. This time it was Diana, Hazel's cousin and Kathy the neighbour who had both met on the doorstep. Pippa introduced Kathy to Diana who thought they might have seen each other at school, though Kathy was only in first year and Diana was older. Diana' mother Carol did not come in. She thanked Charles for having Diana overnight and left. Kathy had been asked to stay too even though she lived so near and she too had an overnight bag. Pippa grabbed the two bags and took them upstairs then she came back down and ushered her friends into the lounge, shutting the door firmly, telling her father that they would like supper at about nine thirty, as they were being allowed to stay up till 10.30pm.

"That's me told!" laughed Charles as he and Fiona went into the sitting room. He had poured their drinks already and they sat back contentedly to watch their chosen film.

Fiona had indeed never seen the film and got engrossed in the determination of Harrison Ford to prove his innocence in the murder of his lover. The denouement where his wife was found to have introduced his semen into the lover's vagina in order to have him arrested for her murder, had her enthralled. By the time the film was over, it was just about 10pm so they went into the kitchen to read the instructions Charles had left himself and heated up the pizzas and sausage rolls. The dessert had thawed nicely and they set out all the plates and cutlery on the kitchen table before calling the girls in to eat. They had watched the two short films that Pippa had chosen that day and all seemed to have enjoyed them. No one complained about supper being late.

As they were all sharing the same room, Pippa and Hazel squeezing into Pippa's single bed and the other two in sleeping bags on the floor, they were quite happy to go to bed and Charles and

Fiona followed soon afterwards, Charles going to his own room and Fiona to the guest bedroom where she had stayed before. They had decided not to take their relationship any further until after the shared holiday, as sharing a room with Pippa in Penang would be a bit fraught, if they wanted each other.

Fiona went off to sleep right away. Charles, being nearer to Pippa's room, had to restrain himself from going in to ask them to keep a bit quieter but they calmed down eventually and soon the house slept.

CHAPTER 45

Penny snuggled happily under her new duvet and thought about her party the night before. Salma had been the first to arrive, bringing a pretty table-cloth and napkins as a second house-warming present. Alec's table was a bit marked in places and she had obviously noticed this when she had helped Penny on removal day. Penny had only just got dressed after her shower. She had forgotten that Salma did not go to many parties like this and would not know that 8pm meant about 9pm on the Southside and probably about 11pm in the West End. Her early arrival gave them time to sit and chat about their work. Penny was a hundred percent sure that the triple murderer was Stewart Bolton, having never liked him from first meeting him but Salma was more inclined to think that it was Norma's stepfather, Gavin Gilbert.

"He has no alibi for any of the murders, Penny," she had pointed out, "except ones his wife and kids can give him and the kids were asleep on the third occasion."

They argued, good-naturedly, about this for a while then Penny asked Salma what she thought about the DCI and DS being away at the same time on their summer break. A friend of Penny's in the office had told her this.

"Do you think they could possibly be going away together?" Penny asked her friend.

"I don't think so. He'll be going with Pippa. Whatever you do don't mention it to Frank or he'll start humming, 'Summer Holiday'!" laughed Salma.

The bell ringing cut through their hilarity and Alec brought Frank in. Alec and Phil had been having a beer in the kitchen but Phil came through now and was introduced to Salma who was looking very modern in her tight denims and white crop top. Unbeknown to Penny (and her own mother) she had left the house dressed more sedately, in a salwar kamiz, but the jeans had been underneath as had the top and she had taken the top layer off in the car. She thought it unlikely that she would meet another Muslim at the party tonight and wanted to blend in with Penny's other female friends.

Frank had brought a six pack of beer and a bottle of wine which Phil took from him and put with other drink which was on a table in the hall, bringing one can back in for Frank himself.

"What will you have, Salma?" he said shyly to the beautiful girl and Salma smiled back and asked for a white wine spritzer, something she had never tasted but had heard others ask for. She did occasionally have a drink but usually a Martini with lemonade which she did not think Penny would have.

The doorbell rang again and this time six young folk came into the room. Alec took their coats and jackets and Penny took them over to where Frank and Salma were sitting together on Penny's settee. They had chosen her room for talking and dancing in and Alec's for laying out the food when the time came for eating. She introduced them, "Sue and her brother Pete, Claire and Fay - they're sisters, though they don't look it - Bert and David. This is Salma, the sergeant I work with and Frank, another PC."

The youngsters said hello and chatted for a while about what they all did and how they had met Penny years ago at church where they had all been in the same Sunday school.

"Do you have anything like that in your mosque, Salma?" Claire asked with interest and she and Salma moved off to stand a little apart while Salma explained what happened at her place of worship. Penny had put on a modern CD and Frank asked Sue for a dance while Penny grabbed David and persuaded him to dance too.

Lying in bed on Sunday morning, Penny realised that Frank and Sue had spent a lot of time on the dance floor during the evening and indeed had sat apart from the others while having supper. She would tease him about that on Monday at work. A good Catholic boy dancing with a Protestant girl! Wonders would never cease. She had lost contact with Salma but on occasion had looked for her colleague and seen her in animated conversation with someone. Gordon had arrived quite late, having had to open up his surgery for an injured cat but he too had mixed in well with her friends. In fact the only ones who did not mix very well were Alec and Phil who stayed together most of the evening. Penny supposed that was understandable as neither of them wanted to dance with a girl. The church group knew that Alec was homosexual so the girls would not feel slighted by his disinterest in them. Frank had danced on occasion with each of the other girls, including Salma. Penny, in the arms of Gordon, thought what a handsome couple they made and was glad that Frank had dropped his racial intolerance so far as to not include his colleague in it.

Pizzas and sausage rolls had vanished, leaving only crumbs on the plates, and the biscuits and cheese followed suit along with the cold meats and salad. They had all laughed when Penny came in looking crestfallen, having forgotten to take the frozen desserts out of the deep freeze. She made coffee and tea for those who wanted it. Salma came into the kitchen to help and confessed that she had better have a few cups of strong coffee as the wine spritzers had made her feel quite light- headed and she needed to be OK for driving home. Her mother would be furious if she arrived home by taxi, as that would mean she had drunk too much and her mother disapproved of her drinking at all.

Surprisingly, it was Frank who left first and, unsurprisingly, Sue went with him. Penny smiled to herself now at how embarrassed he had been when she had gone to the door to say cheerio. When she got back to the living room, Alec had come across to say that he and Phil were off to visit some friends in Pollokshaws and it was not long before Salma left, feeling more awake after her coffees and thanking Penny for a good time.

"Your friends are very nice," she had told Penny at the door.

As usual, two people stayed on and on and it was about 3am before Bert and David left. They and Penny and Gordon had started talking politics and before they knew it the time had flown. Apologising if they had overstayed their welcome, the two young men left and Gordon helped Penny clear up.

When they sank down, exhausted, about an hour later, Gordon put his arm round Penny and they sat companionably for a while before he kissed her gently and got to his feet.

"No rest for the wicked, eh love?" he said affectionately. "I've got work tomorrow morning. How about us spending the afternoon together? We could take a run down the coast and have a meal somewhere."

Penny was delighted. She had had some boyfriends in her time but had never felt quite so right in their company as she did in Gordon's.

She had fallen asleep, feeling very contented and, lying in bed now, she looked forward to the afternoon. She must have dosed off again as it was 11.30am when she looked at the clock. She had just enough time to have a bath and decide what to wear. She hoped that neither animals nor people would intervene to spoil her time with Gordon.

CHAPTER 46

Charles and Fiona waited to have breakfast till after the girls had eaten theirs. Ralph Ewing came for both Hazel and Diana and Kathy walked home as her house was in the next road. Pippa, complaining of being still tired, went back to bed. Charles made bacon, eggs and sausage for Fiona and himself and they ate that, then sat in the living room with the Sunday papers. Charles always got The Observer and he had gone out and bought Scotland on Sunday which was Fiona's usual read. They sat in a companionable silence until Pippa got back up and declared that she thought that they should all go out for lunch. Fiona being willing, they set off for The Wishing Well in Eaglesham and found Hazel and her Mum and Dad with Carol Ewing and Diana, having lunch there too. The Wishing Well was too small for them to all gather round the one table for which Charles was thankful as he had only got to know the two Ewing families really well during his last murder case when he had had to arrest Carol's twin sons for the murder of their father and a family friend. This made socialising with them a bit awkward.

Ralph and Sally smiled at him but he could see that Carol was not pleased to see him and Fiona so they were pleased to get a table in the room leading off the main area. Pippa, of course, was disappointed, so when Ralph came through to ask if she could join the other two girls, Charles said she could.

Over lunch of paninis, coronation chicken for Fiona and prawn Marie rose for Charles, they discussed in low voices what had happened to the Ewing family. The two boys, Ian and John had been sent down for only eight and five years respectively, there being mitigating circumstances for the murder of their father, namely the fact that their father had been abusing their sister, Diana. Ian had been sent down for longer as he had killed the family friend who had done nothing wrong except get suspicious of the boys. Diana had suffered the most, having lost her father and then her two brothers but Charles had heard from Pippa that she had settled down well at her new school and had made friends there. She had never liked the boarding school she had gone to previously and had been glad to leave.

Talk then turned to their current murders and they discussed them until they had finished their meal which had ended with a large meringue each.

"No proof that Bolton's guilty, Fiona. Where are fingerprints when you want them?"

"Will you speak to his girlfriend again?"

"I suppose so, though she's churchgoer so I don't imagine she would lie for him."

"Love could be stronger than her faith, Charles."

"I'm not that sure that she's in love with him. He told me she wouldn't sleep with him unless they were married so her faith's pretty strong, wouldn't you say?"

"So you'll release him tomorrow?"

"I'll interview him again and see if two nights in the cells have weakened him. If he is guilty, maybe that will have scared him and he might give himself away."

"Yes, if his lawyer lets him speak."

"I'll have a word with her first. Try to make her see that his keeping quiet isn't helping him."

They sat in silence for a few minutes.

"We'll have to go back to our diets, Charles," Fiona said, licking her fingers to get the last of the cream.

"I know. We can't have rolls of fat for the holiday."

Charles paid for the lunch, not allowing Fiona to pay for any of it and they picked up Pippa on their way out. She had had sandwiches and chocolate fudge cake and Charles refused to let Ralph pay for her.

"See you tomorrow, Hazel," Pippa called from the door.

Georgina and Jane, sitting at a table at the back of the tearoom, kept quiet and did not draw attention to themselves. Georgina especially, was glad to see the DCI leave. She had told Jane that Stewart had been interviewed the day before. Jane knew that but wanted to know more.

"I don't think the police believe Stewart," Jane said, looking worried. "They seem to think that I could have given him a false alibi for the first murder and he was alone for the next two."

"But you wouldn't lie for him, would you?"

"No. I'm very fond of him but I don't lie."

"Is he at The Swan just now? Do you want to go over and join him and Barry?"

"He isn't there. The police kept him overnight."

"Oh, Jane. That's awful."

"He got a friend of ours, Sarah Cox, who's a lawyer, to go in and be with him during the interview. She called me. That's why I know where he is. I rang Barry to cancel their lunch and he asked if we would meet him in The Swan at about 1.30. Is that OK with you?"

Georgina saying that that was fine, the two of them paid for their lunch and walked across The Orry to the pub. Barry was there and had kept two seats for them as it was crowded as usual. Barry kissed Georgina and then did the same to Jane. He went to the bar and came back with a shandy for Georgina and a fresh orange and lemonade for Jane.

"What else did the lawyer friend say, Jane?" asked Georgina, after they had told Barry what had happened.

"She wants me to go to the police station tomorrow morning with her, to try to convince the inspector that Stewart was with me the night Norma was killed."

"And he *was* with you Jane?" Barry asked anxiously.

"Of course he was!"

"I feel awful. It was me who landed Stewart in it. Mary McGregor told me Norma had mentioned his name and I had to tell them when they came to ask me if she'd spoken to me at the clubhouse the night she was killed."

Georgina looked stricken and her two friends hurried to reassure her that she could not have done anything else.

In the cells at the police station, Stewart had been brought some breakfast. He managed to nibble at the toast and drank the tea gratefully. He had spent an uncomfortable night, both mentally and physically and expected to have to stay all day and another night before he saw his lawyer again.

The door opened and a constable came in and picked up the tray.

"OK son?"

The kindness in the man's voice brought sudden tears to Stewart's eyes and he hastily got out his handkerchief and wiped them.

"What happens next?" he asked.

"DCI Davenport will see you tomorrow morning. He'll probably have your lawyer with him. He won't keep you unless he has some definite proof of your guilt."

"He can't have that. I'm not guilty!"

Kevin Collins spent the day with Lucy. No one seeing him, would have known that he was anxious over the interview the day before. He felt he had handled it well and it was true what he had said. Why on earth would the girl have got into his car? She did not know him and after two murders, she would surely never have got into a strange man's car. However, being a suspect at all, was not pleasant.

Gavin Gilbert had discussed his interview with his wife, Jan. She knew that he had been with her on the night Norma had been murdered and was aghast that anyone could think he would have left his two sons on their own.

"Though I went to bed quite early that first night, Gavin. I know you didn't kill Norma but you could have left the house later and if they ask I'll have to tell them that."

Fiona thanked Charles for her lovely time with him and, saying goodbye to Pippa, picked up her overnight bag and went home. Pippa went up to her room to lie on her bed and do some reading before getting her school clothes out. Charles sat downstairs and racked his brain for what had been niggling at it since Fiona had left.

Georgina, Jane and Barry had one more drink then went their separate ways. Barry had asked Georgina to come out with him again that night but disappointingly she seemed to view him as a Saturday night date and no more and she said no. Jane was beginning to realise how strongly she felt for Stewart and determined to visit the police station first thing in the morning.

In his small cell, Stewart was more cheerful, having convinced himself that the police would have to let him go the next day. They surely could not have found proof of his guilt.

Kevin had not told his daughter about his interview. She was a very honest girl and if the police spoke to her, she would tell them that he had collected her quite late last Tuesday and that she had gone to bed after the pictures leaving him on his own and able to leave the house once she was asleep.

Donald Kinross received a phone call from Sheila Ferguson.

"You can tell Olive this is about tennis, Don but I'm phoning to tell you that it's over. We're moving to London soon. Larry told me last night."

She rang off before she started to cry. Don was surprised at the feeling of relief he felt.

Sunday progressed slowly and the murderer's spirits stayed high.

CHAPTER 47

Another day, another funeral. Davenport was going to be busy with Stewart Bolton that morning and he had asked Fiona to attend Mary's burial at the cemetery in Thornliebank. He had spoken to Mrs McGregor. Although her husband had been cremated and his ashes had been scattered in the Garden of Remembrance at Linn Crematorium, she had told him that she wanted to be able to visit her daughter's grave.

"At least Bruce had had some life, Inspector, and he had been so ill that his death was almost a relief but Mary...well her life was just beginning."

She had broken down and hung up the phone, ringing him again once she had composed herself, to give him details of the funeral.

"Will your father be there, Mrs McGregor? I know he doesn't keep well."

"Father-in-law, Inspector. He offered to come and stay with us when Bruce died and he's been such a rock. I never knew my own father and he's been just what a father should be and such a great granddad to Mary. He will be at the funeral. It's at 10.00 at Thornliebank Cemetery. Will you be there?"

Davenport had explained that he had urgent business elsewhere but that his DS would certainly attend.

Now Fiona was waiting outside the cemetery, for the hearse and funeral cars. It was a wet day and the skies were leaden. She could hear the swish of tyres on the wet road as people drove past. It was almost 10.00 when the hearse drove past her and through the gates, followed by the limousine bringing Mrs McGregor and her father-in-law. Some other cars followed them and Fiona switched on her engine and drove into line. The little procession wound its way through the graveyard until it came to a freshly dug plot. The cars stopped and everyone got out, some in raincoats, others with umbrellas which they immediately unfurled. Fiona had forgotten to bring an umbrella but one of the other mourners came over to her and offered her shelter under hers.

"Come on under here with me. I'm Mary's form teacher." She introduced another woman as Mary's Guidance teacher. They all shook hands and Fiona told them who she was. They had no time to say anything else as the minister was starting to speak.

Fiona stood across the open grave from the immediate family and looked round. There were only a handful of folk attending, one of them a young lad whom Fiona guessed would be Neil Smith from the tennis club. When the service was over, Fiona made her way across the grass to Mrs McGregor.

"Mrs McGregor, Mr McGregor," she smiled at the elderly man, "I'm DS Macdonald." The woman had been weeping but the man was dry-eyed.

"I hope you catch the villain who killed Mary," he said with a venom which she suspected was out of character for this gentle - looking man.

"He's killed three times, Sir. You're not alone in hoping that we get him soon," she replied.

"Would you come back to the house, sergeant, please? We knew there wouldn't be many here. We have no other immediate family and Mary was too young to have acquired lots of friends so there's food and drink back at home for the few who have come."

Fiona said that she would be pleased to come and turned back to thank the woman who all this time had been holding the umbrella over her. The woman spoke to Mary's mother, as did her colleague and both said that they would have to be getting back to school. They escorted Fiona back to her car and as she was getting in, one of them spoke to the young boy who was passing.

"Neil. Good of you to come. Are you going back to school? Can we give you a lift?"

"Thanks, Mrs Gordon, but I'm going to go back to Mary's house. Her Mum invited me.

Back at their Waterfoot home, Mrs McGregor busied herself getting teas and coffees for the dozen or so people who had come back. Fiona went to stand beside Neil.

"Neil, I'm DS Macdonald, the DS involved in the three murder cases. It was nice of you to come."

"Well I liked Mary. She had just started to go out with me the night she was...killed," said Neil, swallowing hard in an effort not to cry.

Mr McGregor was sitting in one of the armchairs at the side of the hearth and Fiona went to sit beside him. He looked so frail and vulnerable that her heart went out to him.

"Mr McGregor, I'm going now. I would suggest a small brandy if there's any in the house."

"Thank you but don't worry about me. June's a doctor. She'll make sure I'm looked after. I wish I could be stronger for her right now. I'm useless like this."

"Mr McGregor, you're all she's got now and she loves you so much. I know from what she said at the cemetery."

His eyes filled up and he looked down at the tea cup he was holding. His hand shook slightly. Fiona got up and told him that she was sure they would catch the person responsible soon. She repeated this to June McGregor as they stood at the outside door and, walking down the path, she devoutly hoped that what she had said to both of them was true.

Back at the station, she accepted a cup of coffee from her boss who had returned from another visit to Stewart Bolton, in his cell downstairs. He had let the man go after warning him not to leave the city. Stewart had, on the advice of his young lawyer, spoken to him this time. He had denied ever having sex with Pat Harper. He had, he said, never even been in her house and he asked if the police could not confirm this through finger prints, or the lack of finger prints in this case. He had paled when Davenport had told him that he could have wiped fingerprints off, before leaving that night.

"I never killed Pat, Inspector and I never killed Norma. I talked to her occasionally. She was obviously getting interested in men but I didn't encourage her and I didn't even know Mary McGregor and have no idea why Norma might mention me except to look big."

The young man sounded genuine and all his brashness had gone. At this moment, Jane Green came into the station. She reiterated that Stewart had been with her on the night of the first murder.

"I wouldn't lie for him or anyone," she stated firmly. Davenport had thanked her and Stewart picked up his possessions from the desk and left with Jane and his lawyer friend. Davenport told Fiona now that he had doubts that Bolton was their man.

"It's a gut feeling as usual, Fiona. Was there anyone at the funeral from the tennis club?"

"Just young Neil, the boy she went out with that night. I don't think anyone else at the tennis club knew Mary. She didn't play tennis, though her mother told me that Norma had tried to get her daughter to join. I know you have this idea that murderers often attend the funeral of their victim but not in this case, Charles."

"Something's worrying at the back of my mind, Fiona. You know that feeling that you should have spotted something?"

"Since when?"

"Since last night."

"Come on, let's go out for lunch and stop trying to force this thing to come to the front of your mind. It'll come when you're least expecting it."

They had lunch at their usual pub and returned to find that there had been a phone call from a Mr Harper.

"He said he was Pat Harper's ex-husband, Sir," said Bob. "He left his number."

Davenport went to his room and rang the man, suggesting that they meet somewhere. Mr Harper had rung from work but suggested that he come to the station after he finished work at 5.30.

"I work in Shawlands," he said. "Not far from the station. My daughter gave me your card. That's where I got the number from."

He arrived just before 6pm and Davenport, alone now in the station, ushered him into his room.

"Thanks for coming, Sir. How can I help you?"

"Well, Debbie said you were asking about the man Pat was having an affair with when I ended our marriage and if she had had any other affairs since. I never discussed it with either of the girls, Inspector. They were too young to be told really and they never showed any interest as they got older. By the time they went back to seeing her on occasion, she was living alone."

"I understand, Sir but perhaps you could tell me now."

CHAPTER 48

Charles was sitting over his breakfast coffee. Something had come to him during the night and he was pensive. The weather had changed from yesterday and the sun was shining brightly through his kitchen window when Pippa came into the room. She had a book clutched in one hand and her schoolbag in the other.

"Another Chalet School book finished pet?"

"No Dad, it's an Agatha Christie. It's one of Hazel's mum's collection.

"Was it a Poirot or a Miss Marple?"

"Poirot. Dad, do you ever get all the people into one room at the end of a murder case and tell them who the murderer is?"

"No pet. Is that what Hercule Poirot does?"

"Yes. In this book he hadn't any proof and he told Mr Hasting, his friend, that he hoped that the murderer would give the game away. Well, those weren't his words but that's what he meant and the woman did admit it in the end."

Davenport was quiet in the car as he drove Pippa to school and went on to the station. He rang for an appointment with Solomon Fairchild and was closeted with him upstairs for some time before coming back down and calling his team into the Incident Room.

"I want you all to get busy on the phone and contact the following people. Some you won't get till evening but I need them all contacted. They are all to be at Greenway Tennis Club for 7.30 pm tomorrow evening. He detailed various people to each of them and, looking mystified, they all went to work as Davenport left the station.

Penny having successfully contacted Kevin Collins who had not left for work, bumped into her DS in the corridor. Being Penny she did not stand on ceremony but asked Fiona why the boss wanted to see all these people.

"I'm sorry PC Price. I'm as mystified as you are. I got Stewart Bolton as he'd decided not to go into work today."

"I got Mr Collins. Salma is trying Donald Kinross and Frank is ringing Mr Jenkins' house."

At that moment Salma came into the corridor having seen the other two in conversation.

"I got Mrs Kinross and she said she'll pass on the message to her husband. Have you any idea what this is about, ma'am?"

"Not a clue."

They went into the room where Frank was hanging up his phone.

"No luck. No one's answering. I'll try the Gilberts."

Here he was successful, getting Jan Gilbert just as she was about to take the boys out. She promised that they would get a baby-sitter and would both be there at 7.30 tomorrow. Penny sat back down at her desk and rang the Laird house, getting Mrs Laird who promised to pass on the message to Georgina. The others heard her say:

"No, Mrs Laird, just Georgina, not Henrietta."

They had no luck with David Bentley, Paul Lawson or Mr Harper. Fiona's phone rang and she sprinted up the corridor to answer it. She returned to the others.

"The boss wants Neil Smith as well."

Avril Smiley was at home and agreed to come the next evening and Neil's mother promised that her son would attend.

"He's a bit upset still," Mrs Smith told Salma. "I put him to bed with some paracetamol and when I looked in a while ago, he was sound asleep."

"So just Brian Jenkins, David Bentley and Paul Lawson still to contact?" Fiona said.

"And Pat Harper's husband!" Penny reminded her.

Fiona grinned and looked, in Penny's opinion, years younger.

"Looks as if the boss is planning a Hercule Poirot denouement!" she said.

Seeing three mystified faces, she explained that Agatha Christie's Belgian detective nearly always called all the suspects together at the end of a case and eventually accused the guilty party.

"Does that mean the DCI knows who the guilty person is?" asked Penny eagerly.

"I hope so. I imagine he'll tell us before tomorrow evening."

All the remaining folk were contacted later in the day. They all agreed to come to the clubhouse.

Davenport did tell his team and told them to be prepared for the murderer to try to escape.

So it was that at 7.30 the following evening, the tennis members congregated upstairs in the clubhouse. Davenport had also invited Pat Harper's husband, Mary McGregor's mother and grandfather and Norma's mother, father and stepfather. There was an excited buzz as the police team entered the room, then the place went silent. Davenport had asked Avril to set out seats in a two half circles with the relatives of the murdered people in the outer circle and the tennis members in the inner one. The only people missing were Stewart Bolton and Kevin Collins.

Davenport took his position in front of the two half circles with DS Macdonald by his side. Penny went to stand behind those seated and Frank and Salma stood at the doorway.

Davenport cleared his throat.

"Ladies and gentlemen, I've called you all together to tell you how far we have got in our investigations. As some of you may know, we arrested Stewart Bolton at the weekend and called Kevin Collins in for interview then too."

There was an excited murmur of voices and Brian Jenkins was heard to say that he would not believe that his friend Kevin could be responsible for three killings.

"You're correct, Mr Jenkins. Kevin Collins is innocent and probably just late."

At that moment, they heard feet pounding up the stairs and Kevin Collins came in, looking hot and flustered.

"Sorry, Inspector. I got held up."

He sat down in the empty seat beside Avril Smiley.

"However, Stewart Bolton did not find it so easy to convince us of his innocence. We had only his girlfriend's word that he was with her on the night of Norma Lawson's murder and we've since spoken to her and convinced her how wrong it is to lie for him."

Georgina Laird looked round her neighbour at her friend Jane who would not catch her eye.

"Norma went into the clubhouse that night with someone she knew, someone she was pleased to be with. Tests showed that she had been sexually aroused before being raped. She must have taken cold feet and been dragged back into the changing room and raped then strangled with the murderer's bare hands."

There were sounds of distress from Jan Gilbert and Davenport apologised for hurting her.

He continued, "The murderer was also having an affair with Pat Harper. Pat must have shown in some way that she knew what her lover had done. She allowed herself to be tied up for their usual sex games but the game turned serious and she was pushed face down into her pillow and smothered.

Stewart Bolton had no alibi for that night.

On the night when Mary McGregor was murdered, Stewart's only alibi was that he stayed behind after match practice to talk to the other men but we know that Mary and Neil went to the local cafe for a drink and that Mary was standing at the bus stop a good while after match practice stopped."

"But Inspector, why would Mary accept a lift from a man she didn't know?" her mother cried out.

"I don't suppose we'll ever know, Mrs McGregor. Maybe Stewart offered to explain why Norma had mentioned his name. He's a good-looking young man and she might have been taken in by his looks."

"How was Mary killed, Inspector?" The old man looked determined to find out. Mrs McGregor nodded in agreement.

"Mary was not sexually assaulted. She was strangled with something, we don't know what, and her body put over the wall into a field.

We suspected you at first, Mr Kinross, as plenty of people could tell us that Norma had flirted with you at the American Tournament and you apparently have a reputation for womanising."

Donald Kinross looked sheepish. He was glad that Olive had not been invited tonight and sent the Inspector a grateful look for not mentioning Sheila by name.

"However you had an alibi for the night of the second and third murders and we were sure that all the murders were committed by the same person."

Davenport paused and looked slowly round at his audience.

"Then we wondered about you, Mr Bentley, as you had said that Norma was a pretty girl but you are obviously very much in love with Nancy, engaged to her and busy house-hunting on two of the dates."

David Bentley blushed.

"DS Macdonald, over to you," said Davenport.

"Next we thought about Norma's father. He had been in contact with Norma, unbeknown to her mother, and had invited his daughter over to the house he shares with his current girlfriend but it was too much to believe that he would kill his own daughter just to stop her pestering him to let her come and stay with him."

"How could you try to lure her away from her home here?" Jan Gilbert spoke out.

"I didn't, Jan. That was all her idea, honest."

Paul Lawson looked stricken.

"Gavin Gilbert, Norma's stepfather, was next to be suspected," Fiona continued. "He had taken her out by himself on two occasions. He could have assaulted her, flattered her into thinking he loved her and lured her to the tennis clubhouse. He had no good alibi except his wife saying that he had been at home with her and he had no alibi for the other two nights either. But, would a mother give a false alibi for her daughter's killer? No! And added to that we later found Norma's tennis club key under her bed so they would not have been able to get in. Our thoughts turned again to Stewart Bolton. He had a key and remember, he had no alibi for the night of Pat Harper's murder, nor for Mary McGregor's and it would be easy to convince Jane, his girlfriend to lie for him.

"I feel so awful about telling him that Norma had mentioned him in the clubhouse that night," Georgina's eyes were bright. "I thought I knew Stewart so well. Oh, Mrs McGregor, I'm so sorry. I'm so sorry."

"It's my fault too," Neil was on his feet. "If I hadn't left her alone at the bus stop..."

"Sit down, Neil," said DS Macdonald. "Don't blame yourself. You said that Mary persuaded you to go. You weren't to know that someone was watching you both, hoping that Mary would be left alone."

"And if her bus had come before yours, she might still be alive," added Georgina.

Davenport gave a slight nod to Penny who disappeared and returned with ...

"Stewart! We thought you'd been arrested!" shouted Georgina. "Was it all a mistake?"

"Sorry to be late, Inspector. Carry on."

Davenport nodded to Fiona who moved aside for him to continue.

Stewart sat down beside Georgina who patted him on the arm and smiled at him.

"No, Stewart wasn't arrested, because Norma wasn't raped by a man who didn't ejaculate and Pat wasn't murdered by a man who smothered her after their sex games and Mary wasn't killed by a man who thought he had been named by her. How did you know, Miss Laird, that Neil's bus came after Mary's?"

Georgina laughed. "Just a guess, Inspector. If Neil's bus had come after Mary's, he would have seen who abducted her."

"Neil told me that he turned the corner and was just passing the stop when a bus pulled up so he caught it even though it was only for a few stops. A lucky guess, Miss Laird? Surely if you had 'guessed' you would have 'guessed' that he had walked home!"

Georgina Laird looked annoyed.

"So I guessed wrongly. Stewart must have seen Neil get on the bus and driven up to Mary's stop and offered her a lift."

"So you're blaming me, George. Thanks."

Stewart looked angry.

"Well it must have been you. You had no alibi for that night, the Inspector said so."

"What about you, Miss Laird? Do you have an alibi for that night, for any of the three nights?"

Davenport's voice was cold.

"Me? You're joking. Rape a teenager, smother Pat, strangle Mary and tip her over a wall. You have to be joking, making a sick joke."

"No, it's not a joke. Where were you on those three nights?"

"I'm leaving."

Georgina rose and made for the door but Salma stood in her way. Frank came to her other side.

Davenport went inexorably on; his voice louder and colder than any of his team had ever heard him.

"I put it to you, Miss Laird, that you were flattered by Norma's attention. She didn't just speak to the senior men; she spoke to the senior women, you in particular. She agreed to meet you at the clubhouse. She had no key. As I said, we found it later on her bedroom floor. You used your own key to open the door, didn't you? You started fondling her and she responded but when things got more intense, she panicked and ran for the door. You pulled her back, got her down on the floor and took her virginity the way dykes do."

Georgina bristled.

"Dykes, Inspector? Your homophobia is showing."

"I have no objection to homosexual acts committed with a consenting adult but Norma was a child, so it was paedophilia, Miss Laird."

Davenport visibly pulled himself together and continued.

"Then of course she ran, probably saying she would tell her mother and you once again pulled her backwards, this time choking her with your hands. You have very strong hands don't you, Miss Laird, tennis player's hands."

Georgina's hands clenched at her side but she remained calm.

"Pat Harper had seen Norma with you. Perhaps she recognised a threat to her position as your lover. She mentioned it to you on the Tuesday night when you went home with her after tennis practice."

"This is all nonsense, Inspector."

"Is it? So why was it that Pat's neighbour told me tonight that she had heard loud noises coming from Pat's house and that it must have been on a Tuesday as that is her scrabble night and her TV isn't on? I put it to you that on Tuesday evenings you and Pat Harper had sex and that you often used fluffy, pink handcuffs to tie each other to the bed. A tiny piece of this pink fluff was found tonight in your car which PC Selby opened once you were in here."

Georgina's eyes were wild as she glared at Davenport. She tried to shrug off Frank's hold on her arm. Salma tightened her grip on her other arm.

"You stupid man, always assuming that it was a man who was clever enough to commit three murders."

"When you met Mary at the clubhouse, what happened? Did she hear your name and remember that Norma had mentioned you. Did you wonder what Norma had told her?" Davenport asked.

"The silly little cow asked me who George was and when I asked why, she said that Norma was always talking about him. I pointed out Stewart to her and said he was George."

"And of course she had no problem with getting into a girl's car, did she?" said Davenport.

Georgina laughed. It was not a nice laugh.

"She was grateful, stupid girl. I went up Floors Road and she was puzzled, naturally, but I told her I had to drop something off to a friend who lived there. I stopped the car and drew her attention to something outside her side of the car. I got out and pretended to look and she got out too and I put a scarf round her neck and pulled it tight. I'm strong you know, so it was easy, once she was dead, to get a wee, thin thing like her over the wall."

Mr McGregor rose from his seat and made for the woman. Penny came from behind the group and caught hold of him. All the aggression went out of him suddenly and he almost collapsed in her arms. His daughter-in-law took his hand in hers, as he sat back down.

Davenport spoke again.

"Georgina Laird, I'm arresting you for the murder of Norma Lawson, Pat Harper and Mary McGregor. You do not need to..."

"Oh forget the police routine crap."

With a quick shove, the woman pushed Salma and Frank away and bolted for the stairs. At the bottom she yanked at the door but it would not open and Frank caught up with her and encircled her tightly in his arms.

Davenport spoke from the top of the stairs.

"I had Norma's key, remember. I locked the door. Stewart and Kevin were already in the clubhouse, primed to come in when I wanted them to."

The young woman's face, turned up towards him, showed a vicious sneer. Salma joined Frank and with, Davenport's key, unlocked the door and led the woman out to the waiting police car.

The assembled audience was sitting, stunned. Davenport thanked Jane Green for letting him say she had lied for Stewart.

"I had to hope that you wouldn't deny that tonight."

Jane smiled.

"I didn't deny it because it suddenly struck me that I would have lied for him, if necessary."

Stewart, eyes shining, took her in his arms.

"You know Jane, maybe being married to you wouldn't be so bad after all."

Davenport thanked them all for coming, adding that he was sorry to have made such a drama out of it but he had been sure that Georgina Laird would not have admitted anything, had he approached her in the normal way.

Although naturally upset, they all assured him that it had been worth it to catch the killer. Joe Harper thanked Davenport for not including his daughters whom he hoped need never find out that their mother was a lesbian. Looking sombre, they left the clubhouse just in time to see the police car pull out of the car park.

Back at the station, Davenport filled in the missing pieces of the jigsaw.

"Something was troubling me after Saturday night and then during the night on Sunday it came to me. DS Macdonald and I were watching 'Presumed Innocent' on Saturday night..."

So engrossed were his young team that even Frank did not pick up the fact that his DCI and DS had been together.

"...Harrison Ford's wife introduced his semen taken after they had had sex, into the vagina of his lover who was found murdered. It came to me that the lack of semen in Norma Lawson's vagina need not have happened because her rapist did not ejaculate but because her would-be lover did not use a penis.

Pat Harper's husband had come to see me to tell me that he had divorced Pat after he discovered that she had been having an affair with a woman. If you remember, it was only Georgina who told us about Pat having a boyfriend. The two daughters couldn't tell me because they didn't know. They had only started to visit their mother after the affair ended.

I went to see old Mrs Jackson and when I asked her if she had good hearing as she had admitted hearing loud noises from Pat's bedroom, the one on the far side from Mrs Jackson, she said the TV must have been off and it was only off on her scrabble evening which was a Tuesday."

He paused and Penny rushed in.

"Was that all, Sir?"

"Well, Jane had said she was puzzled that Pat never invited her along on Tuesdays. Not a big point but taken with the other things, it made sense. Jane had also made the comment that Georgina went through men like hot dinners whereas she had been going out with Stewart for months. She told me this to prove that Stewart had been understanding about her refusing to have sex with him so was hardly likely to have instigated a sexual relationship with a teenager. I think we'll find that Georgina Laird got rid of boyfriends before they wanted sex with her.

"It was lucky Frank finding that bit of pink fluff, Sir," said Salma.

Frank sat up straight.

"But Sir, I didn't find any fluff ! I didn't break into her car tonight."

Davenport grinned.

"I told one wee white lie, team. I'm sorry about that. I hoped that by lulling her into thinking that we had arrested either Kevin or Stewart, then throwing her by having them turn up one after the other, she might make a mistake and she did when she mentioned the buses but I thought that might not be enough and it might not have been, hence the wee lie."